PRAISE FOR
DORELLA

"Different and thoroughly enjoyable."
—Lawrence Watt-Evans

"A very satisfying novel."
—Mike Resnick

"A delightful story. A truly fine debut."
—Dave Wolverton

"*Dorella* is a lot of fun. Seldom has the struggle between good and evil been embodied in such an appealing heroine. The sorceress Dorella is at once intriguingly nonhuman and touchingly human. A delight."
—Nancy Kress

For John (Jack) and Shirley
Who have always been there
MG

For Dad,
Who had to leave early
CM

DORELLA

MARK A. GARLAND
CHARLES G. McGRAW

BAEN FANTASY

DORELLA

Copyright © 1992 by Mark A. Garland & Charles G. McGraw

A Baen Books Original

Baen Publishing Enterprises
P.O. Box 1403
Riverdale, N.Y. 10471

ISBN: 0-671-72136-4

Cover art by Darrell K. Sweet

First printing, September 1992

Distributed by
SIMON & SCHUSTER
1230 Avenue of the Americas
New York, N.Y. 10020

Printed in the United States of America

Part One: DORELLA

1

There is timeless darkness, complete absence, total immersion; yet there is something—vague, ethereal, seemingly near and yet so insubstantial it must be very distant.

All that remains clear are memories: the terrible effort, the untenable results, pain, frustration, horror, and . . .

Anger!

A thirst of anger no amount of vengeance could ever quench.

2

From the moment the crow had awakened her, Dorella felt it would be a watch-worthy day. She had always paid attention to her instincts, otherwise she could never have lived so long. Nevertheless, she decided not to dwell on her apprehensions. Mornings had a way of running off and leaving one stranded in the middle of an unused day; and life, no matter how long, was too short for that.

Breakfast was cereal and toast with jelly. She fed most of the toast to the crow. Returning upstairs she put on a simple blue-and-white summer dress, lamenting for a moment her self-imposed moratorium on trailing blacks, then checked her appearance in the bedroom mirror. She was pleased. She didn't look a day over fifty, and though she no longer aspired to great beauty, she could still insist on handsome.

"Well, what do you think, crow?" She turned towards the bedroom window when there was no response. The crow looked noncommittal.

"Crow!"

The bird shuffled its feet and glanced over its shoulder, as though it half-hoped another such animal might be standing behind it. Dorella narrowed her gaze, clasping both hands behind her, rising on her toes. The crow jumped, flapping off into a tree just outside the window.

Dorella shook her head. "You are the sorriest crow I have ever had!"

She heard squawks of protest from a cautious distance.

In the living room Dorella paused at the wide bay window that dominated the front of the house. Five human-bodied statues stood a few inches apart on the wooden sill. One with a head like a lion, another an ox; one a wide-eyed bird, another an equine; the last was a fat-faced rodent of some sort. Their solid surfaces seemed to change colors, shifting from shades of gray to brown, brown to black, as if the warmth of the rising sun caused some subtle change in them. The brilliant, gemlike eyes sparkled with reflections.

Dorella had kept little over the years, but these would always be with her.

Closing her eyes she gestured, spoke the words, taking only a moment.

When she looked up again she saw children on the sidewalk in front of the house. They were waiting for her. Fine children, she thought. Sweet children. Perfectly delicious—"delightful"—children, she corrected herself, the word was "delightful."

She went to the stairs and called out to the crow, warning it to leave everything alone while she was out. She could hear the television come on even before she left the yard.

3

"Tell us again about the guy who you said invented telescopes," Paul asked. He was a small boy with blond hair, green eyes and a mind that was always asking questions. He had a smile that made him worth answering, despite having no front teeth (he insisted they were coming in).

"I think before long there will be nothing for your teachers to do," Dorella said, smiling, walking. They had nearly covered the two blocks between her home and the corner of Harris Street.

"How about those Nosemen in the boats?" said Paul, raising his voice over the noise of traffic ahead.

"They're Norseman," Eric corrected, "and she told us that story last week." Eric stood a head taller than Paul. He had far too much black knotty hair and too little meat on his bones. Being almost eight, Eric was at the first of many ages when confidence in one's own worldly knowledge becomes absolute. Dorella overlooked it.

"Very well. Tomorrow I'll think of something new for both of you," Dorella said, patting each of them on the head. They ducked with embarrassment as they joined a handful of children to wait for the bus in front of the Steak and Breakfast Diner.

Dorella received warm greetings from the other children, then listened quietly as the conversation drifted. She loved the light drone of their voices, cherished their foolishness. In their presence she felt a deepening sense of warmth, an unaccustomed peace. Strange how it had gone undiscovered for so very long.

She saw a man approaching on the sidewalk. Young, in his thirties perhaps. He wore dark blue trousers below a rumpled, brown, canvas-style jacket. His face looked weathered, with a slight puffiness about the eyes and a dark tan that matched his hands. The clothes looked as if they had not been laundered in a long time. Dorella tried to see into him, to find his center, but saw almost nothing. She learned only that he made her uneasy, and he must be watched because of it.

He stopped and bought a paper from the newspaper box on the corner, then stood there examining the headlines.

"Where did you get them, Dorella?" asked a small voice. A hand was pulling at her dress. She realized the children had been talking about her.

"Get what, Paul?"

"Those funny statues you have in your front room," Eric said for him. "And you bought 'em, what else?"

Dorella laughed. "Oh, no, Eric. You can't buy anything like that. They're rather special. You might say they were given to me—three of them, at least. Two of the statues were gifts by way of my sister. I've had them for . . . for a very long time."

"I didn't know you had a sister," one of the other children said, a girl of about nine.

"I don't. Not exactly, anyway. Not the way you mean."

"Well, you can have mine," replied another child, a boy. The girl made a face.

"So what kind of animals are they?" Eric asked.

"I can't say," Dorella said. "They are what they are."

"I think they're great," said Paul.

"I think they're weird," said Eric. "But I'd like to buy one off you."

"They're not for sale," Dorella replied. "A great price was paid for each of them." *And, protected as they were, no price nor human hand could have them now.* "I have some other things you might like, though." Dorella glanced up at the stranger, who still held the newspaper, not reading it. He looked away as Dorella's eyes met his, folded the paper, and went into the diner.

"Sometime I'll show you. Okay?" Everyone nodded, if somewhat hesitantly.

The children lined up to board the bus as it pulled to the curb. Eric and Paul waved as they got on. Dorella waved back.

When the bus was gone, she turned and entered the diner. Now she was free to chat with her adult friends, who were another constant delight.

She looked carefully about the room as she crossed to her usual seat at the counter. She saw the stranger seated alone at the far corner table. Again he looked away.

"Good morning, Dorella," Mrs. Santorelli said. She was waiting on a good-looking salesman, who never seemed to eat very much. Next to him sat a single girl who worked at the jewelry store down the street and who ate even less. At another table were two robust men, one larger than the other, who delivered office furniture; everyone said they ate too many eggs, even Mrs. Santorelli.

Of all the regulars, however, Dorella's favorites were the two fat, aging sisters, Betty and Bess. They never tired of discussing ex-husbands, friends, neighbors or each other; or of bragging about their children. And they never ran out of new places to shop.

This was a world Dorella had never known—or never

noticed, perhaps—and she was strangely enchanted by it. Such beautiful nonsense, she thought. These people, like the children, were an unexpected luxury of more recent times. Changing times.

She had lived near neighborhoods before, of course, but never *in* one, never as part of one. Over time she had managed to find herself on every major continent, had learned and forgotten languages, found and lost the cultures that spoke them. Each bit of knowledge had been gained for the sake of convenience and facility, each move made most often to alleviate nuisance or boredom; especially boredom, since during the last few centuries at least, she had rarely faced any real danger or menace.

Since escaping to this world more than four thousand years ago, her race had known no peers; but she had begun to see how the lack of community among them had kept her people from ever developing a common direction or purpose, had led, at least in part, to their continued decline. For much of their years this had left no impression on Dorella, or on her sister, come to that. That, of course, was when her sister and others of their kind had still lived in fair numbers in the world. That was before time and true solitude, war and ignorance had taken such an endless toll.

She had been drifting, growing old. The way was not as well-lit as it once had been, but here, now, she could see her way by the light of those around her. She had even let some of the gray start to show in her deep black hair.

"Bess says she's got a new flame," Mrs. Santorelli said.

Bess smiled towards Dorella. "We've just met, really."

"And now *he's* sobered up and *she's* getting worried," Betty chuckled.

"Well, I think it's wonderful," Dorella told her. "If you get married again I'd like to come."

"Oh, I wouldn't let you miss it," said Bess. "I'm

thinking of proposing to him this weekend, maybe. I'll let you know just what happens."

"You sure you can let it wait that long?" Betty asked.

"Jealous!" Bess snapped.

The two furniture movers got up from their meal. The thinner man approached Dorella, said, "I wonder if I could ask you a favor?"

"Your back bothering you again?" Dorella asked. He nodded. "It's no trouble," she said.

Dorella had him stand in front of her, facing away, then she moved her fingers along his spine, speaking low under her breath as she did. He began to sigh with relief. The physical things had always been the simplest.

"No kidding, Dorella," he told her, "I don't know what the hell I'd do if you weren't around. Are you married?"

Dorella pretended to blush, shook her head no.

"Well, *you* are," Mrs. Santorelli scolded from behind the counter.

"Just a thought," the mover said and he made his way towards the door.

The salesman was leaving too, and the jewelry-store girl.

"You tell her," Betty said in a raised voice, turning to Mrs. Santorelli, pointing to Bess. "I paid yesterday."

"I wouldn't get in the middle of that," the salesman warned, grinning.

"Some people flip a coin, then leave it with the tip," Mrs. Santorelli suggested.

"I'll buy for both of you," Dorella offered. "That will settle it."

Both sisters protested at once and started digging through their purses. Dorella, turning away, closed her eyes and said a few barely remembered words to herself. It was a very small thing.

"Oh, no!" said Bess, setting items on the counter. "I must have left my wallet home. I can't believe it."

"I—I don't seem to have mine either!" Betty said.

"Well, that does settle it then," Dorella announced. She plucked the check from between them, handed Mrs. Santorelli a few bills and waved her off. Then, to Betty and Bess, "Let me know if they turn up when you get home, girls."

Dorella fought to control her smile, then frowned as she got up and looked around. She saw the stranger still sitting at his table. Still he bothered her. She could not focus on him, as though something were preventing it. She began to wonder if within him he might not harbor a Dire—foul, lesser demons that were known to possess human beings from time to time, to drive them mad. But they had been all but absent from the world for hundreds of years. And a Dire glowed with a scent, an aura, that Dorella should have been able to sense, especially now, concentrating so hard; yet there was no light in him at all, a curious nothing. Dorella was not a stranger to the dark, and she knew that the opaque ones were always certain trouble.

4

"My mother says you're probably lonely. That's why you talk to kids," said Paul.

"Actually, I used to be lonely," Dorella told him. "I never knew it, though. I never even considered it. Not until lately, anyway. But now I don't think I am; I have you guys."

"Who used to be your friends?" Eric asked.

"I . . . I didn't have any. I didn't even like children," Dorella said, and she glared down at them.

"Oh," said Paul. His expression wilted.

"She's kidding," said Eric. "She likes everybody."

They came to the Harris Street corner. The skies were threatening rain, the morning was cool. All the children wore raincoats or jackets. Eric kept unbuttoning his, but Dorella made him do it back up.

"I told my mother you have a crow at your house," Eric said as they waited for the bus. "She said it must be a parrot or something."

"Just please tell her she's right," Dorella said.

"But I've seen it," Eric said. "It *is* a crow."

"Well, you may be right," Dorella said. "I believe parrots are supposed to talk, and that bird will never be able to do anything like that. I'll look into it."

"You ought to get a big dog to protect the place," Eric told her. "We've got one. My mom says there's all kinds of crazy people around these days."

"I'm afraid that's been a problem in other days, too," Dorella said. "Anyway, my lease doesn't allow dogs in the house." She smiled. "I'm not worried. I have you and my neighbors to look out for me."

She tried to take notice of the streets again as if for the first time, the small wooden and aluminum-clad houses, the pretty mowed lawns and the silver maples along the sidewalks. Not unlike the streets of other cities in other times, in other lands. American neighborhoods were spread out and diverse in style, and full of those miraculous TV satellite dishes! It all seemed to wear out much too quickly: the buildings, the communities. Somehow though, she felt strangely confident that a solution to this would be aptly found. Humans, especially these days, were like that.

In fact, this neighborhood was almost too nice. She had always preferred to live among people of simple means. There, among the poor, acceptance had no price and questions were few. It was easier to go unnoticed, unchallenged by those who might suspect.

Paul said the bus was coming. When Dorella looked up she saw the same man who had troubled her thoughts since the morning before. He came up the walk, careful not to meet her eyes. This time he passed up the newspaper box and went straight into the diner. When the children were gone, Dorella followed.

The conversation this morning was subdued, reflecting a mood not unlike the weather. The salesman said he thought he might get a regional promotion. The jewelry-store girl was quite pleased. The furniture movers ate quietly. Bess had gone out with her new friend again, but hadn't yet taken any big steps. Betty dared her. Bess accepted. The weekend was named as the deadline.

Just as everyone was leaving, the sun poked through the clouds, spreading warmth. Dorella was pleased; she could not imagine why she never used to like that.

She paid Mrs. Santorelli, then stood for a moment carefully watching the stranger. He sat in the same spot as the day before. Listening, she thought. Watching her.

He had coffee, and Dorella noticed him wincing as he finished his cup. An ulcer, perhaps, or just too much sugar. For a moment his eyes came up to meet hers; still she could see nothing but darkness in them. *I should remove them from their sockets*, Dorella thought. *I should turn you into a . . . into . . . into the "authorities,"* she corrected herself. What you did these days was contact the "authorities."

Dorella noticed the stranger getting up to leave just as she went out the door. On the walk home she was sure she was being followed.

5

As soon as Dorella reached the house she summoned the crow. It listened patiently to a brief description of the man at the diner. On Dorella's command it set off through the open kitchen window. In minutes the crow returned, squawking excitedly; unable to speak, unable even to invoke its own true name, at times it was easily understood. She followed the bird out into the street, up the block, down the back street. At one corner she saw a man in blue and brown, disappearing around another. She held no doubt who it was.

Back home, Dorella set about the task at hand. She had always been vigilant, cautious. The things most important to her were already protected. Now she must also think of herself. She had needed no such defense in many years; no armies sought her aid, no kings wished her dead, no true wizard had challenged her for hundreds of years—there were so few of them anymore. And nobody was burning anyone at the stake nowadays, thank the stars. In fact, there should be no reason for such inconsistencies at all.

Still, there might be someone, a middling, dabbling, misguided apprentice of the ancient arts. Certainly the stranger at the diner was not "he," if indeed "he" existed, but emissaries could easily be culled from such transient stock.

The spell she used was an old one, but effective. She had seen it work three times before. Her sister had used it twice. She worked it carefully, until her nakedness felt clothed, until she felt safe, and ready.

6

This morning Paul and Eric had prodded Dorella to tell them about a lengthy ordeal involving several gallant knights of Old England. When they reached the corner, the other children became an instant audience. She had been talking a very long time, recounting an especially perilous quest, when she noticed the clock on the bank across the street. The bus was late. It was then that she realized the watch-worthy stranger had not shown up at all.

At first Dorella thought he might have moved on, or run out of money, or perhaps gotten himself arrested. Then, there was a far more likely possibility.

She closed her eyes in concentration and listened. In a moment her mind's ear heard the screeching frantic calls of the crow.

Dorella excused herself suddenly and hastened around the corner. She made straight for her home, leaving the children wide-eyed at the corner. There was no time for explanations.

When the bus came she was a block away. She never thought to wonder whether everyone had gotten on.

7

The sun was well above the houses now and Dorella was sweating as she reached with her keys for the lock. The front door was ajar and no longer locked as when she had left. She hesitated to open it further. The sudden piercing double cry of the crow made her rush inside.

She found the man standing in the center of her living room, wearing the same blue trousers and brown jacket, glaring at her with his flat black eyes. He held a wooden kitchen chair in one hand, in his other a small serrated knife. The crow lay on the floor in front of him, one broken wing folded over. The man threw the chair down and took a step towards Dorella.

"What is it you want?" Dorella demanded.

"I'm going to take you off, lady," His voice was low, full of gravel. He began circling to the left. Only then did Dorella glance at the bay window. A plastic trash-bag lay on the floor below the sill. *He wants the statues, or someone does,* she thought.

They were all still there, held in place by a spell twice renewed the day before. To move them would mean moving the house itself. She looked back and saw him about to lunge.

"I have something for you," Dorella said, raising

her hands. She said a few words beginning the spell, speaking in the ancient tongue, reaching out through the universe to draw upon the fabulous power that lay within the tiny cracks that were the fractures of creation, the edges of space and time. The stranger doubled over in pain.

"Something special."

He went down to his knees, starting to cough, holding his abdomen. His pants grew suddenly wet with a dark stain Dorella recognized as blood. A spot of red trickled from his lips as well. It was an ulcer after all, thought Dorella. The physical things had always been the simplest.

The respite was short: the thief rose in spite of the pain and came at her again. He was strong, Dorella thought, driven now by a blind rage and hatred that was always as strong as all but the most powerful spells. And perhaps there was more. Perhaps he benefitted from some type of spell himself. If so, it was a shabby one and no match for her own. It would be hard to kill him by sorcery now, but she did not need for him to die.

She completed the spell just as he lunged again, bringing the knife down. She put both arms up to catch each of his wrists and stumbled back under his weight. Even as their bodies touched, he began to change.

The knife blade clattered as it bounced on the floor. The air became heavy with the smell of sulfur and hemlock as a thick mist formed at the ends of Dorella's outstretched hands, enveloping the stranger, consuming him.

Slowly the mist began to clear. Dorella wavered slightly, weakened, and brought her hands back to cover her face. She wiped the sweat from her forehead, then bent down and picked up a darkly colored object: a figurine with the head of a jackal and the body of a man.

On shaky legs she walked across the living room to

the bay window. After rearranging the statues there was room enough for one more. She placed the sixth one on the sill.

As Dorella turned around she saw Eric and Paul standing in the doorway.

8

Dorella bent over and picked up the crow, stroking its feathers smooth. One of its eyes opened slightly. She recalled the terrible battle her sister had fought against a wizard even Dorella could not have destroyed had not her sister already weakened him. Still, Dorella had been too late to save her; too late to do any more than preserve something of the essence of her sister, Alibrandi, inside the body of a crow. A poor solution at best, but one which would buy her time. A place where someday, somehow, perhaps . . .

Dorella looked up at the boys huddled unmoving in the doorway. "You are not to tell anyone about this," she said calmly. "It will only be between us."

Paul looked about to burst.

"Please, Paul, try not to."

"I won't say a thing," Eric said. "I . . . I just have to ask you. I have to know what you did to that—"

"I know," Dorella said, shaking her head. "I am only kidding myself. It has already lasted much longer than I could have hoped. I'm sorry."

She ushered the boys outside and gave them each a note saying they had been helping her and had missed the bus. It took a number of lies and promises to get them to go. Dorella did not shed a tear.

There would not be time to visit other friends, to fix a back, to open wedding invitations, or to learn whomever it was that may have discovered her. It would not take her long to pack. It had never taken long. She could easily disappear by afternoon.

Part Two:
LEST DARKNESS CALL

1

Over time, a very long, long time, there is more. Other thoughts seep through this consummate rage: the memory of the spell, carefully woven into the iridescent opaline crystal he had worn, a spell built to perfection with patience and great amounts of cautiously expended energies; a spell strengthened and tailored through the years and designed to work only at the moment of his death, should such occur. A reliable spell, he recalls. No—infallible.

How many had never possessed the presence of mind to work such a mechanism of safety for themselves? How many had gone as far as to question his own wisdom in those endeavors—*save that work*, they'd said, *until you are old and bored and nearer the need for such spells and*—gone, of course, most of them. He'd seen them perish one by one. And how many since?

Since when?

Since . . .

Thoughts of his death and defeat wash him in renewed anger, yet he is buoyed somewhat by the realization that the crystal would, after all, be a dull and muted place in which to reside, that his circumstances clearly indicated the spell has worked.

2

Whispered voices carried from the next aisle as Dorella placed a leather-bound, fourteenth century volume on mystic healings high up on the sixth shelf in its coded slot. She almost couldn't reach, even on her tiptoes. Height had always been a bothersome thing.

Another book remained in her hand, a tattered volume written by an obscure researcher early in the eighteenth century. The work concerned itself with a single spell supposed to enhance one's longevity. She had glanced through it briefly, examining the various versions, mildly amused. The author had undoubtedly gone to his timely grave never knowing that the last page contained the words exactly right, save for the order of the final line.

The first chapter discussed the probable potency of such spells when correctly used—in fact, Dorella had not looked a day over fifty in several hundred years.

"You have to come tonight," someone was saying, almost pleading, though not quite. "I'll expect you, I promise."

"I'm not sure I fit in," someone else replied. Even hushed, Dorella recognized this second voice. It belonged to a short, slightly plump, engaging sophomore from California named Alison Kimbrough, who worked part time at the university library just as Dorella did. A nice young girl, Dorella thought, and smart, and especially easy to talk to . . . usually.

"I've been reading the books you mentioned," Alison was saying. "I never understood. I never knew there was so much to it, so much relevancy. The group—everyone—they seem so involved and devoted. I wonder if I could ever be sincere enough."

"You could be perfect," the other someone said, a young man Dorella didn't think she knew. "You already are."

For a moment there was only the sound of restless breathing. "We're your friends in truth," the young man said. "What we offer is nothing less than everything! A new and different life; power, purpose, an end to isolation. Even now you are not alone, not ever truly alone, dear beautiful Alison. You will see, we are the way. You will believe."

"I want to," Alison blurted out. "I mean, that is, I'd like to be—"

"I'll tell you what. Let me send Kathleen or someone around to the dorm to pick you up. Someone to go with you, share the experience with you. How would that be?"

"That would be . . . nice."

"Wonderful!"

"I'll be in my room. I'll see you when we get there."

Dorella placed the other book back and came around the end of the aisle just as the young man turned towards her. He was a most average-looking boy of about twenty-one, with smallish features, a thin frame, and very short blond hair that lay flat against his scalp like animal fur. He wore a baggy, dark pullover sweater and white trousers. His deck shoes made slapping sounds against the tile floor as he walked away, glancing curtly at Dorella as he passed by her. Dorella looked a question at Alison.

"A friend of a friend," Alison explained. Nothing more. Dorella noticed the book in Alison's hand, "The Satanic Bible." She perked an eyebrow. "You've joined a group that reads this?" she asked, pointing.

Alison fidgeted, nodded, just barely. "It's a . . . club."

"Oh?"

"Yes." She turned away. The look in her eyes was distant, sullen. She had returned only four weeks ago from a trip back home, where she'd been tending to her Grandmother's estate. Alison's family, her mother and father, had been killed years ago in an auto accident. No fault of their own, she'd said. Just blind bad luck. A rock slide while driving through construction in the hills. An act of God, she'd said. A bitter act of God.

She had taken the money from the settlement and gone to stay with her Grandmother, her only living relative, until she'd grown enough to go off to school, and come here.

When they met, Dorella found Alison to be extremely quiet and self-involved, at least at first. Then, slowly, they had become friends. Good friends, in time. But the Grandmother's death had taken Alison hard. The girl had been an island since she'd returned.

"Are you sure you know what you're getting yourself into?"

"Oh, sure," Alison replied, restless, staring at her shoes. "Something . . . special. Something I can really be part of. For a long time. Forever, maybe. Daniel says—"

"And who is Daniel?"

Alison's gaze followed the departed visitor. She seemed to hesitate. "A guy, that's all. Just a guy in the club."

"He does the club's recruiting, I see."

"Well, he's—he's the president, sort of."

"I think they call it 'High Priest.' "

Alison looked at Dorella with narrow eyes. "So what?"

"Of course. So just go and enjoy yourself. You know what's going on, I'm sure. You're a big girl."

"That's right." Watching shoes. "I'm making friends."

"Boy friends?"

Alison darkened still further.

There had been a boy, the latest one, Jack something-or-other. According to last accounts he was still "around," but Dorella had looked into his eyes one night, not long after the funeral, when he had come by the library to talk with Alison.

He was giving Alison some freedom, he'd said; some time, he'd said; a little room to breathe, he'd said. Miles and miles of it.

"No," Alison muttered. "I've just gotten to know some of the girls so far. But things change. Sometimes for the better. It depends on your definitions." She looked at Dorella then, a hostile expression. "Maybe I *need* another friend or two."

Dorella weathered the remark. In the few months since the semester had begun they'd talked a great deal together, about people and places, literature and legacies, life, death, loneliness. Some nights they went on for hours, on others the talk simply faded to silence, a moment shared without benefit of words. Alison had known loneliness for a very long time. For Dorella, it had been a slow learning process.

She didn't want to spar further, regretted having begun.

"It's something I want to do—I mean I'm *going* to do," Alison said. "I've never been very religious. The older you get, the more things happen to you, to the people around you, the more you start to wonder about . . . certain things.

"They have a strong bond between them. Their own laws and concordat. They know exactly who they are. And they have strength. I've seen them together, in meetings, in ceremony, doing . . . things." She put her palms together, made a joyous expression. "Incredible things. Daniel knows the secrets of the universe," she went on. "They worship—"

"I am aware of who and what they worship," Dorella said. "And why." She shook her head and sighed.

"They seek kinship with the darkness, the powers of the negative universe. They chase a destiny they think is theirs because they find it attractive, mysterious, overwhelming, but they do not truly comprehend the source of that power or what it really means, the destruction it can bring. Not until later."

"No," Alison said, shaking her head furiously. "I've seen wonders at the gatherings. Daniel knows. He understands the way of things. Last week he cast a spell all his own, and a vision appeared before us. An animal, I think. Hovering, transparent. Daniel says—"

Dorella placed a hand gently on Alison's arm, waited until she found the young girl's eyes. "There is great power in the universe," she said, "and from many sources. Power to be gathered, remembered, stored; used by some, and misused by others; wonderful natural energies, and terrible alternate kinds. Here, there are volumes all around us filled with information and theories, ages of revelations on the subject. Many, perhaps most, are books of pure conjecture, or samples simply of ignorance and lies. Adult fantasy. Some, perhaps only one or two, holds truth. Think, Alison, do you believe Daniel knows which is which?"

Alison thumbed the corners of the tattered volume in her hands. Black curls fell across her forehead, hid her face. She seemed tense. "And you're so smart, right? Lady Buddha. You sound like a mad professor." She didn't look up.

"That isn't what I mean."

Alison screwed her face up, raised one eye. "You could tag along with me, you know. It might do us some good." She seemed to soften. "I'm not bent on being in this all by myself, you know."

Dorella wanted to remind Alison of her new companions. She decided against it.

"But you do still want to do it?"

"It's such a hard thing to explain. Maybe if you went, if you met them. It isn't what you think. It's not

what anybody thinks. Please, they want others to
come. Daniel—"

"Enough Daniel," Dorella began, then found herself suddenly amused by the whole idea—she and
Daniel trading secrets—as though he had any. She
banished this in favor of more sensible thoughts. "I'll
keep this in mind," she said.

"Yeah, thanks a lot." Alison checked her watch.
Dorella saw the numbers read eight-something. "I've
got to go. I'm certain you won't mind."

Dorella only nodded. "Good night."

She watched Alison leave, exiting the balcony section of the library, walking up the main aisle, checking
the "Bible" out at the desk before she went. Witches,
Dorella thought. She had been called worse herself,
times before. But *modern* witches! Of course they
were perfect for this town. The university library contained a huge occult collection, with everything from
Sinclair's "Satan's Invisible World" to Glanvill's
"Saducismus Triumphatus" to various reprinted versions of the "Grimmories," the handbooks of magic.

There were hundreds more. The dark brotherhood
could feast on such works. Indeed, the library's repu-
tation was largely what had drawn Dorella here some
months ago. There was always something to be learned,
of course, but she most hoped to discover a means for
unlocking the spell that immured the one life she
could not reach—the one she someday must—if
indeed enough of Alibrandi still survived.

Dorella knew well the secrets of power, but her
greatest knowledge lay in understanding the ways of
matter, the weave of creation: the whole. Though
many of her kind had been absorbed—and many lesser
folk of this world after them—she had remained one of
those who never allowed the darkness any claim on
her, never succumbed to its lure. Instead she had mas-
tered the many skills her mother had taught, and
learned to reach out from within herself to tap the
wondrous sources of power that were, in fact, the very

seams of existence. As three generations before her had done, so she did. In time she had made strong her heart and mind.

That the universe was not easily tapped or tamed was an inherent fact. That some found other, easier means was a thing accepted. Provided, of course, one knew, or had been taught, the many truths involved.

She fancied herself no tutor, but Alison was a nice girl; something Dorella was pleased simply to notice these days, since in the past, human beings had somehow seemed more trivial, less distinguishable. Dorella had come to notice, too, that many of these people had something which she had never possessed, something her own kind had never been wont to acknowledge—each other. And while that had its drawbacks, it often seemed to create a rich, palpable spell all its own that warmed the earth and lit a path through the world as no magic ever had.

Alison was possessed of great humanity, of a very special self. She had shared these things with Dorella, and Dorella had been charmed by that, had come, almost, to need her companionship. To need people . . .

A weakness, she worried. Or a small gift in her gaining years. Though even now she must remain on guard. Perhaps now especially, she thought, pausing a moment to reflect on the newest statue in her small collection.

But she must also act. So, she thought, if Alison needed someone to talk to, she would likely come to me, and if she needed help—

The trouble, she reminded herself, was that people were a most capricious lot, their minds ruled by minor flows and currents which formed patterns more complex than all the world's weather. Alison might never come to her for help at all, or to anyone else on earth. She might go straight to the devil instead.

Alison's affairs were quite properly no more Dorella's business than the fate of governments or the level of the tides, but such things could become enormously compelling.

Dorella finished up early and made her way off campus. She was again intrigued by the ways the world had changed over the centuries, and by the ways that it had not. All of man's great architecture was little more than a dim memorial to their passing, all their hopes as small and distant as starlight, and this against the inexorable darkness and mighty workings of time. Still, there was a certain, elusive value . . .

It came to her that she'd never cared much for what the world of darkness had come to these days, and especially what passed for witchcraft.

She neared her apartment, the upstairs of a two-family city home chosen in part because it was within walking distance of the college; she had never learned how to drive, and one simply couldn't go sailing about on cloud cover in today's world, even with props. She fumbled in her bag for her house keys, found them hard to locate at first. Such a nuisance, she grumbled, and waved the deadbolt aside.

Alison *did* need a friend, she thought.

Truly, there was no harm in simple information. Was there?

3

As she put on the living room lamp, Dorella was greeted by a sharp squawk from the crow.

"I have a small task for you," she told it. The crow bobbed its head, shuffling its feet back and forth on the upholstered ridge of its chair-back perch. "I want you to go to the dorm where Alison stays, then wait there. Follow her when she leaves. I'll wish to know where she goes, as soon as you're sure." She reached out and gently touched the animal, stroking its back. The crow chirped in short, raspy notes, bobbing its head.

It could fly quite well again. The broken wing had healed nicely with time and a bit of help from Dorella—physical things were always the simplest. The attack, however, had taken its toll. Dorella longed more than ever to find a means to free Alibrandi, to make her whole again, to have her sister back. Well past the age when most of her kind grew away from each other, Alibrandi and she had remained close. Close enough to make the pain and frustration of separation almost impossible to face—it was easier to eschew the loss.

She was haunted now by concerns over who might have enlisted the blank-eyed interloper and cast the spells he wore, over his interest in her statues, and whether someone might be seeking proof of her existence.

She went to the window behind the little sofa and pulled it open, then glanced back at the bird—who danced about still more but did not rise.

"Go," she bid it. "I will not repeat myself."

The bird seemed unimpressed.

"At least there are never living witnesses."

The bird leaped off the chair, but landed in the open archway leading to the kitchen, where it commenced making a trilling sound that could have easily come from a round white steeple dove. Dorella eyed the creature with vexation. She held her temper; there was the slightest trace of her sister in the creature's eyes, a rare, precious trace; she knew that when she looked again it would be gone.

"You haven't found yourself any dinner?"

The crow hung its head, more cooing sounds in its throat.

"Don't tell me you can't do for yourself. You are simply too lazy to bother even with cupboards. And stop that pathetic babble before I find a more agreeable place to keep your vocal cords."

She brushed past the bird into the kitchen and pulled out a loaf of white bread, then opened a jar of peanut butter and spread some on half of one small slice before folding it over. The bird leaped onto the table and devoured the combination. Dorella put out a cup of milk. The crow tipped its head, considering, doubtless recalling breakfast.

"The only way you'll get cream again today is if I chose to drown you in it."

The crow drank hastily, then scrambled into the air, flapping through the doorway. It found the open window and was gone.

She ate her own dinner then, a heated can of vegetable soup, some wheat bread and butter. The simpler tastes had always done her well. When she was done she sat with books from the library and read, looking for that single, elusive stalk in a vast and grassy field. The crow caught her dozing when it returned, scratching on the windowsill. She awoke and hastened to let it in.

Dorella listened carefully of necessity; her ability to interpret crow had never been more than fair, and the bird's own crow was but passable at best. So far as she could determine, the place where Alison had gone featured a Wiccan gathering of some sort, though the level on which this particular group worshiped was still in question. As were their ends.

There were honorable souls in the world who drew their strength from nature, who developed their talents by following the ancient methods. They learned to understand the forces that bind the fabrics of creation together. These were the mortal sorcerers, the natural witches. These were people not far removed in spirit from Dorella's own race, who had always found these means and methods to be an intrinsic part of themselves.

Yet there had long been others in the world, those who embraced an evil as old as time, a thing that three hundred years of witch hunting had done nothing to address. The dark dimension and those who inhabited it were more terrible than mortal imaginations could know. Yet foolish people seeking instant power and the promise of immortality went readily, blindly into the anarchy, to touch the blackest, foulest reaches of eternity.

They made high displays, perverting every intimate act, holding black masses, sacrificing living things to the great Death, gathering souls for the damned and paying homage to the demons.

Here they found power that was easily obtained but never easily controlled, and far too costly by any account. Even to the people of Dorella's race.

Many found the pulpit of hell a useful place from which to tear at all that their fellow man had built, to shout their strange politics or defame what others might call true or good or—life. Still others sought ends only they could know.

Dorella was no stranger to the darkness or the light. She had spent a thousand years learning to balance always in the twilight, drawing most of her strength from the hidden cosmic sources her mother, and her mother before that, had shown to her, working hard to touch the universe with the fingers of her thoughts. She had never fallen into the ever alluring, destructive waters of the dark well. For a human being this was, she guessed, not possible.

Even the most evil among the "born" wizards had never truly despised mortal life. It was a fact that they had destroyed thousands of humans in the past, but most had done so in response to requests and promises made by conquering kings, or while fighting the wizards of their enemies, or for reasons of love, anger, jealously—

Reason was not a fuel for the engines that drove some men, however, especially those seeking powers beyond human domains. Such folk became desperate creatures, and they often became very dangerous.

Alison had likely found a tamer coven made up of young materialists and would-be witches, some students and a few odd local citizens caught up in the mysticism or fashionable novelty of the occult—the enticing, alien messages it preached.

Their leader, Daniel, was no doubt well read on the subject, a good orator, perhaps an apt showman. He might be most convincing—and amply rewarded, certainly. Alison, of course, needed something to cling to, a source from which to draw the nourishment of peer involvement and a sense of self-worth: a mission.

Dorella knew she should just let things be, wait and see if any treacherous signs appeared along the way, and more importantly, allow Alison to follow her own course. But certain details bothered her.

The crow told of a gathering involving what had to be an altar, and a location all out in the open, a clearing in the woods where only a partial structure stood. In such a place the proceedings would be well among the elements, instead of inside someone's closed, draped apartment, where the world was far removed. All of which lent a troubling ring of authenticity, and added to her apprehensions about Daniel.

While curiosity had never been much of an asset, Alison *had* invited her to come along, and Dorella hadn't been to that kind of ceremony in at least a century . . .

One peek, she thought. For a friend.

"Lead me to this place," she commanded the crow, "and easy on your way. It seems a fair hike."

The crow took to the air as Dorella opened the door, then waited for her to lock up. As they set off into the brisk autumn night a wind came gently prowling, chilling her as it nagged. She said a few words softly, as if to herself, and the air warmed somewhat around her; the wind found its way to either side.

4

Two miles west of town she came upon a small grassy path which led through the woods, coming eventually to a large clearing that contained the remnants of an old barn. The roof had long ago fallen in. The largest remaining wall faced north and served to block much of the weather. The south wall was missing completely.

Dorella made her way silently through the thigh-high grasses, hidden by the night, pausing when she was close enough to see through a large, weatherworn opening in the timbers of the barn's east wall. A diverse assortment of lighting, ranging from clumps of candles to Coleman lanterns and battery-powered lamps, even a small central fire, all combined to cast myriad light and dark patterns over the faces of the thirty or so people gathered inside the walls.

An altar had been constructed of wood on what was once a low, walk-up hay loft. Daniel stood behind the altar, arms raised, reciting some indiscernible chant. From time to time the rest of the participants would respond in unison.

As Dorella watched she saw someone bring an animal, a small, long-legged creature that might have been a very young lamb or goat, or a stray dog. The animal was held high before the crowd, then deposited on the altar, where two white-haired college-aged men helped secure it. There came a round of chants, people raising their voices and arms, following the priest's lead. Finally Daniel produced a shining, sharply tapering ceremonial dagger, the orthame.

He held it up, calling out in recital above the gathered voices. He examined his crowd of followers a moment, looked to the sky, then brought his arms down. The animal jerked in its restraints. In another moment, following a number of grandly executed strikes with the knife, Daniel retrieved something from the creature and held it up before the congregation. The heart, Dorella guessed. The animal had fallen still.

She watched the assistants work to drain and collect the creature's blood into special basins, which in turn were used to fill a number of waiting goblets. One by one, the brothers and sisters did partake.

Dorella found Alison among them, observed carefully as she went with the others to the altar. Alison seemed to stay towards the rear, letting others go ahead of her; she seemed in a trance, whether self-induced by a part of her mind that could not rationalize some things, or by the proceedings, Dorella could not guess. She let the cup come to her lips. Dorella was too far away to see if she actually swallowed. Yet even from here, she could sense the revulsion in the girl.

Dorella let a frown find her lips as she began to face the probability that the worst combination of facts was true: the little coven in the woods was far too serious in their business for the good of anyone, and Alison, much as Dorella had expected, was having trouble attempting to become someone she was not, despite her enthusiasm. All the while wishing, of course, with typical human perplexity, that she somehow still could be!

It was impossible to see Daniel's eyes from her position, to see what sort of images burned within them, so Dorella could not be sure what he was, or had become—or might yet be. She could only be sure that he hadn't taken Alison completely—yet. The rest would simply have to wait.

A few of those gathered wandered off as the ceremony decentralized. Alison went to stand at a crumbled partition off in a bundle of shadows, apparently waiting for the girl who might have been Kathleen, and for Daniel himself. Dorella breathed a heavy sigh. The three of them came away together, talking.

Time to go, Dorella thought, to ponder a course of action. To think . . .

She might help Alison by conjuring some lower form of reptile into a fine young prince—"doctor"— what you did these days was turn them into "doctors," she reminded herself, or "investment brokers." Which, so far as she could see, was infinitely less satisfying.

If she was going to try to find some comfort or true companionship among the human race, she was going to have to learn how to live as one of them. To understand them. She must gain the experience.

Since considering the idea that normal human beings might be worthwhile creatures, she had made a few friends among them, people who made her a part of their lives, if only briefly. They had left no doubt in her mind that the experiment would prove worth the trouble. She had every confidence that Alison would, too.

5

"I don't think you understand."

"Is that one statement, or two?" Dorella asked. Alison turned a corner, guiding the little Colt up a narrow side street, cutting through the city's old West End on her way to the new Northern Mall. The population inhabiting the street corners and doorways as they passed reflected the dim poverty of the neighborhood, menacing, desperate. Alison leaned across and depressed the lock button on Dorella's door after pushing her own.

"It's hard for you to see," Alison said, then paused, apparently trying to think of the best way to phrase her thoughts, or perhaps to identify them.

"Try just telling me. Say whatever." Dorella made her voice sound calm, nice.

"I keep wondering what the world has against me? Why it is I'm not supposed to have anything, no home, no family? Why one jerk after another walks all over my life like I had 'DISPOSABLE' written on me somewhere? I don't have low days, my life is a landmark depression."

She held the steering wheel tightly in both hands, stared out the windshield. "Don't you see, nobody gives a damn about Alison Kimbrough, and nobody ever will. There isn't anyone, except maybe you, and we know you're only willing to go so far." She shut up, waiting for a remark. Dorella made none, which seemed almost to aggravate the younger girl.

"So maybe I *should* do something like this," she went on. "Join people who will make a difference, who feel the way I do about this world, and maybe the next. Daniel can change my life."

"One way or another," Dorella said. She looked away, out the window. *Where do you begin?* she wondered.

They came to a stop in a narrow intersection. The buildings on all four corners were boarded up, broken down. To the right, out Dorella's window, stood a small storefront bar. Half-lit neon beer signs hung in the windows. An old, stooped man stood out in front smoking a cigarette. He held it up in front of him, devoted to the curling smoke, shivering.

Out along the crosswalk a young black woman shouted at no one at all, arguing with ghosts. Just beyond her, near a stripped down VW, a man with eastern looks quietly spoke with someone in the window of a graying wooden two-story.

A boy in his early teens, dressed in pale jeans and someone else's giant green army coat, approached the car. Dorella could see the dark hollowness in his sallow features, a dull pain in his eyes—eyes that kept rolling back up into his head all out of focus—this in combination with a high swing of his left arm and leg, an odd, autonomic type of movement that served only itself. With every other step, the boy seemed about to faint and vault some unseen obstacle all at the same time.

"So sad," Alison was saying, watching the boy with a winced expression. "I feel so sorry for people like that."

"Feeling sorry is becoming something of a hobby for you," Dorella noted.

"You know what I mean. I've seen that kid before, when I've come through here. I don't think he has anyone at all, and I don't want to know what he does for money. I'm sure those are the only things he has to wear. I've seen him in dumpsters looking for discarded cans and bottles, or food."

The boy stopped a few feet from the car, eyes rolling down to focus, his spasm ending. He stood peering in through the windshield at the two women, blank.

"He comes out and stands there just that way sometimes, when I get this light, looking, like he's never seen a human being before. You wish there was something . . . I don't know. Just something."

"I see. So you mean he's not bright and attractive and healthy and going to college or anything."

Alison glared at her. "What the hell is that supposed to mean? You've made yourself my analyst now? Are we in 'Pedestrian Philosophy 101' or something? I didn't bring you along for abuse. I can get that anywhere."

The light changed. Alison mashed down on the throttle and the little engine strained to respond.

"I was only . . . talking to you."

"You know, Daniel said not to trust anyone, not to talk about the—club. I thought you'd look into it with me, or at least discuss it. Maybe he was right."

"Maybe."

Alison drove in silence. They rode the bypass for a while, then got off at the mall exit and quickly found a spot in the mammoth parking lot. She shut the car off and sat a while, staring at the dashboard. Dorella sensed a calamity of emotions in Alison, felt the distance between them growing wider. As most young people did, the girl saw herself as very nearly the center of things; her people, these people. She couldn't imagine anything going *too* far, turning out *too* badly for her, anymore than she could believe one of her only reliable companions, regardless of circumstances, would not share her newest interests, or bear her now-told sorrows.

But there was more, there beneath the obvious. Underlying shades of thought and feeling Dorella could not easily read: hatred, or was it only fear? Emotional things had always been some of the most difficult. Alison breathed a sigh.

"I don't mean to step on you," she said. "I know better, I guess. I'm not being fair."

"I only want you to be careful what you step *in*."

Alison looked at her, then looked away. Dorella reached for the door. Alison turned back and stayed her hand.

"They're having a get-together tomorrow, Daniel and some of his fav—his best friends. At someone's house. I'm invited. I'd like you to go, just for company, and so that you can get to know him. You'll see. There's something about him, and all of them. I promise they won't hurt you or anything."

Dorella smiled in spite of herself, then forced a more dour face. "Why me?"

"I don't know," Alison said right away, as though she'd been expecting the question. "Things are happening so fast. In two weeks they're having a major ceremony, something special. They've been talking about it for days. I'm going to be re-baptized in my new name, two other girls, too. Maybe more. Daniel is going to do some very serious work, I don't know precisely what, but it promises to be incredible. They say he has fantastic powers, and he's going to share them with us. Something about freeing us from the limits of our corporal being. Immortality! *They* all believe in him completely. I—I think I'm beginning to—I think I do, too."

"Why do you tell me these things?"

This question seemed less anticipated. "Why?" Her face knotted up. "Why shouldn't I?"

"Of course."

"What the hell does that mean?" Suddenly obdurate.

"Just 'of course.' "

Alison pursed her lips. "I *am* going. I don't expect you to try and talk me out of it."

"I'm certain I'll do no such thing."

"Good!"

Silence. Alison screwed her face up again.

"I damn well have to tell *somebody*, don't I?"

"I know," Dorella said. Alison took a breath.

"Kathleen is okay, but she's distant, and always wants to talk about ... I just don't want to go by myself. I mean ...

"Look, you're supposed to be my friend, and they want more members, so you can at least see what you're missing. If they think you're the right type ..." There was moisture at her eyes, a softening to the line of her chin. "Everything is so goddamned fucked up," she said, thinly, teetering. "I—I don't suppose you'd ever consider it."

Dorella let her thoughts digress, tossing choices and scenarios in her head like a juggler. *Human events are not truly your affair*, she cautioned herself—again, as she had done so many times. Perhaps too many times to listen.

Alison seemed genuinely to need her, or someone, and by some strange evolution of fate and spirit, Dorella seemed to need her too.

"I might change my mind."

Alison looked at her and smiled, blinking too much. Dorella reached for the door, pulled the handle. "Let's get inside," she said. "I'm going to need something special to wear."

Alison hid her face, wiped her eyes. Dorella pretended not to notice.

6

The meeting was in an old house converted to apartments off-campus which offered a huge, unused attic. They arrived to find Kathleen and four other girls from the college sitting on the floor, facing each other, talking. A lamp for reading had been set up over Kathleen's shoulder, materials lay in a pile beside her. Daniel stood near the door, just hanging his coat on the back of a chair.

"I'm glad you're here," he told Alison, smiling

gently at her. "I see you've brought along your friend. I wonder why?"

"Well, she's here to—"

"I can speak for myself," Dorella said, touching Alison's arm to silence her. She saw Alison look at her, a glimmer of apprehension in her eyes. *Not to worry*, she thought. "I'm here because you are, my lord."

Daniel's small mouth formed a hard grin. He looked at Alison, who weakly smiled, then back to Dorella. "I see."

"I do not see, at least not as you," Dorella said. "Teach me what I live to know."

Daniel seemed to delight in her words and turned towards the others behind him. "Kathleen, come here a moment, please."

The other girl got up at once and strode over. Daniel huddled with her a moment, then turned back around. "We'd like to talk with you a while, learn about you, tell you more about us." He pointed towards a table at the far end of the attic, half hidden by a partial wall that worked to divide the big room. Dorella nodded agreement, averting her eyes in deference to them both. Again Daniel looked pleased.

"You may take Kathleen's place with the others," he told Alison. "We will join you soon enough."

Alison went as directed, glancing shyly sidelong at Dorella as they separated. Dorella smiled softly at her, and winked.

7

Daniel floated between the table and the central gathering. Kathleen was incessant, drilling, prodding, manipulating the conversation. She was very good, Dorella noted, an apt interrogator. So Dorella told the young concubine exactly what she wanted to hear.

Dorella had convinced many similar minds of grander illusions times before—minds far shrewder even than

Kathleen's. The girl's mind was consumed by a single purpose and therefore inclined to be easily pleased in accordance with it. Even with all Kathleen knew about her subject, and with all her guile, she was at best parochial in Dorella's eyes.

Daniel sat with them from time to time, a cautious observer. He seemed to remain aloof, saying as little as possible, listening mostly. He was no fool, Dorella saw, for by maintaining distance he retained a degree of mystery, even with Dorella. She thought to probe his mind and attempt to learn his deeper secrets, but there was the chance that he knew the spells to warn him, and it was much too soon for that. She could see enough at just a glance to know there was nothing good in this man, and something breeding, growing within him that, even this far removed, smelled very foul indeed.

Dorella's main concern was that Daniel might have acquired the ability of true sight and be able to "see" the difference in her, just as she could spot talent or other aberrant characteristics in those which she encountered. She met his gaze solidly several times, let him stare into her for clues until he seemed satisfied. While she in turn reached far enough into him to gain more knowledge. Still, she dared not do too much.

As the night wore on they began a question-and-answer session that delved deeply into their occult beliefs. Dorella said all the right things, offered just the right amount of astonishment whenever it was called for, and finally told them the very darkest secrets of the coven she had belonged to in the city where she had recently lived—a fine fiction that left Daniel and Kathleen very nearly astonished themselves, and begging for details. Dorella kept it short.

Daniel finally brought Dorella out to join the others, introducing her as their newest member, praising her beliefs and accomplishments, extolling her aspirations.

Before the night was through she nearly had Kathleen jealous.

"You're such an eccentric," Alison said afterward, as they walked to her car. "I had no idea you'd been in one of these things before." She'd grown completely silent towards the end, hadn't looked at Dorella in almost an hour.

"Neither did I," Dorella said.

"What?"

"You wanted me in, didn't you? So I could go with you, share in your odd little adventure, for whatever reason. Well, I'm in."

Alison looked at her with blank eyes. "You didn't have to run for president. Some of the things you said—how did you learn—"

"I read a great deal!" Dorella snapped, her tone by itself ending the conversation. "Now, please take me home."

8

The walk was no longer than it had been two weeks before, though it seemed so. Dorella finally reached the clearing and the old half-barn wondering whether she was of sound mind or becoming instead a deluded old fool slightly before her time. For now she tried to put such thoughts out of her mind. They would only make things more difficult.

At the barn the darkness was nearly absolute. Clouds obscured the stars and moon. A thin frost stiffened the highest parts of the field grass. She gathered slight warmth from the air, light from those memories of the recent day that still lingered in everything around her. After waiting a moment, making sure she was alone, she made her way to the short loft and the make-shift wooden altar.

None of the trappings were present, the pans or chalices or candelabrums. But something was there, hidden beneath a scattering of grasses and hay which lay all around the loft—hay too crisp to be of any vintage.

Carefully Dorella brushed some of the straw away to reveal freshly painted markings upon the old boards, a line which became a circle surrounding the altar, a five-pointed star drawn inside it, characters signifying the many names of God, from English to Greek to Hebrew, written along the edges of the circle and at the points of the star. The pentagram was carefully constructed to allow ample room for the altar and a person or persons to be contained within it. Depending upon one's objectives, such devices were usually necessary in calling up demons, and useful thereafter in keeping them confined—or, if one preferred, keeping them just that far away—protection for the many, or the few.

Dorella sighed wearily. Daniel had done plenty of homework, that was certain. She tossed the straw back in place, then went behind the altar and retrieved a pendant from the pocket of her coat. The natural warmth of stored primal energies within the dark red-and-black flecked fire opal was something she could feel the moment she touched it. She placed the stone beneath the straw a few feet back from the altar, just inside the circle of the pentagram, then set about building the spells she had intended for it to hold, carefully accessing the power they would require.

She had only scant knowledge of what might transpire when she returned here a few nights hence. No way to be certain whether Daniel was nothing more than the deviant weekend psychotic she believed him to be, or a mortal menace to himself and those who followed him.

There was just the slightest chance that Daniel might actually tap into the nether world, might be able to draw some of its power to him. Dorella had not faced that power in hundreds of years. She hoped she wouldn't now, even feared it, in fact. In any case,

forethought had always been worthwhile, and caution
the first step towards indemnity.

Besides, she had no intention of making a spectacle
of herself, or spoiling the quiet life and persona she
had been accruing here. To live as she intended, she
must remain anonymous. She wasn't about to lose
everything over nothing.

The air grew colder around her, causing her to
shudder. When she was finished with her work she
took a moment to renew her warming spell, then covered the pendant over and stole quietly away.

The crow waited for her as she left the barn and
headed towards the wood. It tried to make conversation. Dorella ignored it, letting her thoughts run. She
wished she still knew of someone who could see even
a small bit of the future. How could one work without
the proper tools?

The walk home was a longer one still.

9

Most of those in attendance were repeats from the
previous ceremony: the students, a few men and
women from the local population. Many of the women
were gaudily, suggestively dressed, heels instead of
warm boots, overly painted faces, coats occasionally
opened to reveal little or no clothing underneath. One
unusually muscular girl wore no coat at all over a
heavy but sleeveless sweat-shirt. From time to time,
Dorella imagined, the coven engaged in other, indoor
ceremonies of a more intimate nature. Which was no
surprise. Hell loved play.

The men were split in appearance between the latest club and occult fashions to styles that dated back
to the sixties. Up close, the pair of tall young men who
were Daniel's assistants, his lieutenants, were oddly
striking. They wore brightly dyed leather and small
alloy earrings, all topped off by chemically created

albino hair that was cut short on top and grown long at the back. Even their eyebrows were snow white.

Candles and lanterns burned everywhere, giving an unreal, cheaply animated look to the proceedings.

Kathleen, beautiful tonight in a full-length black and white and gray gown, stood in front of the altar to one side, silently watching. Daniel himself stood center behind the altar wearing a long black robe with sleeves that hung down almost a foot at the ends. He read verses and spoke loudly to his followers, his expression one of impossible confidence: the perfect candidate for mayor.

As the first rituals progressed, Daniel called upon all present to sing chants of ambition and praise. At last, one of the albinos took the floor and made a rousing speech, condemning half of the physical universe for unclear reasons, praising some of the rest, tagging key points to the spiritual self. It was quickly apparent that he knew remarkably little about anything he said.

Finally, with the night's festivities rising to an energetic peak, pans and chalices were arrayed about the altar, and Daniel produced the orthame dagger.

Daniel began reciting a sermon, working from notes, driving the crowd on with a nearly brilliant vigor. He paused then, and began anew, reading from a fresh page. Dorella hardly heard at first, then the words began to draw her attention.

". . . this night, and will call forth a great power, a creature of eternity, from the world beyond our own. With him we will evoke a new reality and allow the forging of a glorious pact, a thing to transcend life and time and death. We will be allies in a greater realm, partners in its glory."

His face glowed with excited energy, his expression was wild and heated, boiling as it flickered in the candlelight all around him. A thousand shadows cavorted as the crowd waved its arms and cried out its approval.

"Each of you will share the secrets of the universe, each of you will be eternal with me."

Dorella glanced about, observing the faces of the others while Daniel raved. They seemed as completely caught up in Daniel's self-propagating revelations as he was, their eyes filled with partisan awe and dark fascination. She'd seen like faces oftentimes before—not entirely real—spellbound. She saw the same things now in Alison's eyes, but also, barely hidden from the others, a glint of something else. . . .

A frightened young girl.

When she turned back towards the altar, Dorella saw several people stepping up onto the platform from the right and dragging a wildly struggling figure in their midst, a boy in his early teens, all bones, his eyes rolling back into his forehead as his limbs twitched and strained in strange contortions. They removed his army coat, the rest of his clothing. They wrapped him about the chest in a length of black cloth, leaving his genitals exposed.

Alison grabbed Dorella's arm with both hands. "It's him!" she blurted, barely keeping a whisper in her voice.

"I know." Dorella leaned near Alison's ear. "I'm not awfully surprised. It's customary to use someone like that boy, someone who won't be missed by anyone: addicts, prostitutes, beggars, runaways. Though whenever possible, many covens prefer to use babies conceived by members and born especially for use in the ceremonies. Which, from a certain standpoint, is quite sensible. The dead infants are then—"

No!" Alison yanked Dorella's arm, squeezing down hard, beginning to tremble. "I can't believe any of this. What are you saying? Where did you get that stuff?" She froze suddenly, staring at the altar, at Daniel and the orthame. "They wouldn't do that, would they? I mean, there was talk, rumors, you know, but I . . ." The whisper had faded, falling silent.

The albinos held the boy up before the altar for

display, his dangling, jerking form white and pale from the cold, stiff with terror. Daniel proclaimed him a sin of God, a disease of man. Kathleen led the crowd in a new round of chanting, until Daniel finally raised his hands and commanded the boy be tied prone across the plane of the altar. The lieutenants pulled the boy backward and secured him in place.

"A gift of flesh and blood, the offering of a soul," Dorella explained further, trying to keep an even tone, trying not to get too close, too emotionally involved for her own good, or Alison's. "This sort of thing is required in any attempt to secure the sort of pact Daniel is seeking. To murder is to break the highest commandment, and so the most sincere demonstration of the depth of one's commitment. In many ceremonies fresh blood—again, ideally the still-warm blood of a human infant—is used for—"

"Dorella!" Alison almost screamed the name aloud, seemed to catch herself just as she spoke. She had Dorella's arm in a tourniquet hold. "Just listen to yourself! How can you stand there reciting as though you were quoting from some book back at the library? What kind of person are you?"

She stared at Dorella, who truly wondered for an instant, what she should say to this last question.

"We have to say something," Alison whispered, her voice a harsh quiver now, the sound of a throat contracting. "We have to *do* something!"

Daniel had the sacred orthame dagger in his hands and was holding it high over his head. He continued chanting, paying homage, swearing allegiance to the dark lords—traveling along the only accessible route to great power for his kind, those without born abilities or the will to learn and accomplish the ways of nature.

Dorella listened intently to the last few phrases of Daniel's recital, which seemed a composite of words drawn from several texts, but with heavy reliance on the Satanic Bible and the ancient saducisums. All of the bits were extremely potent and competently delivered. He called to the demon world, honoring them yet again, asking for one demon in particular whom he called Arynome. He finished with perfection, getting all of the words exactly right, even to the order of the last line. For the first time in several hundred years, Dorella felt a part of her insides clench.

"To be truthful, I've seen all I care to see," Dorella said, having lost most of her desire to know the evening's outcome, and having a particular disaffection for even the least of hell's creatures in any case. "In fact," she added, being perfectly candid, "I really don't think we should stay. So unless you feel you must—"

"What!" Alison somehow found it in her to paint one more shade of horror upon her features. She opened her mouth, let her jaw hang nearly limp a moment, then struggled to get it working again.

"We can't just leave," she gulped. "Even if they'd let us, which I know they wouldn't, we—we—" Abruptly she began to sob, then fought to hold it back. "We have to do something about the boy!"

Dorella saw Alison's tears threaten to overcome her as those around them chanted and roared, Daniel and the two albinos leading them along. Ceremonies like these had gone on for centuries, and man had been abusing man far longer than that, killing each other, destroying all manner of lives. *What in all of that is my responsibility?* Dorella asked herself, almost desperate now, trying to rationalize. How was this some fault of hers, that she should "do something"? In past centuries she had been granted great wealth and distinction for far lesser troubles than these. Fairer times, those, more easily navigated and put aside. Now, though, one whim of intervention might carry severe consequences. What did Alison expect of her? What did she think?

Alison had apparently suddenly lost much of her interest in the coven, which was all or more than Dorella had ever intended in the first place. As for not being able to leave, that hardly seemed a likely possibility, especially if it was done covertly. But the girl may have something in mind, a solution that would not put them at risk yet produce some positive effect. It was at least worth asking about.

"What would you suggest we do?"

"I—I don't know."

Dorella frowned, shook her head. "Come then, the boy should not be up to us."

Daniel was shouting Arynome's name to the blinding accompaniment of electrically ignited flash cans positioned about the loft, each loaded with small amounts of fast gunpowder and magnesium. The crowd was worked to a frenzy. Daniel kept on, calling out above the noise of the faithful as a newly gusting, whistling wind began to blow out of the night, rustling through the barn, tugging at candle flames. He waved the dagger like a painter's brush, a magic wand.

"Now." Dorella said, looking up, feeling the wind, feeling the knot inside her grow tighter. "We must go now!"

"No, I can't. I have to do something!"

"Come and receive the gifts I offer!" Daniel bellowed, and opened his arms.

The air forward and left of the altar took on a strange, shimmering quality as the wind grew to near gale force. Daniel glanced down, seemed to size up the boy's deeply ribbed chest. Then Alison let go of Dorella and bolted for the altar, screaming at Daniel with all the breath in her lungs.

She leaped, then slammed hard against the front of the altar, groping wildly for the dagger—and missed. She snapped her head side to side, trying to throw salty tears out of her eyes, swung again, missed. Daniel fixed her with a withering gaze, then cast a glance to his right. He stepped back and held his arm out of reach while the two albinos grabbed Alison and pulled her to one side, holding her there.

The wind filled with a stench like long-dead animals

and hot sulfur. Something was materializing within the tower of shimmering air a few feet from the altar. All at once, the demon was there.

10

In his present incarnation Arynome stood nearly seven meters tall. His skin was the color of charred raw meat and covered thinly all over with course black hairs. He had scuffed black hoofs instead of feet, long bony hands and dangling, knotty fingers, with great yellow nails that hung from the tips. His chest was like a wine barrel that seethed below a round, fat head that resembled a grotesque blow-up toy—over-inflated and ready to burst. His face and arms were riddled with ghastly black holes of many sizes, and he was most definitely male. The wind began to die.

"Here, great Arynome!" Daniel cried. "Here is he who has summoned you. Hear what I will say."

The demon glared down at Daniel, then seemed to briefly eye its whole predicament. It made a hissing sound, a cacophony of punctured truck tires, then made it change, straining and fine tuning until the noise ranged down and became a low, reverberating drone. With this the demon said, "Then, little man, speak quickly, for it is you who shall be first destroyed."

"Here me," Daniel said, undaunted. "I offer you the living heart and soul of this young boy." He paused for just an instant, glancing at Alison. "And those of this young, lovely girl. Both yours this night, given you along with the promise of many more to come, and myself in the bargain, when such time shall come to pass. All this in return for our agreement made and fulfilled."

Daniel signaled the two albinos to bring Alison and tie her upright to the altar close beside him, hands pulled back over the legs of the boy. They tore her coat away, leaving her in just jeans and blouse.

"My terms are simple," Daniel said. "Power over agreed-upon aspects of earth and sea, over men and creatures to specified ends, that I might accomplish all our goals. Last, the promise of a kingdom of souls in your endless domain that I might rule from the day I choose to die, a day on which we will also agree. I seek the powers of darkness from a master of that realm, I reject the light for new truth.

"Great Arynome, these things you can do and more. Yet they are all I do ask. May my offer be seen as worthy."

Daniel fell silent. The demon stood considering for a very long moment, eyeing first the altar, then the persons gathered around it, and finally the crowd beyond—which, just then, managed to fade back noticeably towards the open end of the barn.

Dorella tried to partially hide herself behind the rotted remains of a horse stall that jutted from the wall just to her left. Even there, the demon might sense her presence, and she knew that if the beast laid eyes on her, some form of recognition was all but certain. She would then be forced to attempt to flee or to confront the monster, to destroy it or be destroyed. Even victory would not ensure Alison's safety, and would ruin any rekindled hopes she had of living a humanlike life here, of being part of the smallness and texture of that life she had come lately almost to relish.

It was clear Daniel had arranged things exclusively for his own well being. The pentagram enclosed only himself and his two lieutenants, leaving the crowd nakedly exposed to the demon's murderous wrath should it lose interest in him. Demons, once aroused, typically sought instant retribution, and the least resistant path to it—and only *then* managed the wherewithal to rejoice in their freedom. To such a creature Daniel was, more than anything, a petulant nuisance.

Many grim possibilities came to Dorella's mind as she watched Daniel try to succeed where many greater and cleverer men had failed—greater *beings*, she thought.

It came to her that it should not be possible for Daniel to breach the barrier between dimensions on such a grand scale, to draw a demon of Arynome's magnitude into the world. Unless something had changed. Unless . . .

There was no time to wonder. No place to run. She had to do—something. She had to act, she had to try.

She began to concentrate on the pendant hidden close behind the altar, still there beneath the straw at Daniel's heels, while something like a smile came to sit upon the demon's black lips.

"Come," Arynome said, curling a finger at Daniel. "Walk with me now and we will discuss this fine agreement of yours. I am intrigued."

Daniel looked about nervously, taking a reassuring peek at the lines of the pentagram. "I will not leave the circle," he proclaimed.

"But I am a reasonable being," Arynome soothed. "Why should I treason one so devoted as you? Have I not great pride in my wisdom and vision? Have I not aspirations? Would not sparing you be an investment?" The demon leaned towards Daniel. "Not all accounts of these like matters are true, I assure you. Give me these lives as you have promised, and I will not harm you. Then give me the secret audience I request of you, and I shall surely reward you."

An intense grin bloomed across Daniel's face. He turned, arms outstretched, towards his followers and declared the moment of glory to be at hand. He looked down at Alison's shivering body beside him, arms bent behind her over the edge of the altar, her knees buckling as they lost the struggle to hold her up against the pain of her position. "And you," Daniel said directly to her. "You will have the privilege of paving the way before me."

His two lieutenants came closer, preparing to deliver

the sacrifices outside the pentagram directly to the demon once Daniel had finished his task.

Dorella took a breath, cleared her thoughts and spoke the words, softly, a whisper no living ears would ever hear. As she did, a glittering figure appeared just behind Daniel, almost upon him—a beautiful young woman about Dorella's size, but without the traces of gray in her full, waist length, shining black hair, without the harsher lines that encroaching middle age lends to one's countenance.

She wore a long, satiny black gown with a diving neckline and thick sash, finely embroidered with gold lace, that circled her waist and fell from her shapely hips on one side. A delicate, black lace shawl covered her shoulders. Three roses, one black, one magenta, the other purest ivory, adorned her hair. At the center of her breast, on the thinnest of gold threads, hung a pendant bearing a deeply-hued fire opal.

Dorella was taken aback for an instant by the girl's youth and radiance—she almost didn't recognize the image herself. She couldn't help but smile.

With the demon looking on, Daniel raised up the orthame one last time, changing his stance as he did so as to place Alison's torso squarely under him—all but blind to everything else going on around him. Dorella wiggled her fingers, animating the simulacrum, sending her splendid agent three steps forward.

The demon sighted the image just as it grabbed Daniel by both his shoulders, and too quickly for anyone to act, planted one foot to the right and heaved. Daniel stumbled sideways, whirling his arms to catch himself. He regained his balance almost instantly— just one step outside the circle of the pentagram.

Daniel screamed when the demon seized him, a scream which quickly fell silent as the demon reached into the High Priest's middle and gutted him in a single motion. The horrified cries of the coven members came to replace Daniel's own as most of them turned and ran for the opposite end of the barn, with

Kathleen and both albinos pounding closely after them.

Dorella's simulacrum was busy at the altar removing the restraints on Alison and the boy. Freed, they scrambled down from the loft, terrified beyond reason, leaving the only safe spot in the barn and moving after the others. The boy was shivering terribly, convulsing uncontrollably, rolling his eyes. Alison, sobbing, trembling, struggled to help him walk. She found her coat at the base of the altar and tried to pull it around them both.

And for a moment Dorella thought it might all work out. The demon had fed its appetite for vengeance and human flesh; the words and deeds of Daniel no longer held any power over the beast—or Alison, come to that. Arynome was free to return to the nether world, or to go into the night and become someone else's problem. She and Alison could then get on with their lives. And with all of that, no one would suspect any connection between herself and the events of this most unpleasant evening.

Her thoughts were broken by a chorus of newly terrorized voices that rose just then from behind her. The fleeing crowd was gathering at the far, open end of the barn, pointing, screaming to one another as they tracked clumsily backward.

At first Dorella saw nothing there, but when she looked again, this time without her full, born vision, using only her physical eyes, she could see the illusion of a ten-meter-tall steel wall which the demon had conjured across the opening. Alison and the street boy stood on the open ground at the center of the barn, only meters away from Dorella's crouched, half-hidden position. They too had stopped, and the demon's eyes were squarely upon them.

Alison, however, much to Dorella's consternation, was looking not at the demon but directly at her. She began calling to her, waving, with the boy hanging on her, beckoning Dorella to follow them out, asking Dorella if *she* needed any help!

The foolish girl is so concerned with my safety, Dorella marveled, *that she neglects to consider herself. Even the boy came first! What kind of person was this? What manner of the heart did she possess?*

The creature made a sound in its throat like falling rock. At a leisurely pace it began to move away from the altar. Dorella fought an intoxicating mix of emotions, anxiety and frustration, pain and affection, and—hope. They came to muddle every attempt at rationalizations, and they felt alien in her ages old, once sober and indifferent heart. She felt almost—human.

Caring, she had learned, could be a terrible thing—to want something insatiably yet find it too costly or difficult to have—the life of a sister, or a friend.

Any sensible mind would have reasoned that the demon was only being true to its nature, responding to a situation which it had no part in creating and every reason for exploiting. Moreover, Dorella had seldom indulged in any great fits of fondness or malice towards any creature, even one so foul and grotesque as this. *None of my business,* she thought. *If only it could be that simple.*

She saw the demon nearly upon Alison and the boy, saw the brave, terrified look in Alison's eyes, and she was transported to a field in her past, a burning, desperate moment, bent over her dying sister, looking into eyes filled with the same mix of gallantry and fear—and in her mind, Dorella came to understand that the one emotion surfacing above all others at that moment was rage.

She stepped out from behind the little wall and called out the demon's unholy name. Arynome paused in mid-stride and turned to look upon her. His pointed tongue appeared between his glistening, open lips. Wildness danced in his slate eyes.

"You have had enough fun," Dorella told the thing.

"Leave these people as they are. Leave this place and be satisfied."

"You are not one among them," Arynome proclaimed, pointing a knotty finger at her accusingly.

Dorella nodded dully. "As you say, Demon, now do as I say."

"But you must know that I am not . . . 'satisfied,'" the beast cackled, purposely hissing at every "s."

Dorella frowned, brazen, almost. "You know precisely what I mean, repulsive one. Must we nitpick?"

The demon circled back towards the altar, an assortment of moods contorting its gruesome features as it looked Dorella over more carefully. He was an old demon, Dorella guessed, wary by virtue of experience, and would know well the pitfalls of haste. Abruptly he seemed to arrive at some special revelation. He spread his arms and said, "You may think to drive me away, minute lady, but you cannot hope to be any match for all of us!"

Immediately Arynome was flanked by two pairs of demons identical to himself, all snarling in chorus. "You are now outnumbered, five to one," they all recited. "Terrible odds, so it is *you* who must do *our* bidding!"

Dorella dared not look away, even as the crowd screamed anew, even as she heard Alison crying out, the voice of someone lost to her own cognizance. Dorella reached a hand beneath her coat and slipped it into one of the very large pockets on the front of her new dress. She withdrew a fair-sized, plain white candle and held it up before her. Again she spoke, drawing what little energy she needed from her own stored inner strengths. The candle's light grew into a pallid white brilliance like that of a dozen full moons. The four newly arrived demons grew dim and seemed to disappear.

"An illusion of light for the illusions of darkness." she said. The demon searched the air to either side with eye and claw, found nothing. Crimped, angry lines spread across his tight features. "You'll have no jest with me, old woman!" The voice was thunder, almost deafening.

Dorella smiled. "But, my dear demon, with you it is such a small task."

Arynome's whole head turned a deep, raging purple. The huge body began to shake as the creature drew a double-barrel breath and raised up its arms again, cocking them back like a boy preparing to swat flies. Slowly then, a sound grew from somewhere inside the beast—or from somewhere much further away—like the hiss it had made earlier, but mixed with the noise of jet engines and locomotive brakes.

As Arynome's trumpet reached painful proportions the wind began again to blow, growing so strong Dorella had difficulty simply remaining upright. Then the demon struck, eyes dead-set, arms thrown forward towards her, channeling all its powers into a single killing blast of blazing energy drawn from the very fires of hell.

But Dorella was gone. In the scattered, dancing light of the few lanterns still lit, a confusion of shadows mingled and jumped. Shadows that could easily hide the true reflection of a shifting being's essence—at least for a moment.

Then Dorella was there again, appearing behind the altar exactly where her simulacrum had stood seconds ago. Her graying hair whipped about in the ebbing winds, the strong lines of maturity etched clearly on her finely carved face. She stood bathed in lantern light, plainly visible. Her coat was gone now. Her dress shimmered with the energy of cosmic fires drawn from the edges of the visible universe, burning yet black, like fireworks reflected on night waters.

Now the demon wasted no time. He threw forward once more, pouring forth a terrible column of netherblaze that warped the very fabric of space and time along its path, bending the lines between dimensions. Yet even as he did, Arynome could see the image of

Dorella fading the way his own illusions had, leaving him to watch in astonishment as his column of fiery energy funnelled into the red-and-black stone pendant the image had worn about her neck.

Like water spiraling down a drain, the blazing river disappeared and as it did, the pendant took on a fearsome spin. A whistling sound began to emanate from the pendant, rising ever higher as its spin rate increased. It glowed with a deep red, burning hue all its own, heating the air and earth around it.

Arynome took a few cautious steps back from the altar, peering at the little trinket in wonder. Then, without any indication, the pendant burst. All the power it contained came streaming out—an intense blue-white rivulet that spewed high into the air like a fountain and fell all around the great demon in a perfect, fiery circle of multidimensional energies, a furious marriage of opposing forces never meant to exist, held together by the iron force of Dorella's spell: a fire to burn the flesh of demons.

Dorella suddenly stood beside the altar again, now holding a lantern high above her head. She held out her free hand, palm open to the sky, and slowly made a fist. As her fingers clenched tight, the bright ring of flames began to shrink.

"Now, demon, you will vanish yourself back whence you came or I will surely make a roast of you!"

Arynome's hide was already beginning to boil. Panic and agony raged in the hell creature's eyes and brought high screaming sounds from its throat. Dorella raised her fist slightly higher, shouting final notice, then threw open her hand. The ring drew instantly into a thin pillar. As her arm fell to her side there was only the empty night and the light from scattered lanterns.

Dorella looked out to the people still huddled together at the opposite end of the barn and pointed above their heads. "There," she called out. "Look now with your own eyes, and not those which the demon had lent you!"

When they saw that the wall had vanished, most of the group gathered themselves up and ran into the field, blind to any specific direction, not one among them looking back. A few of the students, six in all, did turn and walked slowly back towards Alison and the naked boy.

Dorella stepped down from the loft and went to join them all. She wore her own coat again. She carried a blanket in her arms, which she lent to the boy.

"Come," she said to him. He shied away as she moved to touch his face, his sides, talking briefly to herself just under human hearing. It was a small task. Physical things had always been that way.

The boy's eyes rolled down into focus. He held them level upon Dorella. He clutched the blanket about himself and took a step forward. Then another as the group moved with him. Then a third as perfect as the rest. His eyes filled with tears and he hid his face. Dorella looked at Alison, whose cheeks were as wet as the boy's, and saw that a warm smile was adding itself to the girl's features.

With a very deep breath, Dorella reached out and hugged her, tightly as she could, for as long as she could. Finally she pulled away. "You should all go home now," she said. "There is nothing here."

Alison looked at her. "And what about you?"

"I wish to be alone, just for a while, out here in the cool and quiet. I hope you can understand that, please. It is all I ask."

Alison opened her mouth to object. Dorella cut her off. They would want to know so much. Who she was, or what, and how she had done everything they had just been witness to—so many things they could never be allowed to learn.

"Please, no argument for now," she asked. "And no questions just yet. Not until I've rested. In the morning, all of you, come to my home and I will explain many things. *Everything.* Again, this is all I ask."

Alison looked vexed. "Dorella, please . . ."

"Just go, just for now," Dorella urged. She smiled grimly. "Please."

"I'm—I'm sorry," Alison blurted out, her expression despondent now, confused. "For everything."

"No, don't be." Dorella shook her head. "I was only minding my own business."

She turned Alison and the boy towards the open field. "In the morning," she prodded, and pushed them gently from behind. "Now do as I say."

Alison nodded dully. The group turned with her, mumbling among themselves, and walked heavily away. They left the barn, collecting one of the lanterns on their way, and faded off into the starlit field. Alison kept looking over her shoulder. Dorella waved her on.

A crow, almost invisible against the surrounding darkness, drifted lazily down on the still air, wings flapping twice as it lit upon Dorella's shoulder. The lantern light gave the bird's feathers a soft, oily sheen.

"Where were you when I could have used you?" Dorella asked. The crow clucked nervously, carefully padding its feet on her coat. It gave a penitent shrug.

"Never mind," she said. She could feel eyes upon her from somewhere far out in the field, where the glow of one lantern traveled nearly out of sight. Going home. Practically, truly gone.

A few of them would sleep. Some would come early tomorrow to see her, begging information. *A few hours,* she thought. *It would be long enough.*

Alison would be the greatest loss. The greatest in ages . . .

Perhaps a postcard one day, someday, from someplace else. Perhaps only a soul remembered.

Dorella lowered her lamp and looked into the glass, then spoke and the glow went out.

Part Three:
THE ROAD TO EDIFIEN

1

"A newly uncovered well," the young apprentice said, a bright, bony man who lately seemed to find his life almost solely in his work, a quality Altez found most acceptable. "They say the well itself dates back hundreds of years. Perhaps thousands," the young man added.

"Fascinating," Altez said, looking at the stone, pressing the jeweler's loupe to his eye. "A most remarkable piece." He turned it over several times, searching his mark. "We'll make a cut here," he explained, "along the axis, and get a better idea."

The old jeweler set the stone up carefully, then took the mallet and cutter in his hands. With a single practiced strike he split the stone almost exactly in half.

He heard his apprentice scream, or perhaps it was himself. The stone was burning, smoking, *alive*. He watched the light turn to darkness. It was the last thing he ever saw.

2

A troublesome man of about forty-five got on the bus in Middle Falls just over the New York border. He stood near the driver for some time reconnoitering. He was not quite six feet tall, with graying hair, nice slacks and a heavy tweed winter overcoat. The moment his eyes found her, Dorella felt a twinge somewhere deep inside.

She tried to see into him, to look below the surface at the images in his mind. What she saw was quite ordinary, a man, like most men, an individual essence. She sensed that the man was looking for something special, but what man she had ever encountered was not? Indeed, what human being?

He had an angular, intelligent face, cleanly shaven and sporting a thin mustache, a long, straight European nose, a rounded brow that slid under a gray woolen motoring cap. He smiled. Dorella nodded cordially, seeing no reason not to.

Then he was coming towards her, working his way up the aisle, swaying as the bus pulled away. He came to a halt as he reached the aisle seat beside Dorella. She realized they were still staring at each other—and blinked.

"May I?" he asked, tipping the brim of his cap, showing off two gold and jeweled rings on his right hand. Fresh snowflakes still melted out of sight all along his sleeves and shoulders. He smelled of wet wool and thick cologne.

Dorella picked up the plastic animal carrier she'd placed on the empty seat and set it on her lap. "Very well," she said, neutral, looking him up and down, still not satisfied with her appraisal. There was nothing specifically wrong, other than the mixed way he made her feel.

The bus lurched over separated pavement and he

flopped ungraciously into the seat beside her. "Gene Packerson," he said. "Thank you."

"There are other seats," Dorella pointed out. "What do you thank me for?"

He grinned evasively. "Well, this one looked especially nice."

He had a pleasant smile, Dorella thought, if somewhat trained in appearance. He stood up and placed his single carry-on bag on the package shelf over head, bracing against the seat as the bus took a curve. "Excuse me," he said when he brushed her with his hip, and smiled again. Once more Dorella nodded.

"Sales," Gene said after that. "Mid-Western Industrial Pumps. We're trying to do some business in the northeast. I hate to fly. Can't anyway, not to about half the stops I have to make."

"I see," Dorella said. Out the window increasingly heavy snows were falling on the farmlands and wooded hillsides, covering everything in white. She looked briefly at Packerson again, then turned away. He had the most unsettling aura about him which refused to go away; too slight almost to bother about, but there nonetheless, and a part of her could not overlook it. Caution, of course, was easily removed yet difficult to add. For the moment, she went back to watching the weather.

"So, ah, how about you?" Gene persisted amidst a volley of throat clearing.

Dorella didn't look at him. "Well, I like to fly alright. I just don't like airplanes."

Gene Packerson said nothing for several miles after that.

3

The child was seated beside her mother, across the aisle and two rows up. Seven or eight years old, Dorella guessed, with her mother's blond hair, long, with a white barrette at the back, and soft, light-brown eyes. She wore corduroy coveralls with a white Pooh-bear print blouse underneath. Her mother had on a lovely red sweater, a nice perm, a few too many pounds. The little girl finally managed to drop her comb into the aisle. She left her seat to get it, then deftly found her way two seats back, where she grinned sheepishly and asked Dorella what she had in the cage.

Dorella turned the animal carrier so the side with the big wire-barred door faced the girl. "This is a friend of mine, more often than not," she said, trying to sound as disarming as possible. The child was simply scrumptious . . . or rather, "adorable"—that's what you called them these days—"adorable." She had to mind her choice of words, especially . . .

Gene tried to shrink back into his seat to let the girl see around him, then he tried leaning forward, then he stood up altogether. "Be back in a minute," he said, and pushed off towards the john shaking his head.

"It's a beautiful bird," the girl said, drawing near.

"They're from Australia," Dorella explained. "It's called a cockatoo. They have to be kept warm, which is why they allow me to keep it on the bus." They hadn't really, of course. The terminal workers, like the driver, had seen an empty cage when they had looked, but spells as contrary as that were difficult to maintain for very long.

She watched the girl admire the parrotlike, mostly white bird, with its yellow tail feathers and top knot. This was an old and easy spell. A simple trick of illusion even a human student of the ancient arts could have managed. People always found exotic birds fascinating, always acceptable, so that was what Dorella let the passengers around her see. They would not be so quick to accept an old black crow.

The bird, knowing nothing of all this, grew excited by the sudden outbreak of attention. It began bobbing its head and strutting on the carrier's makeshift, woodenstick perch.

"And who are you?" Dorella asked.

"Tricia," the girl replied, clutching her small hands together in front of her, bending at the knees to talk to the bird. "What's the Catoo's name?"

"Cockatoo," Dorella corrected, "and 'bird' will do well enough, since this is the only one about."

The girl's mother was suddenly standing over her, looking down, eyeing Dorella meticulously. She noticed the bird and raised an eyebrow.

"You have a charming daughter," Dorella told her, gazing at the youngster, thinking that she meant it. They were a wonder, these human children, in ways she had overlooked for far too long: riches never counted.

"She shouldn't be out of her seat," the woman said.

Dorella smiled, nodded. Well, perhaps where she was going, or some place after that, there would be little girls like Tricia, or even little boys, in a pinch. Children like those she'd found not long ago in a town quite common but for them. Perhaps, in a place where she could fade into the regular surroundings and reacquaint herself with the local folk, she would even find another friend, like Alison . . .

If she was careful. After a long, long quietus her world seemed suddenly filled with anomalies. She still couldn't understand how it was possible for someone like Daniel to summon a demon so fearful as Arynome. And the bleak intruder she'd battled just a few months ago, the more she thought about him, seemed so dull and unresourceful, she could not believe he could have been working on his own. And if someone was looking for her, for whatever reason, she had managed to leave a trail of transformations, deaths and demon battles any layman could follow. It was almost as if . . .

There would be a time to find the truth, of course,

she simply had to stay alert for it—had to be ready with the proper questions.

She looked wistfully at the crow, the house where her sister dwelled in a semi-cognizant, slowly deteriorating limbo, and was again reminded that some questions—such as how to undo the spell cast upon her sibling—had been posed for centuries, and that Alibrandi still awaited the answer. "If only you were really . . . *here*."

"What?"

Dorella realized she had spoken this last thought aloud. Tricia was looking at her with big eyes.

"Nothing," Dorella said. "I was just thinking of someone."

"Who?"

"Oh, family."

"We're going to see Tricia's father for the holidays," the girl's mother said. "In Philadelphia. It'll be nice, even for me. We're talking again a little, if you know what I mean."

"It's nice to know where you're going," Dorella said, putting on a grin. "Even a little."

"Who are you going to see?" Tricia asked. "Do they live in Philadelphia? I bet Daddy hasn't ever seen a bird like that one! Maybe you could come to his house? With the bird?"

Dorella let the questions roll off her mind. "No," she said summarily. "I'd like to, but . . ."

"Excuse me again," Gene Packerson said, back from his task. He slid into the seat with a nod to Tricia's mother.

"Come on," the woman said, taking Tricia by the shoulders, steering her back up towards their own seats. "You can talk to the nice lady later on." She smiled warmly—sincerely—at Dorella and they moved away.

You allowed them to live when they talked like that, Dorella thought. Even in the old days.

4

"Awful storm," Gene said. "Probably a little lake effect mixed in with it. I understand they get a lot of that upstate. You're not from around here, are you?"

"No."

"Where then?"

The snow was falling so heavily Dorella could barely see the edge of the road, and nothing of the countryside beyond. A fierce and building wind pushed curved walls of airborne snow around and drew long white veils from the drifts and mailboxes. Gusts rocked the bus with grabby fingers. She noticed they were traveling quite slowly now, almost a crawl.

"I'm from Europe, originally," she replied. "I haven't been back there in—in ages."

"Folks still there?"

"No. Not anymore, and not many then."

"Here then?"

"No."

"So where are you headed?"

"You ask a lot of questions."

"Oh, I'm sorry," Gene said in a ho-hum voice. "It's just that I want to know something about you. Who you're leaving behind, maybe, or who you've got waiting for you somewhere up ahead?" He paused a moment, appearing thoughtful. "You see, in the sales game you don't rely much on luck. You have to push all the time, make each bit count. Running into a woman so attractive, near my own age, alone, that's a good deal of luck no matter what. So I've got the urge to push, to watch out. For once, I guess I ought to just relax instead."

Humility? Dorella marveled, a sudden onset of manners, and still that stay-nice smile. He was being conservative, easy—sweet. She had agreed to let him sit beside her in the first place because something about him piqued her interest, and maybe partly, because she was bored or lonely or just in need of a diversion—all of these. As she looked at him now, and listened to him talk, and saw the way his eyes never left her, she began to wonder at her motives—and to see his more clearly.

Something about him was affecting her, adding ingredients to liven the mixture of her emotions, and that wasn't necessarily all bad.

"You're doing all right so far," she told him, turning strategically back to the storm. She caught a glimpse of a farmhouse on a knoll near the road. A car came sliding past, making its way around the bus, starting to fishtail. She watched as it spun full about and slid backwards away from the bus into the shallow ditch along the side of the road. The car's emergency flashers came on as the bus rolled by. Snow was already filling in the car's wild tracks.

"I'd like to make a lasting impression," Gene was saying. "Find something we have in common. If I can. For instance ... I'm single." He made it into a question.

"Well, then we both are."

"Honest?" He held up his left hand, scout's honor. Dorella nodded, grinned at his puerile manner. "Okay," Gene said. "Next we can maybe find out what your name is?"

"One of us already knows."

"Right." Gene averted his eyes. "You don't want to talk, that's fine. I understand."

"Oh, no," Dorella said, putting her hand on his arm. "I'm just not used to ... to this. Shining knights used to ride up on horseback. So simple then. Please, I'll be good."

He turned and she made a shy face, banking on the result. He brightened enormously and put his hand on top of hers. It made her feel good in a way she had not often known; a way, once or twice, talking with a foolish bunch at a small diner had made her feel, or spending an evening in a college library talking to Alison, yet with all of that, something more.

She let the feelings come to her, let them fill her while she looked into her would-be lover's clear, mysterious eyes. He was nothing but human she knew, but here, now, so far removed from the past and all its meanings, that hardly seemed to matter.

"You may call me—Alibrandi," Dorella said, sparing her own true name out of cautious habit, just for a while. The bird in the cage began to jump about, squawking, sounding, Dorella knew, like a very loud parrot to all those seated nearby.

"Lovely name," Gene Packerson said. "And your crow seems to like it, too."

5

Dorella furnished Gene with a vehement glare as she realized what he had said. He shrank back noticeably, startled by her expression. Then everything moved sideways.

People screamed and cursed and cried out to one another as the oncoming car slid in and out of their lane. The passengers on the right side of the bus spilled into the aisle while those on the left, Dorella and Gene among them, fought to keep righted in their seats.

Dorella saw the road ahead out her window, then the road behind as the bus came full circle and began to shake and rattle as waves of deep-felt shudders ran its length. A row of snowy-faced trees walked out of the blizzard and met the bus broadside, stopping it with a crushing jolt, buckling the right side of the bus in a half-dozen places and cracking most of the facing glass.

The engine had stalled. Cooling air blew softly from the vents throughout the bus, the only sound for several moments. The lights were dimly lit. People everywhere started to moan and move, climbing up from the floor and from between the seats, looking around, checking themselves over and wincing at injuries.

Four women, all wearing real-estate pins on their jackets, began helping people ahead of Dorella to gather carry-ons and purses and companions. An old woman near the front of the bus was holding the fingers of one hand, crying, bent slightly forward; a young girl who could have been her daughter was trying to make the woman attempt to wiggle them.

Dorella found herself to be quite all right. She checked the crow, who appeared no better or worse than ever. Then she remembered Gene Packerson—

No simple human being should have been able to see beyond the illusion she had placed upon the animal, unless they were possessed of magic themselves, or somehow enchanted by it. Which meant they might also be securely protected against it. Against her powers of sight.

Such as a person sent to look for her. A new agent, though this one was much improved from the first. She had felt something in him, had thought it to be personal attraction. But she felt very differently now, the way she had some thousand years ago as she had watched her sister die, the way she felt leaving the diner for the last time, or leaving the college. A pain no magic could touch. How had he done this to her, and why?

She had been completely deceived by someone whose intent had been only that, someone who placed no apparent value on the feelings of others and surely, that being true, had few feelings himself. Magic could not heal a wounded heart, but it did well to avenge one.

A pig, she imagined. Mr. Packerson would make a very fine pig, and with very little effort. She tried to recall the exact spell.

Packerson got up just then, mumbling something,

and went forward along the aisle. With that Dorella noticed that several passengers had gathered in the middle of the bus and were huddling over a small figure. She leaned out around the seat in front of her and saw that it was Tricia.

The girl's mother was bent over her where she lay crumpled on the floor. Blood soaked down her hair from just above the right side of her forehead, staining the shoulder of her blouse. Her mother had propped Tricia up with one arm. Tears filled her eyes as she called softly to her daughter, almost pleading. Tricia's eyes would not open. She made no sound.

A young woman on the other side of the huddle put a coat over Tricia's legs, then seemed to check the girl's breathing, nodding positively as she did. A young man in a denim jacket with the words "Grateful Dead" sewn on the back came to join the group, reporting that the driver was on the radio and help would be arriving just as soon as they could get through.

Everyone seemed to glance out the windows at once, reconfirming the strength of the blizzard. A chilling gust of snow-filled wind rocked the bus just then, adding testimony to their predicament. Rescue could take a very long time, Dorella thought. She looked back to the young girl, frail, tiny, so still; her mother shaking and sobbing as she held her close, terrified. Dorella sensed the girl was sinking, life ebbing away.

Even a hundred years ago she might not have concerned herself with the matter, would had been instead a mere spectator to such "trivial" human events, but she had come to see these boldly struggling beings who shared—indeed now ruled—this world as much more than amusements, the way her forefathers had. Since leaving the college she had thought about denying this, about trying to leave the pain of closeness and concern behind like everything

else. She saw now that it was a hopeless endeavor—
that such times had passed, or evolved . . .

She placed the animal carrier on the empty seat and
climbed into the aisle, stepping up close behind Gene
Packerson. He was standing there, quietly, watching
with his hands well into his pockets. Dorella tapped
him on the shoulder and he jumped.

"Could I see you for a moment?" she asked, gestur-
ing towards the presently deserted rear of the bus.

Packerson shrugged, nodded, then came along.
They stood near the lavatory door well away from the
others.

"Tell me who you are," she said firmly, locking eyes.
She tried again to look deep into his mind. There was
nothing there, other than a wan sort of pleasantness,
which was altogether too pat. There should at least be
some slight apprehension, she decided, some of the
fear she could sense in everyone else present. She
realized his eyes must be as a window that had been
colored over, like painted glass. He seemed able not
only to see through simple magic but also to be
shielded from it, seeing yet unseen.

"But I've told you, I'm Gene Packerson."

"No, I want to know who you really are, and why
you've come looking for me."

Gene spread his hands and made naughty puppy
eyes. "I really don't know what you mean."

"You had better come to it," Dorella muttered
coldly, "or no man beyond a barnyard will ever see
the likes of you again."

Packerson seemed to puzzle at this. "What's gotten
into you?" he pleaded, almost convincingly.

Dorella held her hands up before her, palms open,
facing the man patty-cake style. She summoned all the
strength she could muster, deciding it should be just
enough. "I trust you have led a fulfilling life, Gene
Packerson."

Something like recognition abruptly filled the other's eyes. "Wait!" Gene stole a glance towards the

rest of the passengers. The bus driver, a short, stout Hispanic-looking man of about forty had come back and joined everyone else. He was bent over Tricia, who seemed unimproved.

"You don't want to try any of that stuff right here, do you?" Gene asked. His face was a package of straight lines now, his stare suddenly piercing. "You don't know a thing about me. You have no way of knowing what I'm capable of. People could get hurt. So could you."

At this a thin smile traced Packerson's lips. Dorella sneered at him. "My questions go unanswered," she said. "Who are you? What do you want of me?"

"I am a student of one more powerful than you can comprehend, a sorcerer of many ages, a being whose greatness stems from the very essence of eternity to transcend time and fulfill—"

"My comprehension is most adequate, thank you. Does this gleaner of modesty have a name?"

"Oh, now, you wouldn't really expect me to betray *that* to you?" Gene said, as condescendingly as he could manage. "Though he will be happy to learn of yours." He seemed to gloat. "In fact, few things are more important to him."

"Not much of a mission."

Packerson looked more like a salesman again, shallow, a wide, cheeky grin. "It will do," he said.

"You're such a good little boy, aren't you?"

Packerson darkened. "I warn you again, I am not somebody you want to—"

"You are nothing at all."

"I have my means. Talents upon talents."

"Shapes and images, no doubt. Illusions."

"And more!" Packerson boasted. "I am well protected from the likes of—"

"May I suggest you shape yourself into something too small and insignificant for me to notice, and begone! Take to the road. Ply your talents on the weather if you can. I have no time for you and even less pity. I intend to go and help that little girl at this moment, which is your only true good fortune."

"The fact is, deep inside you're frightened of me." Packerson's face was becoming the window his eyes were not. Dorella crossed her arms tightly, angrily in front of her, considering him. "If I lay eyes upon you when I have finished," she said, "then so help me it will be your end!"

Packerson shrugged. "I have what I came for, while you, dear lady, have nothing—aside from a lot of empty wind. My information will be proof to him that I—"

"Proof of your great stupidity, and his," Dorella answered, cutting him off again. "Your master chooses fools. You found only a bus. You know only a name I have chosen to give you as a trinket. You know less of me than of yourself, and you, dear sir, are a most simple issue at that."

"You're just covering!" Packerson raged, drawing looks from some of the other passengers now. "You suspected nothing before. Your name is exactly as you said."

"My name is none of your business."

Packerson bit his lip hard. His eyes twitched as emotions percolated behind them. Once more Dorella followed his gaze to the other passengers. The driver was attempting to apply first aid to the child's head. Someone had gone out to the baggage compartments and retrieved a number of suitcases. People pawed through them, adding layers of clothing to themselves and each other. A few of the passengers contributed items to Tricia, while everyone else was beginning to huddle together in clumps against the invading cold from outside.

"You will tell me your true name," Packerson said, growling almost, "whatever it is. Otherwise some very unpleasant things will happen to these people you seem so concerned about. I don't happen to share that weakness. There is no lever for you to use against me. You might talk tough, but you have limits, or you wouldn't have been fooled by the deflecting spell I wear. The same spell that protects me from the simple tricks and illusions that are the stock and trade of witches such as you."

He watched Dorella for a moment, fingering his chin, then seemed to relax. "You can't be sure, can you? Use your powers here and even if you are successful these people might suffer for it. So I'll explain this just once more, and you pay attention, okay? Tell me the truth or I start trouble. Touch the girl before I get what I want and the same thing happens. It's called check and mate."

Dorella closed her eyes, covering them over with the tops of her fingers, then drew her hands slowly down over her face as she sighed. Strange, she thought, that she would somehow feel compelled to help the little girl and keep these others from harm, even at possible risk to herself, while Gene Packerson—a human being himself—felt no such obligation.

Dorella had been raised to find humanity an inferior species, compelling as a whole but insignificant as individuals. Over time, though, she had begun to wonder if it wasn't partly the other way around.

There were legends of alliances, sacred and not, of worship and fear, honor and glory. Stories remembered from childhood of her own ancestors, thought to be gods by the Mycenaeans, the Greeks, the Romans, sorcerers and witches by later men, stories of matings with humans, and periods when her kind had lived among mankind, for reasons she was perhaps only now beginning to understand.

"Very well," she said, turning away from the man. She went straight to her seat and put on her coat, then pulled the cloth covering over the animal carrier and gathered it up. She turned back briefly to Gene.

"Good-bye," she announced, then spun and headed for the front of the bus. Before anyone could say or do a thing she was down the steps and pushing the door shut behind her.

6

Dorella had already disappeared into the storm by the time Gene Packerson got himself bundled up. He pushed his way forward, ignoring the calls and broken questions of the other passengers.

"You're both going to freeze to death out there," the driver objected. "Please, stay on board."

"Only one of us is going to freeze," Gene told him and pressed on.

7

When she was well out of sight, Dorella worked her way off the road, stepping high, wading through knee-deep fluffy white snow. The wind tore at the exposed flesh on her face and hands and bit through her coat. Snow gathered wetly on her wind-whipped hair and melted through her stockings, while cold melt dribbled down her neck and new snow filled her shoes.

Beyond the ditch, she crossed a fence made of stubby wooden posts and strung with a single steel wire. The wire carried within it a small current of positively charged electricity, the white energy that was the basis of the "new" magic of man. Like lightning, she thought, which had always been a powerful weapon against negative forces, but remarkably ... domesticated.

Pausing, holding her free hand out, she spoke to the wire—a somewhat difficult spell which was largely improvised on the spot, changing the old to suit the "new." When she was done a sprout of energy flowed out of the fence and spread to surround her like a shimmering balloon on a string, shielding her, warming her.

Dorella moved away, trudging another twenty meters

further out into the drifted field, as far as she dared go from the easy comfort of the wire. Here she set the animal carrier down, pulled the cover back, and opened the metal door. The crow stood quite still, clinging to its low perch. It peered out nervously.

"Come," Dorella told it. "You must earn a bit of your keep." The crow ventured forth, and with an awkward bounce, landed on the melting ring of snow at Dorella's feet. She waited until its errant gaze finally rose up to meet her.

"Our friend enjoys the art of shaping," Dorella said out loud, "and claims a mastery of illusion. He should learn there are many levels of talent, many kinds of reality."

She put her hands on the crow, held it steady, then closed her eyes and spoke over the creature in a tongue unique to her kind. As she had been taught since becoming a young woman, she reached out from within herself, using her mind, making her heart the focal point, the talisman through which she worked.

She touched the universe bit by bit. First the snow and earth and wind around her, then all the world, then beyond, pushing out into the galaxy, searching again for the rare, incredibly powerful cracks in the mantle of creation, the seams and edges left over from when the universe was formed. They were not something seen but rather felt. Invisible lines, cosmic strings of intensely concentrated mass-energy, each a door to the thousand trillion degree fires of the birth of existence.

Throughout her life she had searched for these ideal sources of power, stretching herself out past the edges of the galaxy to discover them. A few of the cracks she knew were tiny, closed loops that could be quickly and safely tapped. Others, the longer open-ended strings were more perilous, and had been known to burn the very souls of those who dared to touch them.

Once, she had come upon a massive, open crack between the galaxies that seemed to run wider and farther than any she had ever imagined—a source of primal power she knew could easily kill even the most trained, most experienced user. The temptation to touch it had been nearly overwhelming—intoxicating at first, but it was a thing beyond all control. She had run away from it and never gone back.

The loops were the most prized, and her people had always sought to bank them for when they might be needed, to carefully establish paths that would make this possible. Dorella now followed her own special path to a specially chosen, favorite loop, one used a very long time ago, in a very different battle. Slowly, cautiously, she focused on the string and began to access its violent energies, skillfully drawing them to her. Nearly enough then, she thought, more than enough now.

Dorella pushed these things away from her conscious mind and journeyed back to the tiny spot on earth where she was anchored. With the life energy of the stars safely contained at her center she opened her eyes on the world.

The crow shook, then was still. It looked up at her with faintly luminescent eyes as she told it what it must do. Solemnly, the bird nodded.

Dorella stood up, releasing the crow, and it took to the air with rustling flaps of its wings, cawing into the icy wind. Black disappearing into endless white, a voice fading over the fields.

Soon a small object that was Gene Packerson appeared on the road and turned. She calmly watched his steady approach. He crossed the fence and stopped some eighteen meters from her, his dark coat blowing about his knees, black leather gloves covering his hands. His hat was tipped towards the gusting winds, and snow clung to that side of him so that he looked much like a giant, oblong pastry.

"Give up your tiny secret," he called out to her, "or die out here and keep it forever." He tipped his head curiously to one side, apparently just noticing the lack of snowfall in Dorella's immediate vicinity, the grass at her feet.

"I hold many secrets," she replied. "But all of mine are truths, not lies. I see both these things in you and need no tricks to tell them apart."

"You are an old woman who doesn't know shit!"

"Oh please, my good fool, I knew you would follow me off the bus. I know that one sent to gather information is supposed to return, not perish with it. I know that whatever things your master has taught you, he did not intend for you to use them towards your own ruin.

"You are a child with an odd toy, and you have come to believe the toy is real. Worse, you choose to believe your own life is somehow more important than others."

"You are the only one who's going to perish!" Gene roared, his face bright red—from the cold or from anger Dorella couldn't be sure. "I see through all illusion, defy any workings you might conjure. I cannot be harmed by anything of yours or touched by your poisoned thoughts. All this was proven by your inability to see. My master has taught me well, prepared me well, armed me well. I see everything, and fear nothing."

"Then you had best watch closely. For my age I move very fast."

"But in fact I have something for *you* to watch. One final lesson."

Packerson moved his arms wildly over his head and his form began to shift, growing larger, longer, wide at the bottom and pointed towards the top. Finally he took on the shape of an overly large polar bear, dull-white and frothing.

The bear stood up on its hind legs, treading air with its massive paws, its snarling face towering nearly four meters above the snowy field. With a resonant roar the beast started for Dorella, taking great swaying strides, reaching out in earnest.

A snow bear should have a suitable playmate,

Dorella thought. She reached out and traced a simple figure in the snow. The figure darkened noticeably, then sat up, a featureless cookie cutout made in the shape of a man. It stood up and marched forward, growing larger with every step the way a rolling snowball gathers size down a hill.

When they met, the snowman stood a full head taller than its furry opponent. It heaved itself at the bear, staggering the animal as it impacted. In seconds the bear had dismantled the creature and turned it into a lumpy, snowy pile, which it then stepped over. Now the bear was almost close enough to lunge.

From within the beast, Packerson's voice called out to Dorella, cackling, almost shrill, mad with self-glorification. "Nothing before me can defeat me. Not you, not your pathetic snow-things. Your chance is lost. Your head will be my gift to Galidar!"

Dorella's breath became a solid thing in her lungs as the name slipped from Packerson's rabid lips. Something deep within her churned, became heavy as iron. In her mind she saw a sudden vision of the terrible past, a clear, vivid recollection of all that was Galidar, and the battle she had won only after Alibrandi had lost—a fight to the death against one more powerful than any in this world.

A great dark shadow moved over the snow, sweeping off towards the road. Dorella paid it almost no mind. The Packerson beast seemed too engrossed in its blossoming triumph to look. Or was he smart enough to guess that to turn away, even for an instant, might spell disaster for him?

Dorella wondered how it could be true. How might Galidar still exist? With her own eyes, she had looked upon his charred remains scattered about the countryside. If something of him had survived, where had he been for all these hundreds of years?

A coincidence, she mused. Or could some modern, accomplished mortal apprentice have taken his name for reasons of grandeur? They were the only answers that made any sense.

The bear reared, paws held apart like waiting cymbals in an orchestra. Saliva ran from its tongue and lips as deep growls boiled somewhere inside.

"My snowman was nothing more than a diversion," Dorella said. "You should be more concerned with what's behind you."

"You call me a fool," Packerson bellowed, "but you won't make one of me! I know your tricks." He stared steadfastly at her.

Dorella shook her head. "Tell that to the dragon."

The big shadow fell over them again. Panic came to replace the animal ferocity in the bear's eyes. Packerson's eyes. He was desperate to turn, stricken by the knowledge that to do so was akin to suicide. Not until he felt the dragon's hot breath did he succumb and glance over his shoulder—in time to see a yellow-blue torrent of fire pour down from the dragon's gaping jaws, fanned still hotter by great, slow flaps of the demon-lizard's massive wings—too late to move.

The dragon was ten meters from the tip of its tail to the top of its narrow, bony head, with a wingspan nearly twice its length. Packerson glared up into the flames, raising his arms in defiance, convinced, Dorella was sure, that his own powers and shielding spells would protect him from this latest "trick" as it had the others. Never knowing, until he began to disintegrate in the ceaseless conflagration, that the dragon was real.

The attack ended quickly. The dragon rose back up into the snow-filled air, looking down to Dorella for approval with molten eyes. In the spot where Packerson had stood there was only a yawning hollow melted in the snow. Flat, burnt field grasses smoldered on the thawed and steaming ground.

Dorella glanced up momentarily at the dragon, then spoke the completing phrase. She reached down and picked up the little animal carrier. From the sky a wiry black crow rustled down, slowing as it drew near, and found its way through the door and back to its perch.

Dorella picked up the carrier, pulled the cover over it again. There was a weakness, old and pervading, already passing from her as she gathered herself. A good feeling, really. Exercise could do that for you, in moderation.

She set off through the snow, releasing the fence of its duties as she crossed over it. She was rapidly impressed by the reality of the cold and the cutting wind as the blizzard found her again.

Drawing her collar tight to her neck she hurried back to the comfort of the bus.

8

Though the bleeding had stopped, Tricia was still unconscious. The driver had done a good job of helping Tricia's mother bandage her wound and they had tucked plenty of clothing around her. They sat now, faces long, nothing else to do. The remaining passengers were balled up in the seats and covered with spare clothing. The bus still provided shelter from the storm, but the temperature inside had dropped almost to match that of the air outside. The driver, full of questions, stopped Dorella as she came aboard.

Yes, she told him. I'm okay. No, I haven't seen the gentleman who was sitting with me earlier. No, I didn't know he left the bus. No, I don't actually know him at all, he had just introduced himself. Yes, I was upset, a little crazy, I needed a way to calm myself so I thought to walk to a nearby farm or—I don't know. Yes, it was foolish. Yes, I hope he finds his way back, too.

The driver explained that the State Police knew where the bus was and that help was coming. They were sending an emergency rescue truck and a local bus behind a county plow. The wait should be a short one.

Dorella excused herself and went to kneel beside Tricia's mother, who was still hovering over her daughter like a protective umbrella.

"I wish she would show some sign," she told Dorella. Her voice was thin and shaky. Her eyes red. The sleeves of her jacket were wet from using them to wipe her cheeks. "It's her breathing," she went on. "You know, so shallow. They say not to let people fall asleep after a head injury like . . . I mean, don't they? But she—she had already—"

The words disappeared. Dorella took hold of the woman's hand. This close she could sense the girl's mind, the beating of her heart. Her life would not wait for the rescue truck.

"Let me try something," Dorella said. "Tricia seemed so fond of my . . . cockatoo. Maybe, if she heard its voice, that might help bring her around. Please."

She looked at Dorella, blank eyes, windows to the pain inside. She nodded numbly and inched backward on her knees, letting Dorella come close with the animal carrier. Dorella tapped affectionately on the cage, mostly for show, then signaled the bird with only a look. It took a breath, bobbed its head, and began to caw at nearly painful volume. A very loud parrot, Dorella thought.

The bus driver sat nearby, looking on, wearing an expression heavy with extra questions. He managed to say nothing at all.

Passengers cupped their ears and looked at each other in amused disbelief as the bird went on. Dorella used the moment to touch the girl's head and find the center of her mind, her essence. She pulled Tricia to her, taking her deep within, joining with her in the very deepest sense, then sailed outward across the plane of the galaxy, retracing her path. Touching the loop again. It took only seconds. Such things had always been that way.

Dorella stood, picking up the cage, quieting the bird. "Well, I hoped she would hear. Perhaps we have helped. She sounds like she's breathing a little stronger."

"Thank you," the woman said, nodding, moving in again. "It's rare to find someone so willing to offer friendship, someone so thoughtful. Everyone . . ." She paused, looked off. "She's all that matters to me in the world you know, since her father—"

She fell into tears again. Dorella tried to comfort her.

"I'm fine," she said, looking back to her daughter. "I'm sorry."

Dorella moved quietly away. She found a seat and settled in, placing the bird beside her. She thought of friends, rare indeed, of the thing she and people, these people and others, seemed to have most in common . . . loneliness. She thought of the times, for a few brief and extraordinary moments, when they had been each other's relief. She thought of her sister, and then of Alison—

I could send a letter some time, she reminded herself. To Alison. A short note on a postcard. Just to make her feel better. After all, who would notice a thing like that? Maybe somewhere, one day soon . . .

But even that would have to wait, at least for a while. Until she could learn the truth about Gene Packerson's most interesting slip of the tongue. Until it was—safe.

Dorella's thoughts were interrupted by a sudden scream. Tricia's mother was holding the girl's body in both arms, hugging her to her breast. The child's eyes were open now, just focusing, blinking to see by the lights which glowed from the power in the bus's big batteries. She coughed once, swallowed. "What's wrong?" she asked thinly, reaching up to touch the bandages on her head.

Her mother rocked on her haunches, cradling the girl's body, sobbing, unable just then to say a word.

Tricia began to look around, her eyes searching the interior of the bus.

"Where is she?" Tricia asked. The driver stood by her now, leaning over. "Where is who?"

"The lady. With the pretty bird. I was just—with her, somewhere, walking in the darkness—and we found stars."

Dorella sat forward in her seat, grinning, in spite of herself. "At least she still has an imagination," she said.

The distant sparkle of approaching emergency lights through fogged safety glass could be seen now to the east. The howling of the winds outside seemed to quiet just a little. People began to talk.

Dorella leaned back to rest, watching her steamy breath rise into the cold air, using no spell at all, feeling perfectly warm.

Part Four:
DEMON RIGHTS

1

Galidar peers down at the splinters of crystal on the table—eyes! he thinks, ecstatic—*eyes!* He smiles, feeling lips, tongue, jaw, feeling physical being for the first time in—

He might never know how long. A very long, long time.

He moves the eyes. Ears call his attention to the side. A very young human male is standing, leaned up against a wall only a few feet away, hands clutched half over his face, a screaming face. *He has been witness, then, to the ascension and bloom of my essence*, Galidar presumes, *to my possession of this body*. Galidar reaches into the energies of the old body he now holds. He fumbles with the memories of an ancient and simple spell intended to remove small amounts of air. This kills the young man.

Galidar moves about, wobbling, tipping, righting

himself, testing the worn yet wonderfully functional systems of the old body, examining every incredible detail of the room. He makes his way to a window and basks in the warm sunlight coming through it, too hot, almost. Rested, he moves back across the room to the old man's small corner desk and sits in the cloth and metal chair, finding the wheels a momentary challenge, overcoming it.

The immense pleasure of new life has begun to ebb. Thoughts of "now" are slowly replaced by contemplations of "later." His mind fills again with impressions of anger and rage and revenge. Yet there is time, he thinks, time for this, time for many things—real *time*.

With a part of his mind that he has always known a special ability to control, to utilize, he enlarges his sphere of consciousness, seeking the limits of this existence, the boundaries of others. He finds the edges of reality easily but quickly learns that the barrier between here and "there," between the positive universe and the negative one, is a much more formidable thing than it was in past times. Few doorways exist; in fact, he finds that he can squeeze through only by forcing his way into the smallest gaps, pushing, pressing.

There could not be many left, he thinks, who draw strength from the nether world, for if there were, the fabric between places would not have repaired the many breaches and paths that constant use by the disciples of darkness had created. Things, he decides, have truly changed.

But he has real *time* now to learn of this, of everything there is to know. Time to stretch and beat and work away at the thick walls between realities. Time to rebuild, to establish new links, to open doors. Time, after that, to change the world.

He has much to do. He begins.

2

The bus station was in the worst part of town. Men without eyes crouched in lightless corners. A woman with a glazed, mottled face and carrying a huge plastic trash bag sat on an outdoor bench, somehow oblivious to the growing cold of the approaching evening. Spent diesel fumes hung thickly in the still air of the open bus garage as Dorella left the lobby, taking the back way out into the streets.

This was the kind of place she had been looking for. It was time, she thought, to get back to living among the less fortunate, often forgotten people of the land. Places much easier to hide in, places that lacked the "community" of the better neighborhoods—and colleges. She had known the finest lodgings and fare that this world had to offer, but for now, perhaps, these streets might serve her better.

The buildings were old, six or more stories, decorative aged brick facing on most of them, a few with hand-worked concrete swirls and knobs along the high false roof lines. Time had crumbled all but the remnants of most of that workmanship.

Art was not strictly a human thing, of course. Her own kind had produced its share of thespians, painters and musicians, but some humans had a flair for these things that was rare and magnificent, or perhaps supernatural—true magic. The odd factor was the lack of value most of mankind seemed to place on some of its very finest works. Human art had never been closely associated with competitiveness as was the case with her own people, yet certain regards were so often absent. For all her years and learning, all her attempts at open-mindedness, Dorella was still confounded by the human race: curiously related, randomly indifferent. Her mother had been right. No one would ever fully understand them, especially themselves.

Cars rolled by on the narrow street behind the bus station, creeping to get around a row of parked busses, windows put up tight. Dorella waited for a gap, lugging her bags in one hand, the cage containing the crow in the other, then tried to wade between them.

She could hear music from inside some of the vehicles, booming bass tones, glaring highs. One car slowed, the man inside apparently investigating her for some unimagined reason. She looked up, standing still in the street, returning the favor. At first it did not occur to her that she was simply in his way until he rolled his window down, leaned out, and shouted, "Hey, lady, make a move."

"A move?" she replied, more than a little suspicious of his meaning.

"Shit or get off the pot!" he roared.

She tried to fathom the comment. He rolled his window back up, blew his horn and edged the car forward, coming within inches of her. She suddenly understood the conversation and hurried out of his path.

Distant laughter resounded from somewhere ahead. A young Oriental boy approached. He was carrying something wrapped in rags tied to the back of his bicycle and gripped a section of a two-by-four across his handlebars. He drew near, then swerved and faded around the corner ahead of the car.

A fortunate circumstance for them both, she thought. She straightened her coat unnecessarily and moved along.

The corner was all parking lot. A car at the near edge of the lot's tarmac sat nose down on its rotors, front wheels missing altogether. The sun had vanished behind the tall buildings nearer the city's center. An aged business district, she thought. But beyond that, in some direction or another, she could find a place to stay. For a little while. There was nothing here.

She looked left as she passed the car lot. There was a smallish, pointy-faced man in a matted gray coat

peeking at her from inside the little ticket booth, his
face cloudy behind the smudged glass. He smiled at
her, a smudged smile, and she smiled back out of
hand. He raised two fingers, wiggled them, a naughty
beckon. She walked on.

Resurfaced buildings gleamed white and brown on
the corners at a main thoroughfare. Traffic was thicker
here. She walked past a very old and crumbling brick
building, first floor windows boarded, broken glass
along the sidewalk, cardboard windows in spots going
up eight floors. Fine mortar fragments bordered the
sidewalk. Half a Frisbee stuck out of the grate of a
rain gutter. People nowhere, she noted.

That was when she heard the baby scream.

3

Three or four floors up, she guessed, though the
sound echoed deceptively in the canyon of the street.
Then another voice was added, a woman's terrorized
shrieks, the word "no" ringing clearly several times.
An older boy could be heard now between the woman's gasps, his small voice heavy with fear, begging
that the woman be left alone. Suddenly, he fell completely silent, as if someone had thrown a switch. The
infant child screamed on, the sound growing thin and
hoarse. The woman began to choke on her own
hysteria.

Dorella passed a doorway, one entrance to the
building. She felt compelled to turn, to go inside and
upstairs and see what was happening, and that didn't
make any sense at all. Perhaps she could send the
crow . . .

Just listen to yourself! she thought. *None of your
business,* she thought. This was not Alison or some
neighbor or even a person she had simply sat close to
on a bus; how far must one take these things? Where,
once you'd begun to involve yourself in the affairs of
humanity, did you draw the line?

She reasoned this might be a fine place to start. After all, one simply could not bother with every passing event, every conversation overheard at any distance. *This is not a world of magic anymore,* she reminded herself. So her own best sort of intervention was likely not appropriate, and people had always created more problems for themselves than the world and all its magic could ever foster or affect. It really *wasn't* any of her business. . . .

She tried to walk on, past the doorway. But the woman began a different scream now that rang not of distress but deep, physical pain. She howled, invoking the names of deities, then her voice rose to a shrill note that pierced the air and sent a strange, unaccustomed chill down Dorella's spine. Dorella observed that on some deep-rooted level she truly felt for the woman, for the children with her, in a way that had heretofore always been reserved for those of her own blood.

The stirrings within her nagged as she tried to push on, chafing inexorably like poorly fitted clothing. She began to reassess the dangers inherent in her newfound closeness to these creatures, to consider the possibility that she might lose all objectivity, that she would never be able to extract herself—that there would be times like these.

Her apprehensions churned in her mind like a volatile broth. The entire issue was so unreasonable.

She decided it was not unreasonable, on the other hand, simply to have a look: a brief, less distant moment of erudite observation . . .

She winced in consternation, shook her head. *There is definitely something the matter with you,* one half of her mind lamented—*humor the woman,* the other half—

She had managed not to argue with herself for fifteen hundred years: a perfect record utterly ruined. With a shrug she spun around and went back towards the building's entrance.

The hall was lit dimly by a handful of ceiling fix-
tures. Stairs rose at either end. A bicycle leaned
against the wall to her left, chained where the plaster
had been broken away to expose a wall stud. She went
past it to the end of the hall, still questioning her
motives, ascending the stairs anyway.

On the fourth floor she moved towards the sound
of the woman screaming, the baby crying. Abruptly
the woman fell silent as the boy had, ending with a
sickened whine that seemed to come from the last
breath in her lungs. There was no other sound from
anywhere else on the floor, but doors, cracked barely
open, drew closed in a mechanical wave as she passed
them by. The baby still cried. Dorella found the room
and stood staring at the closed door, considering.

She tried to concentrate on the persons inside and
was immediately surprised. There were five entities
present in the room, but only four of them were
human.

4

Two emotions, surprise at discovering a creature of
the ages and trepidation over its nature, swept her
mind all at once.

If this thing was what its bitter aura suggested—

Reason enough, in any case, to warrant a closer
look. She uttered a phrase and the door creaked open
wide.

A smallish man of about thirty, wearing a stained,
light blue T-shirt, black jeans and brown, unlaced
work boots stood near the window leaning over a crib.
Dorella could see the baby through the crib's side-
bars, no more than a few months old, its face a deep
purple-red from incessant screaming. The man held

a bloody, broken section of broom stick in his right hand.

Briefly Dorella noted the blood-covered bodies of a woman and a young boy, both lying on the floor in front of the sofa along the right side of the room. She sensed that life remained within them, though weakly.

The small man raised the stick above the child. Dorella spoke, not to the man but to the dark creature she sensed dwelling within him, the Dire.

They turned and glared, four eyes upon her, two looking, two seeing. The Dire laughed from inside the man, silent to the world, loud and grating in Dorella's ears. Evil, odious, often murderous things, she recalled, negatively aligned; they had stalked the earth for countless ages in search of self-serving, self-indulgent mischief; minor spectral demons that did not belong to this world nor strictly to the negative universe, but existed in between them, an errant abomination of creation. Though fair numbers of them once roamed the world, drawing power from the nether world during a time when the barrier between dimensions was less substantial, Dorella had not come upon one in several decades.

A despicable thing, she knew, fighting the inevitable slow attrition of destiny. Eventually, she had thought, the universe would see fit to rid all creation of such beings, winnowing them out as it seemed to have done with her own race, leaving the earth solely in the grasp of the elemental physics that spawned it. For now, it seemed, they both survived.

"Enough," she told it flatly. "Go!"

The Dire eyed her carefully. She waited while it sized her up, doing its best to determine the depths of her powers, and thereby its chances. Having no true biological presence, Dires were extremely difficult to dispose of, and alas, they knew it.

"Why do you interfere?" it asked, which was, Dorella knew, a reasonable question. Not for the first time she found herself wondering the same thing. She fought the urge to enlist the Dire in a debate over the issue—Dires having a similar perspective on creation—but she decided she was not that desperate. Dires had no redemptive qualities anyone had ever discovered, and a notoriously malicious intellect. Still, Dires seldom commanded the power which this one seemed to.

"Be content to understand that I do," Dorella said, "and wise enough to honor my request. I—" The thought caught in her throat a moment. What did she want of this creature? What did she intend to do?

"I do not wish combat with you," she said.

She sensed the creature understood her meaning, that it had tasted the aura and essence of her thoughts as she had tasted its—that they were traveling, for a limited stretch, on the same road.

Reason might then be her ally. Dires, of course, knew little of reason. That didn't mean they could not learn.

"You have great abilities," the Dire told her, using the man's mouth, grinning with his cheeks. "I have no wish to test them. But I object to this harassment! Do I come upon you unexpectedly and threaten you for your spell-working?"

"No," Dorella conceded.

"Do I stand in judgment of you? I do not!" The Dire answered for itself. "From you I desire only to be left alone, a simple courtesy which has been afforded me for centuries, and which has been returned."

"I know all of that," Dorella tried to explain, at odds with the truth of the matter. "But I must insist."

The demon cackled, a sound that made the man's throat twist audibly, then flew out of the human body it occupied, straight at Dorella.

She had half-expected such a move, and had already begun assembling a spell that would rebound the Dire should it attempt to gain entry. She recited the last phrase just as the creature reached her, felt the cold injected venom of its timeless rancor arc violently in her body's cells and nearly penetrate her mind as the spell took. The crow jumped wildly in the cage, nearly pulling Dorella off balance. Nearly.

The Dire hovered in mid-air, a mixture of darkness and bluish light that formed no true body or appendages, deep, empty eyes with no face around them. The man in the dirty T-shirt had collapsed on the floor, unconscious. The Dire spoke to her again now, but directly.

"You meddle where you have no right!" it said, its acrid, piping voice howling in her mind. "You make enemies you would do well to mollify. I have friends!"

"You have fewer friends than you think, as do I, vile one. There are many places to go in this world, many more lives to ruin. Go and discover them. Leave this house."

"What are these people to you?" the Dire demanded once more—pleaded almost, in a tone that smacked of disbelief.

"They are nearby, I suppose," Dorella answered, drooping her shoulders, growing quickly tired now from too much effort and too much analyzing. The Dire drifted imprecisely before her. She looked to her inner self, mustering her resolve, drawing positive life energy reserves from her body and spirit, forming a single discharge, then slapped the sinuous beast with it. Hard.

The Dire screeched in shocked agony, its form crackling like sparklers in the dimness of the room. It fled into the hall, invisible to the people whose heads were poked out of doorways, oblivious to Dorella as she looked after it, her eyes following until it disappeared down the stairs. She had hardly scratched it, of course—Dires were notorious whiners—but the family of this house would never see it again. They wouldn't know to read the papers, to look for telltale signs in order to learn what became of it.

She went to the boy first, touching his injuries, several on the head, a broken collar bone, a ruptured kidney in back. She repaired all that with a few straightforward efforts. The woman was worse off. She had bone-deep bruises along both her arms and legs, her spine was fractured halfway up, her face and skull had fared as badly.

Dorella wondered what had kept the woman up and conscious long enough to sustain so many injuries. Protecting the children with her own body? Foolish against such a clearly hopeless onslaught. Better to play dead. But the woman had disregarded her own safety in order to protect those closest to her, the way Alison . . .

So odd these creatures, Dorella declared to herself. So self-centered at times, yet so utterly opposite at others. It must always have been so, but she had never been so acutely aware of it. Or so impressed by it. What manner of beings? she wondered yet again. Pausing, nearing the end of her strength, she healed the woman as best she could.

The man moved on the floor, coming to, looking at her. She could find his real identity now as she looked into his eyes. He was not a very loving person, she saw, not very bright. In fact he lacked many things, but he was no murderer. She turned, gathering her bags and her crow, and left the room before he got to his feet. The baby's sobs were already trailing off as she reached the stairs.

5

There was a sign to do with free meals. It was a Christian place from the religious symbols prominently displayed everywhere. That seemed to suit Dorella well enough. It was an unlikely place to take a meal, not what her accumulated wealth might recommend, but she valued its obscurity.

Inside she found rows of tables in a single great room. People, mostly men, a few women, were lined up receiving plates already filled from workers behind a chrome and glass counter. They sat and ate, most of them silently, keeping tightly to themselves. As she looked individuals over more carefully, she saw that they were all diminished in some sense, even for human beings. They shone dimly against the backdrop of the universe, barely existing, barely thinking: the coldest embers at the far edges of the human fire.

She fell in line, pushing the bird carrier and her bags ahead of her on the floor, collecting her plate— peas, white rice and spiraled pasta in a meaty tomato sauce. She found her way to the end of the nearest table and sat down.

She tried to talk to people: the older, stick-thin man sitting next to her, wearing an expired suit coat and knee-torn corduroy slacks, who could not seem to stop shaking; the almost fat woman across the table from her, round cheeks with nearly as many whiskers as the old man, wearing a tattered multitude of sweaters. Dorella learned the old man had no money and nothing to drink, and that he wasn't awfully interested in getting ahold of money. The woman seemed quite sober but further away, detached from the world as it existed, a visualizer of something that was less substantial, but was for her, it seemed, more palatable.

She finished the meal and learned that downstairs there were beds to be had simply for the asking, so Dorella asked. The basement was dry and warm. The beds were too soft, but irresistible and quietly convenient. One night, she thought, then she would find a more suitable place to stay.

In the morning she found herself almost alone. She asked one of the workers, a very young girl with already-old wrinkles, where she might find a more permanent place to stay. The girl tipped her head, peeking through the cover of the animal carrier as she did, eyeing the crow with demure amusement, and directed her to what sounded like a suitable boarding house on Route 12. Dorella walked out into the cold morning sun, looking for any remembered faces of the night before, finding none. Then she found one after all.

Across the street the day revealed a renovated three-story firehouse. People stood in double lines at the main doors. Dorella recognized the woman holding the baby near the back of the lines. She looked much better than she had the day before, healing nicely.

Dorella went back inside and asked the girl about the lines. It was a government food program, she learned, limited handouts of white rice, American cheese and boxes of non-fat powdered milk. "You have to sign up," the girl explained, but it was no trouble compared to the rewards. Dorella nodded and left. She had no need of further handouts but she was drawn to the mother and child, vaguely, curiously. The woman wasn't like Alison or the people she'd known in the little coffee shop, or like the little girl and her mother on the bus, gone on to Philadelphia now. They had bright, hopeful lives comparatively—clearer eyes, sharper dreams. Yet for all her failings, she thought, the woman was indelibly courageous, unexpectedly resilient.

Dorella saw an odd appeal in the apparent ability of these people to endure their despondency, to make the best of the worst, or to make of it at least something.

It occurred to her that she must be more equitable in her consideration of people, must make herself aware of the entire spectrum.

She crossed the street and "joined" the line behind the young mother and her child, standing quietly at first, setting her bags down, holding the covered crow, then began with something about the weather. The woman's name was Elizabeth; the baby, named after its father, was called Joel. Joel senior was a diesel mechanic at a truck stop off the interstate exit north of the city. They'd met at the grocery on McCallin and discovered they lived in the same neighborhood—

which neither of them saw as a plus. Elizabeth had worked in fast-food places when she was younger, then had her first child, the boy, then had seen the boy's father go to another woman. You can't make it without a man, she explained, not with kids.

She and Joel hadn't even discussed marriage, since that would mean lost social benefits. She didn't mention the attack of the day before, either. Dorella felt compelled to bring the subject up and offer some explanation that might help the woman cope—surely there were hard, unanswered questions in her mind, in the man's mind. But she sensed they would struggle through it, would move on.

A dark-skinned girl no more than nineteen with dark somber eyes and long, pulled-back hair joined the line behind them. In her arms, cuddled in bright green blankets, she held a baby that looked about the same age as Joel. Elizabeth seemed to know her. They struck up a conversation immediately while the babies cooed at one another. The younger girl asked about Elizabeth's new friend, which prompted Dorella to introduce herself properly to both of them, adding what compliments she could: the girl had genuine beauty in her finely carved features, fortitude in her expression.

Dorella listened contentedly, prodding when the conversation lagged, missing some of the meaning but enjoying the tapestry of the women's slang nonetheless.

A loud cracking noise, once, then again, interrupted their talk. A third crack was followed by the collapse of a man in line no more than a meter ahead of Dorella, and she recognized the sounds as gunshots.

Others in line had apparently reached the same conclusion as they began dropping to the ground or running in any direction. Dorella heard two more shots, saw an old woman who was dragging a two-wheeled cart stagger and gasp, then tumble to the sidewalk.

Then Dorella turned as she heard the young girl behind her scream, and found her clutching at her tiny baby, red blood already beginning to stain the pretty green blankets. Dorella looked up now, to the top of the vacant office building next door to the fire-house. There was a figure there, a huge man even at a glance, perched on the edge of the roof, holding a rifle in his hands. And as she looked she saw something—*tasted* something—that was immediately, unpleasantly familiar. She blocked everything from her mind in order to concentrate on the thoughts that were the true engine of this man. The images she encountered were bitingly clear.

The Dire within the man radiated with furious, violent rage. No, she saw then, as she strained to comprehend the shades of the Dire's glowing emanations, it was *frustrated* rage. Dorella realized she had made a dreadful error.

She could not help feeling that all this was, at least in part, her responsibility. She had spared the Dire, thinking of the demon's rights, thinking it the most correct resolution at the time, thinking that saving little Joel was *her* right, and that her own judgment was clear enough and righteous enough. . . .

She shook off the muddle that filled her mind and focused on the gunman again. The past could not be changed. She was left with the decision to uphold the traditions of her own near-vanished race, or to enter on the side of the race that was taking control of the world with the magic of marvelous technologies. She had been walking a precarious line these last few decades, attempting to keep an equilibrium between the "old" and the "new," and had managed until now to ignore occasions where her attempts failed, where the edges would not meet.

But here was a stark division. Even now, with people dying all around her, it was hard to break with the past, as it had always been. As it always would be, she knew.

She looked again at the young mother behind her, the bleeding baby in her arms. "Shit or get off the pot," she thought. She focused on the Dire once more.

Shit!

She put the crow's cage down, then pulled the door and set it free. The bird scurried aloft immediately, swatting cold air with its big wings, finding purchase, rising towards the office building's roof. It flew into the gunman's face, interrupting him, keeping close enough to prevent him from using the rifle to rid himself of the pest, diving in and out of multiple power lines that ran past the building and split at a double-T pole only meters away.

Dorella took the moment to consider her alternatives. She could not destroy the Dire with her own, natural energies; and here, in a street filled with screaming people and deadly gunfire, she had little hope of taking the time to reach into the heavens and draw from the energies there.

A fog perhaps, she thought, to hide the people and the street from the eye of the—

But that would only stall the inevitable. Again.

She watched the crow duck behind one of the large, cylindrical transformers on the utility pole as the gunman drew down on it. The bullet tore a thick strip of wood from the top of one of the T-bars. The crow swept past the gunman's right side, flipping to brake, then dove from behind again. Fierce threats followed from the big man's mouth as it vanished below the roof line. Dorella smiled at her sudden thought.

Dires were, more than anything else, an earth-bound fusion of negative energy that traced its origins to the darkest depths of the nether world. They were utterly repelled by—

She made her way from the street and hurried around the side of the building. Now, out of sight, she concentrated on the air directly above her, conjuring an image, displaying it on molecules of atmosphere in a shifting arc just beside the roof—a bridge of imagery between the building and the T-bar of the utility pole.

Using as much of her energy as she dared, saving just enough, she lifted herself up through the illusion, almost to the top of the pole, and hovered there, seemingly suspended just ahead of the double T's. She enlarged the image slightly, letting it widen until it not only hid the space beneath her feet, but also concealed her almost completely from the crowd.

Next she called the crow away. The bird seemed only too happy to comply, which left the gunman to glower down at the street once more, taking aim. Dorella called out, again not to the man, but to the Dire within.

She felt the creature's frosted glare as it realized the source of the intrusion. Sensed its bemusement as it observed her precarious stance. "Not again!" the Dire called, using the man's voice, then in her head, using its own.

The rifle came up, sights drawing down on Dorella's floating form, but the man's finger did not move. The Dire was sorting things out, Dorella guessed, remembering who and what it was dealing with, accepting begrudgingly that bullets would likely be less than effective.

"Again," Dorella said, "and always. You will never be rid of me, offensive one. I will dog you wherever you go."

"Why! Why! Why!" the Dire screamed at her. "What possible reason lies behind this insane behavior?"

She considered that a moment. "I don't like you," she said.

The Dire howled in fitful outrage. The body of the big man began to jerk uncontrollably, then fell back onto the roof. The Dire was free again, glowing from the pyre of its rancor, plainly summoning all its powers for a full assault.

Dorella remained motionless as the Dire pounced. Then she stepped back, off the rounded top of the transformer, onto the wooden arm of the utility pole, and let the illusion come to her.

The Dire, committed now, made full contact with the transformer's ringed terminals—white, positive current shorting the negative presence of the raging creature. Nearly 80,000 volts leaped from the lines into the shorted circuit that was the Dire, creating a single deafening crack like a thousand gunshots. Smoke drifted lightly above the transformer now. With all her senses Dorella knew there was nothing else there.

In the street below people were tending to themselves, no doubt curious as to what had happened with the man on the roof, why he had suddenly fallen back while shouting at the phone pole, what the sudden crack had been. The authorities would test him, recommend him for extended psychiatric treatment. Having been possessed by a Dire, he would need it.

A squad of ambulances had gathered below. Dorella watched the young dark-eyed girl getting into one of them with her baby. There was no aid she could render, Dorella knew. People in white and red uniforms carried filled stretchers into the others. Dorella slowly let herself down from the pole, letting the illusion fade, and began to walk. A crow fluttered overhead.

It was a curious thing really, to look down so, to place one's self so high up: a forbidding notion. Best forgotten, perhaps, and guarded against. Or best remembered. . . .

Then her mind came around, racing, suddenly filled with a gathering of scattered thoughts and memories that seemed to be falling into place all at once. Such a powerful Dire, she thought again. *Too* powerful. It should not have been able to so completely control its victims. Not now. Not with—

And the demon, she thought then, recalling her disbelief when Daniel had somehow summoned Arynome, a feat that should have been impossible for all but the greatest mortal sorcerers. Unless . . .

Unless the barrier between this world and the nether region had been diminished in some way. Unless someone had once again opened a path and was drawing . . .

She thought suddenly of Packerson, of the transformed intruder who had come before him. Packerson had spoken a name . . . Galidar.

But she could hardly accept that explanation, anymore than she could accept the endless wars he and his sort had spawned or the world they had left behind, anymore than she could accept her temporary lack of place in the world or her sister's seemingly immutable fate.

She would find another answer, because she knew it must be so. There must be a real explanation. Because the alternative—

No, she thought. It couldn't be. . . .

She headed for Route 12. She didn't feel very good. She didn't feel much of anything at all.

Part Five:
HOME AGAIN HOME

1

For days Galidar observes the world, the many ways in which it has changed, the ways it hasn't. There are machines everywhere, uncounted millions of them. Machines that do things, still more that make things or change things, heating them or cooling them, and all the people of the Earth seem always to be using at least some of these machines.

The old man's house contains a remarkable number of machines and boasts one in particular that shows images of everything else in the world! There is even instant fire and indoor water. All of this is accomplished, so far as he can determine, with the use of no magic whatsoever. It is a new thing, an energy, not magic but a complete alternative to it.

The things that are mostly the same, of course, are the people themselves.

They still fear the unknown, though less than in ages past; they still war among themselves and prey upon each other, though there is apparently much less of the former, and in many ways, much more of the latter. They have conquered the face of the planet, yet strangely they think little of it. At length he finds himself . . . intrigued.

Finally he reaches out, using information gathered from books in the house, from images on the seeing machine that is still the most amazing of all. He uses his own powers, a talent he has always known, and stretches his awareness throughout the world, feeling his way across Europe, across the huge continents to the East and South, finally across the ocean to the West.

There is civilization everywhere, electric machine energy everywhere—and somewhere, in the great double continents to the West, a presence. It is altered in appearance and shrouded by potent dispersal spells, an aura spread over the land and sky. Most would never have detected it. He could not allow himself to miss it.

Strangely, this is the only source of supernatural energy he can find, the only flickering of magic. His curiosity grows intense. But the harder he tries to concentrate on the source, the more vague and dispersed the central focus of the energy becomes. The spells prove better than he thinks.

He is enormously impressed. He is utterly incensed. In order to calm himself he lessens his effort, retreats to nearer shores.

He is physically in a city somewhere on the Iberian peninsula, Spain, he determines. It seems clear though, this is not the place to remain indefinitely. He must move, learn, experiment. He must go to the great continents in the West.

He realizes that the old jeweler's body had been here for decades and has little travel left in it. Still, he estimates, it will get him to the western half of the world. Thereafter, more suitable arrangements would be made.

Slowly, carefully, he spends the next few days using subtle influence and minor trickery to bend a handful of local human beings, causing them to be inclined to his will. Learning as he goes, he arranges for the sale of the jeweler's house and business. He concocts evidence to ensure that a neighbor—a plumber whose pipe wrench matches the newly made dent in the corpse's skull, will be indicted in the murder of the young apprentice once he has gone.

Finally he leaves. He makes good use of another of man's most amazing new machines and boards a flying ship to the west, to a place he has learned is called the United States, a place where the only other "power" in the world, somewhere, waits.

The machine takes him at first to the northeastern shores of the northern continent, where his sense of the second presence becomes blinded almost completely. He perceives that he is too close and boards another machine.

This machine takes him near the southwestern corner of the same continent, to a sun-baked, pleasingly isolated desert. He has always favored warm, dry climates. He favors them still. He learns this place is called New Mexico.

He buys passage on a small carriage machine out into the desert, where he has the driver leave him off. He finds comfort and pleasure in the beautifully desolate land. In the distance again he can sense the other presence. Deep within, he knows there is only the slightest chance that the presence he had found is the One he seeks, but the chance exists, and as long as it does . . .

If it is not the One, the creature will still likely need to die, he decides. If it is the right one, then she will need to die many times. He fights to control his anger, his thirst for vengeance, for fear it will destroy the old body, which he is still dependant on. Another body, he reminds himself. He begins to walk.

2

Dorella put a postcard in the mailbox on the corner. As she dropped it through and let the metal door clang shut, an aroma like smoldering newspapers offended her nostrils.

She toured the neighborhood by eye, accounting for each of the nearby homes lining Route 12; old tinder boxes, most of them, even the pair of houses at the corner with the new aluminum siding, and especially the boarded up saltbox three doors away. She glanced last at the combination home and store-front grocery across the street. Nowhere was there any sign of smoke.

She turned back to the mailbox, pulled the door open, and put her nose to its mouth. Clearly, someone had started a fire in the box.

With a scowl she let go and mumbled a few quickly chosen words. She waited while the box's lower door unlocked itself and yawned open, then reached inside and retrieved her single piece of mail. She let the box close itself up. Someone else's mail was strictly none of her affair.

The next mailbox was three blocks farther south. Dorella set off to find it, grumbling at the weather.

By the calendar it was almost spring, though this morning gave no clue to that fact. Dirty slush lay in the streets where city plows had passed and covered the ice with salt and sand. The sidewalk remained glazed and slippery. Dorella minded her footing and stayed near the lawns to avoid the spray from passing cars and trucks. She was the only pedestrian in sight until she reached the second mailbox.

A car was parked there along the curb just onto the side street, a long white car, a Buick perhaps, though Dorella was poorly versed in the differences. Three young men all in their late teens stood on the walk talking to someone in the car. She couldn't see inside the car.

The nearest member of the group, black-skinned, wearing a thinly brimmed white fedora and a brown wool coat that fell straight to the tops of his padded white sneakers, glanced up as Dorella, sniffing cautiously, dropped her postcard through the mailbox door. He seemed to examine her carefully, making remarks to the others. Next he came walking over. Behind him came the second, white-skinned boy, wide-faced, a strong solid frame and strangely nervous eyes. He had on a pair of jeans and a white corduroy jacket with "KJ" initialed in longhand on the left breast. They both smiled and made sniffing noises not unlike Dorella's.

"Hey," the first boy said, looking at her sidelong. "Maybe you need something for that nose? A little candy?"

"Come on, Ray," the second boy said. "Don't waste it."

"Candy?" Dorella asked, somewhat puzzled by the question. "Why candy?"

"So whatever you wanna do," Ray said agreeably, leaning towards her, his breath on her through bad teeth. "We got the best 'do' there is, right?" He had his hands in his pockets. He glanced up and down the streets, excited almost. He seemed to grow uneasy when Dorella made no reply. His friend was close at his back. "Come on, say something!" he said.

"I don't know," Dorella confided, trying, more than anything, to figure why the one boy ended most every statement by turning it into a question.

"What *do*?" she asked.

"Anything!" He looked around again. "Blow, rock, dust, ice, 'ludes. All cash." He grinned. "We don't take American Express."

"You fellows work at some sort of mining operation?"

"Hey." Ray's eyes went cold. The boy with him tugged at his sleeve. Ray ignored him. "You trying to fuck around with me?"

The third man, black like the first, called to these two from the side of the car: "Ray, KJ, move your asses." He had a short cropped beard parted briefly by a scar that slid below his jaw to the left of his mouth. His hair was shaved nearly off, deep black scalp showing through. He took a cigarette from somewhere inside his black leather car coat, dug a lighter out of a zippered pants pocket. He was shaking so from the cold that he could hardly keep the flame in place. His friends seemed to ignore him.

"Hey," he called louder, sucking hard on the cigarette, as if he expected it to somehow keep him warm. "We got business."

"Come on, Gitz," Ray said, waving the other man off. "This *is* business."

"This ain't shit," Gitz said, chastising. Ray turned his attentions back to Dorella, smiling even more. "You're such a funny lady, right? Real bright. You wanna know how much I like that?" KJ leaned closer, intent on every word.

Dorella looked as far as she could into Ray's eyes, going beyond the shallow reflections to the images that lay beneath. She saw dismal shadows, a mind ruled by hatreds and fears and referenced by poorly formed conceptions, poorly grounded hopes. She sensed these same things in KJ as she turned to him—a common lack between them. But there were no Dires present to blame here, no magical excuses. She looked further, past both of them, and saw something still worse in the staring eyes of Gitz—something hard and empty, like abandoned cars.

"You pay attention while I'm talking!" Ray barked,

dissolving her thoughts. He used the heel of his hand
to shove her shoulder back once.

"The truth is," Dorella replied, putting starch in it,
"I've pretty much decided against that."

Behind them the white car pulled slowly away from
the curb. Gitz moved towards the others.

Ray glared at Dorella, steamy breath rolling out of
his mouth. "I think you're gonna have a problem."

"Get your ass away from that old bag," Gitz said
from behind him, putting a package under his coat.
"We're out of here."

"Not yet."

"Yeah, yet. What the hell's the matter with you?"

"Nothing. Solving a little problem."

"He does indeed have a problem," Dorella reported,
frowning now. "He is a sad, pathetic individual by any
gauge, even for a human being." Gitz grinned, so did
KJ. "But you all know how that is, I'm sure." The
grins faded quickly.

Ray grimaced and pulled open his coat, produced a
single-edged hunting knife, sharp on the good edge,
battered and carved with small circles along the top.
He grabbed Dorella's arm with his other hand.

KJ stepped in then, to intervene, Dorella thought;
but then, seeing the true look in his eye, she realized
he only wanted to keep from missing out on any of
the fun. Gitz seemed content to observe from his
steady stance a few feet away. He blew smoke and
smiled as Ray made his move. Dorella looked away,
reciting a quiet phrase.

Ray appeared suddenly stricken. His eyes tried to
cross, his lips made a stiff pucker while his cheeks
bulged and reddened. He let go of Dorella and
clutched at his abdomen as he bent over and began
to wretch. KJ seemed to lose interest in the assault as
he grabbed hold of Ray, pounding him on the back,
asking him what was wrong.

"Your friend is not well," Dorella said. Gitz raised
his eyebrows, then raised his hand again to take a pull

on his cigarette. He was abruptly surprised to find that it was no longer between his fingers. He glanced about on the sidewalk, even checking the street and the frozen lawn beside him. Finally he shrugged and slipped another one out of the pack.

Ray was on his knees, kneeling in his breakfast while KJ wrapped both arms around him, trying to get him up high enough to attempt a street-style Heimlich maneuver, since Ray himself seemed helpless to dislodge whatever was stuck in his throat.

Dorella backed slowly away, heading up the sidewalk towards home, keeping her eyes on the three young men. Gitz was shaking his head, enjoying a certain amount of humor at Ray's expense, keeping one elbow pressed against the bulge at his side, letting her go.

3

Home for the past two months was a sprawling two-story, two-family house on the corner of Route 12 and Colby Street. Outside, the wooden clapboard siding was painted yellow on the first floor, brown on top, with blotchy windowsills too rotten to hold much paint at all. Inside, both floors contained a relentless succession of rooms, from parlor to den to living room to bedrooms off a short hallway to dining room to a huge kitchen and pantry at the back. The upstairs had been divided into four mini-apartments with a common bath. Downstairs, a wall had been removed making the den and parlor into one large common room filled with sofas, a love seat and a mammoth black and white console TV. The kitchen had been made part of the dining room by removing yet another wall. The rest of the first floor was where Esther Mulvihill lived— and ruled.

Esther was a knotty, skinny, noticeably hunched old woman of seventy years or more. A woman whose clear eyes and permanently furrowed brow led one to believe that the world made no custom of taking her by surprise. She was also a person of many opinions and little social regard, whether anyone liked it or not.

She had converted the place into a rooming house not long after her husband had died and left it to her some ten years ago. She didn't require references or a deposit or even luggage from a prospective tenant. You were required, however, to pass a short verbal examination which seemed direct enough but owed much to subtlety and stealth. Then you had to be able to put up with Esther after that. Which, Dorella had early determined, was no minor task.

Dorella had a room on the southern wall of the house with a view that looked down on Colby Street and the corner. Another of the three upstairs apartments was occupied by an older, somewhat potbellied and balding man by the name of Vincent Reabert. Vince received a monthly Social Security check and a small pension, on which he claimed to get along well enough. He spent a lot of time reading books and magazines of every sort and watching talk shows with Esther in the common room, so he seemed always to have something to add to virtually every conversation. He had an arthritic hip that made him limp just slightly, which he said was from pushing down clutches on the baked goods trucks he'd driven for so many years. (*You know*, he'd said, *the ones with the little elves*. Which, Dorella thought, was most curious, since she had believed there to be no elf colonies still living publicly in the world and since, even when there were, they had never been much interested in baking.)

Vincent's wife had passed away some years ago—a long and dreadful illness, he'd said, nothing more. They'd never managed any children. He had a plain little two-door car the same silver color as his mustache.

Dorella saw simple character in him whenever she looked, a mind seeking level ground.

The third room contained the only other resident,

a young girl in her late teens who, despite looks that were thoroughly Amerasian, called herself Lynn Duffield. She kept three cats and stayed in her room with them much of the time, only coming down to eat, dump the litter box, or go out—usually in the evening. Her hair was very long and black and cut unevenly across the back as though she'd done it herself in a mirror. She had a complexion that never seemed to clear up, a face that was thin and drawn. She often wore colorful, sexy clothing—especially in the evening—though her stick figure lacked the proportions needed to fill some of those styles. She rarely talked to anyone other than Vince, who seemed to have some vague, ambiguous relationship with her.

Lynn never discussed what she did for money, though clearly Mrs. Mulvihill had her opinions.

Vince seemed disinclined to comment, other than to say that Lynn had lived more than once in the streets, had dropped out of school very young, that she had never mentioned any folks. He'd managed to get her interested in reading over the summer. Every Saturday morning he went out, returning about noon with a bag full of magazines and paperback novels from the local Waldenbooks. There were always a few for Lynn.

Dorella noticed that this morning was normal in at least that respect as she returned from her walk: Vincent's car was missing. She went around back of the house and used the kitchen door, found Esther inside cleaning away the bowls and spoons from breakfast—which, like it or not, had been the largest box of corn flakes Dorella could ever have imagined.

"Back already?" Esther said, using a tone that implied there was no right answer.

"Cold again this morning," Dorella remarked.

"It's winter," Esther said.

"Almost spring."

"Nice 'n' quiet for a while with nobody around." Esther began wiping sinks.

"I've interrupted your solitude," Dorella said.

"No kidding."

"I wasn't."

Esther looked at her, wrinkling her nose. "You are a strange bird, aren't you?" She moved half the items on the bottom cupboard shelf to make room for the cereal box. "Sometimes I wonder if all your snaps are fastened."

Dorella realized she'd misread the remark. She tried to talk to Esther as little as possible for any number of good reasons. It was too late now.

"You seem to feel that way about most everyone," Dorella observed.

"No, really. You got this weird look about you, like you're off in some world all your own most of the time. Maybe that little sweetie across the hall's been sharing some of her drugs with you."

Dorella turned the gas on under the kettle, got a tea bag from over the sink. "I've heard you mention that before," she said. "What kinds of drugs? Is she some sort of—healer?"

"Healer?"

"No—doctor! That's what they call—" She cut herself off.

Esther stood with a rag in her hand, temporarily disinterested in the kitchen table altogether. She frowned at Dorella—more than usual. "Are you as blind-sided as Vincent? You mean to tell me—" She shut her mouth, shook her head. "Well, the whole bunch of you gotta be a little below standard is all." She shook her head again and smiled to herself.

"If you feel that way, why do you rent to us?"

"I gotta pay taxes."

Dorella poured hot water and stirred. Esther finished up and tossed her rag on the counter. "Isn't Lynn here?" Dorella asked.

"Went with Vincent, her new 'father,' you know, or her dirty old man, or some combination I suppose." She chuckled privately.

"I think he just feels she needs somebody," Dorella

offered, realizing as she did that she was assigning a relationship to Vincent and Lynn not unlike the one she had had with Alison. It was easy for her to imagine that others might find within themselves the need to care for another less able, or the need to be cared about. To send a postcard against better judgment, in spite of the risks.

For someone like Vincent, though, the only sure risk in becoming familiar with Lynn, in whatever capacity, was having to face the persecution that invariably followed from Mrs. Mulvihill.

"I imagine he's simply taken her with him to the bookstore," Dorella suggested. "You could stand to lend people the benefit of doubt now and then."

Esther looked at her. "As soon as I start taking advice from the weird."

"Or anyone else," Dorella said back, doing her best to limit her scowl, and more importantly, her temper. "You will excuse me," she said and headed into the hall.

"I've tried," Esther jabbed, chuckling again. "But it isn't easy."

The tea in Dorella's cup began to boil.

4

"She knows what time it is," Esther said, flipping the burgers, adding milk to the pot of instant potatoes. She glanced over her shoulder at Dorella, checking her progress with the salad. Dorella finished adding carrots and set the bowl on the table. Vincent worked around her, placing silverware. "I'll just go up and tell her," he said.

"No, I'll go," Dorella offered. "I have to feed my bird anyway." She went to the counter and picked up a small dish containing chunks of cooked burger and a shredded piece of wheat bread soaked in milk.

"Weird as they get," Esther mumbled, a very loud mumble.

"She seems okay to me," Vince put in, smiling at Dorella as she passed. He dismissed Mrs. Mulvihill with a wave.

"Your standards, she likely does," Esther said. "How many people you know keep a crow in their room?"

"The crow was a . . . gift, of sorts," Dorella said, pausing to defend herself. "It is well trained, and at least as well mannered as some people."

"Cute," Esther grumbled. "It's a scavenger all the same, a living garbage can. Pity one of Lynn's cats doesn't eat it or, for that matter, the other way around."

"Maybe I should go out and buy a dog," Vince said, grinning fiendishly at Esther.

"I'll be right back," Dorella said, slipping quickly out of the room. She lost the conversation as she went through the house and ascended the stairs that rose from the common room. She stopped at Lynn's room and knocked on the door. A breathy voice acknowledged her.

"Dinner," Dorella said.

"Okay."

Nothing more. Dorella shrugged and went to her own room. The crow stood lengthwise in its favorite spot on the windowsill—its favorite allowed spot, since Dorella had declared the bed off limits. It jumped about excitedly when it saw the plate in her hands. She set the food on the floor and the bird flapped quickly down to eat it.

"You'd think after feeding you for a few hundred years you'd be full," Dorella said. Her humor seemed lost on the animal. Despite her sister's occasionally strong influence over the creature, it was still largely a crow, and crows, for a fact, were not among the earth's most praiseworthy creatures.

The bird ate voraciously, then fluttered again to the

window, cawing twice, trumpeting its satisfaction. Or gratitude.

Another sharp caw announced that the bird was ready to be let out. Dorella stepped forward and pushed the lower half of the window up, then jimmied the storm glass open. The bird took to the air, swooping off between two houses across the way. Cold air rolled in through the opening. Dorella tugged her sweater around her and waited. Within seconds the bird returned. It hated to go out, she knew, especially alone.

"Try to be good," she said, closing the inside window, "which means keeping your claws off the furniture."

The bird gave a sympathetic nod, or something like one, and Dorella turned to exit the room. As she closed the door behind her she caught the unmistakable sound of feathers rustling through the air.

"One hole in my blankets and you'll be back in your cage," she stated at volume. Wings abruptly fluttered anew. As she passed Lynn's door Dorella knocked again, then waited. She heard only a muffled reply. She knocked once more and waited until the door opened.

"What?" Lynn asked.

"Dinner."

"Food would be good," Lynn said, leaning against the door jamb. Her hair was half in her face, her eyes were empty, like her smile. She had a bruise on her right cheek that was turning purple. Dorella asked about it.

"Oh," she said, touching it with her fingertips. "I fell over one of these goddamn cats." A gray and white tom chose that moment to poke its head out between the door and Lynn's leg. Lynn looked down at it, grinning, then frowned and sent a kick in its direction. The cat dodged and ran.

"Shit-head," Lynn called it. She looked off then, gazing about the room as if she had misplaced something. The look held a certain familiarity.

Dorella had seen people and creatures of many kinds make use of mind potions and mood-altering mixtures derived from various plants—used by royalty and commoners alike, and in every civilization. Some of her own ancestors had been highly regarded for their talents with such concoctions, from blissful formulas to enhanced wines, from opiates to more exotic recipes. She had never passed judgment on these activities. She had always instinctively avoided or countered any attempts to cloud her own mind, and since the rest was really none of her affair . . .

She looked upon Lynn mostly in that same, detached light, noticing her inconsistent state without connotations. But she wasn't so certain that was good.

"Are you enjoying what you're doing?" Dorella asked honestly. Lynn looked a question at her. Dorella tried to rephrase, asking about her experiences, and began to get through.

"Sure," Lynn said. "Often as I can. The price is right."

"I have no idea," Dorella confessed.

"Sure. Good shit costs. *Any* shit costs, you know. But I get unlimited free samples." She smiled tightly, then began to giggle. "Like working at the fruit stand, they let you eat the apples." A bigger giggle now.

"Sometimes, I suppose—"

"Come on." Lynn shook her head no. "That's how things work. Get whatever you can get, any way you can get it. So I do."

The room behind Lynn was a mess, clothing on the floor, blankets dragged off the bed. It reeked of cat piss. Lynn moved away from the door and put on one shoe, then set about looking for the other. On a small wooden table near the window there were four Barbie dolls, each one bent to a sitting position and leaned up against the wall. A cardboard box full of tiny doll clothes stood on the floor beside the table. No Ken.

"I've always thought that the workings of the world were a bit more complicated," Dorella said.

"Sometimes, if you ask them right, people will just give you things. Valuable things, in fact," she added, thinking it through. "I don't know why really, but I'm trying to understand it. I will, sooner or later."

"No, no," Lynn came back, wagging one finger at Dorella tick-tock style. "They just want what you got to give. You give, they want, you give, they want. That's it. Otherwise they give you shit."

"Not everybody," Dorella insisted. "I've met some people who were very—"

"Everybody's always an asshole!" Lynn declared, almost shouting. Then the hard lines melted and she giggled again.

On the bed stand lay a few envelopes, an open pad of paper, some pens with the caps missing. A few lines of script were scribbled on the pad.

"Writing a letter?" Dorella asked, trying a fresh tack. Lynn didn't answer. "I've just sent a card to a friend of mine," Dorella added. "Someone a bit like you, in certain ways."

Lynn looked up but didn't focus. "Yeah, that's nice." She lifted a ski jacket off the floor behind the door and discovered her other shoe.

"I think so," Dorella said.

Lynn's face clouded, became unreadable. She chewed her upper lip a moment. "The letter's for ... for them," she said, nodding towards the dolls. "They can't write, you know. You can't expect them to ..."

Abruptly, a shade of clarity returned to her face. "Bunch of shit anyway," she announced. "I wanna eat."

"Who do you write to when it's just for yourself?"

Lynn stood in the doorway staring at Dorella. "What kind of question is that?"

"You know, people know people; something else I've been learning. Family, friends, somebody. I just wondered."

"Are you always such a pain in the ass?"

She pushed past Dorella into the hall, hiding her

eyes. Dorella followed her down to the kitchen. In the brighter light it was apparent the girl had been struggling with tears.

"She's toasted again, isn't she?" Esther said, looking sharply up from her plate.

"Esther!" Vince said tersely, glaring.

"Oh, what!" Esther insisted. "Look at her. Half gone and you know it. She's been that way so long I don't think she knows what real life looks like anymore, or what *she* looks like, or she wouldn't look so bad. Not to bring up what her bed partners look like. Or how many there are. Or how many of them even pay."

Lynn had her face buried in her arms over her empty plate, sobbing in waves now. Dorella eyed her in a clearer light. She'd always known that some human women made a practice of allowing men to have sex with them in return for money or barter. From time to time, certain male members of her own race had been known to make use of them (and certain of the women had likewise fancied some human men). But Dorella had never known such a woman closely, and hadn't thought of Lynn in exactly that way until just now.

"Then you're a whore?" Dorella asked, quite honestly.

Lynn's sobs ceased for an instant. She raised her red eyes to Dorella, then dropped her head back down and wailed all the louder.

"For God's sake!" Vincent shouted at Dorella. He got up and went around the table to where Lynn was seated. He put his big weathered hands on the young girl's shoulders and gently squeezed. "You think she's happy? You think if she had a home she could remember, or anyone at all, any *place* at all, that she'd be running drugs and doing—doing whatever, for those downtown bastards? People aren't born all messed up."

"Maybe they are, maybe they're not," Esther said,

waxing philosophical, gazing at the ceiling. "You never know."

"You don't know her, Esther. What she's been through, living on her wits for years. The facts are a lot of guys came back from Southeast Asia with new wives and new kids, then dumped the whole bunch when the novelty and craziness wore off. Some of those girls weren't able to keep their babies, even when they wanted to. She's been telling me the way it's been for her. It isn't so hard just to listen."

Even Esther remained silent for a moment, joining the others as they stared at the table.

"You know why she's living around here?" Vince continued. "Where she came from it was worse. She finally got up enough guts'n'smarts to get the hell out of the city. She wants things to get better. She's trying to change, for crissakes. It just isn't done like *that*!"

"Nobody has it easy," Esther said then, putting her fork down, taking everyone to task with a short visual review. "No one I ever knew firsthand, anyway. If you plan on walking through a pasture, you'd best just figure a way to keep from stepping in the piles, if you know what I—"

"What the hell are you talking about?" Vince snarled.

"Simple," Esther replied. "Your lot in life is what you make of it, that's all. Why, back during the depression—"

"Hold it! *I* was around during the depression, too, don't forget. This is a whole different thing. We all clung together back then. Families were tight. Families helped other families. Nothing like now."

Esther looked at him. "Why?"

A look of exasperation swept Vincent's face. "Okay, I'll bite, why?"

"I'm not gonna tell you."

Vince swore an oath under his breath.

"I would like to know why," Dorella said. Both Vincent and Esther paused and stared at her. Finally

Vince seemed to dismiss the entire topic with a shake of his head. He turned back to Esther. "I'd like to give this girl a hand instead of a kick in the pants, that's all. She just might be worth it."

Lynn was beginning to get herself under control. She sucked in a fairly solid breath and turned, looking up at him over her shoulder. "Thanks," she said.

"And I think she means it," Vince said.

"So sweet," Esther taunted.

Vince and Esther glared at each other with laser eyes for a moment. Lynn turned directly towards Esther. "We've been talking," she said. "I've got money enough for a while, and they'll never miss it. I don't want to wait anymore."

"I said I'd serve as sort of a coach, or whatever she needs," Vince explained. "Keep her from coming apart and running out to the streets again. Until she can get clean, anyway. And I can keep the wrong people away from her, or her from them." He pulled Lynn's hair back out of her face, then smiled. She didn't turn.

"We're overlooking the fact that she's on something right now," Esther said, disparagingly. "Seems to me in order to quit something you have to start by not doing it."

"This is the last of her stuff," Vince said. "There isn't going to be any more. That was our deal." Lynn nodded along to his words. "I double checked her room this afternoon. I think she's telling the truth. I bought her everything she'll need: books, magazines, cards, games, some doll—things, chocolate. You know, she's never learned to play pitch, so I'm going to teach her."

Dorella had been content to sit and absorb the entire conversation so far, trying to be more equitable in her consideration of people, making herself aware of the entire spectrum; but parts of this were too intriguing for her to risk misinterpretation. "Is Lynn physically dependant on the . . . drugs?" she asked as Vince paused for air.

All eyes turned towards her. Vincent shrugged. "Sure, but up here too," he said, tapping at his temple with two fingers. "That's the hard part."

"Well," Esther said, "I've got this damned addiction to eating dinner every day. Silliest thing." She went back to her meal. Dorella watched Vincent return to his own seat, taking Lynn's plate with him. He filled it with burger and potatoes while Lynn stared at the tabletop. Vincent reached towards her silverware. Dorella stayed his hand.

"I'll get it," she said and fixed it for her. Lynn ate small bites silently.

Dorella had no idea what it might be like to put one's self through physical and emotional traumas of the sort Lynn was apparently intent on facing, but she sensed it would be best if the young girl were allowed to get through it without any unusual, unnatural tricks and assistance from her, no matter how helpful they might seem. It was a thing Lynn must do for herself. Alone for the most part.

Perhaps, Dorella thought, feeling suddenly almost sorry for herself, concerned anew over the strange events of recent months—finding a vision of ancient war and dying briefly flashed upon her mind's eyes— perhaps, sooner or later, it was always like this, no matter who, no matter what.

As she finished her meal, cold thoughts remained in her mind. She needed answers to the questions that followed her now like wolves in the winter, questions that seemed to come to her with more and more of her life attached to them each time they were raised. She needed to learn the truth about the demon, the Dire, the men who had come looking for her—the truth about a battle fought more than a thousand years ago.

5

In the desert he finds an old man walking. The man is painted with fascinating colors and seems lost in thought. Galidar intrudes on those thoughts and learns that this is an earthly man of small magic, of ancient practices and natural ways—that he has come out into the desert in meditation. He is of a people who are descended from a human tribe who roamed this land even in Galidar's time. They are a people steeped in tradition and bound to the earth, in touch with its subtle aura. These days, Galidar learns, they call themselves the Navajo.

The body is not excellent by any measure, but it is better than what remains of the old jeweler; and, Galidar imagines, there may be certain built-in enhancements. He decides that it will do.

With a concentrated effort, Galidar drains the old jeweler of the very last small amounts of energy within him. In this moment of transition a whirlwind of memories boil unbidden into his conscious mind, a jumbled summary of his existence, then, now, and to be. But again a single image of battle dominates, an unchanging conspiracy of fate.

So perfect, he thinks, was the carefully laid trap, the power patiently gathered and stored, all to end the existence of Alibrandi. One of the few children left among their kind, her combination of youth and ability had posed an impassable threat. Yet of all those he had helped to their deaths, she had proven one of the most difficult.

From the crest of a small hillock he had lain in wait. He had seen the jaws of the trap close around her— then seen her somehow survive—even as he'd poured more and more power into the spell. Until at last he could no longer sustain the effort and was forced, slumping back, to release her. When he again had the strength to stand, he looked down on Alibrandi, her motionless form. He sensed her fading spirit and knew he need only wait. So perfect—

Until he sensed another presence, close, powerful, upon them almost before he could manage to conceal his aura and slip back down out of sight. The girl's sister, he determined—apparently, unexpectedly coming to her aid. He watched as she bent over the fallen form of her sister, tending to her; he realized there would be no other chance.

He attacked only to find his spell deflected by a powerful warding spell. He bore down, summoning all his reserves. He tasted failure and with it a strange spell he could not identify somewhere in the air around her. His strength failed. He could sense no presence in the body of Alibrandi anymore and great power gathering in her sister as she faced him. He knew then that there was nothing to stay for, no hope, no chance. He took the crystal into his hand and spoke the final words.

So perfect . . .

The memories fade with the last of the energies of the old jeweler. Galidar thinks again of the task at hand, that of completing the spell that for a time will ensure his needs. He feels the change. The jeweler dies. The Navajo medicine man dies, almost—then lives.

6

"I've seen this movie before," Vince said. "Isn't there anything else on? '60 Minutes' maybe? Something?"

Part one of the Disney Sunday movie was just beginning. A trio of tiny, plump fairies were setting about raising Snow White in the woods, where they thought she would be safe.

"You don't like stories about magic, I take it?" Dorella asked quietly.

"You wish life was that simple, don't you?" Vince said. "Most of the time I have trouble just believing there's a God. Not that Lynn couldn't use a Good Fairy or the Good Lord or whatever. Me either, far as that goes." Vince eyed his fingernails absently. "Never seen evidence of either."

"Up to smiting God now, are we?" Esther said as she came into the room. She sat in the love seat under the reading lamp. "He don't make house calls, you know. Big stuff, nothing little. That's how he works. The whole trouble is that nobody wants to get involved anymore. Not even God. Are you going to whine all night or we gonna watch TV?"

"At least you've got your children," Vince said, pointing to the TV set. A framed 8 X 10 photograph was propped up atop the center of the cabinet. Three well-dressed men, all ranging in age from their late thirties to mid-forties, stood arm in arm smiling confidently at the world: Esther's sons. She had other, older photos of them around the house, which showed the boys at various stages of growth, but this one was more of a centerpiece, a main attraction. This photo appeared rather recent.

"I have *pictures* of children," Esther corrected. "The boys are content to live their own lives. They haven't come around since that picture was taken, matter of fact. Must be three years now, and that was the first time in years. The oldest lives in California, the middle one married a girl from Worchester, so of course there they go; the youngest went into the Air Force and never came out. Not yet, anyway. He's stationed in Germany. Likes it there, I guess. Seems they don't any of them like it here."

Esther's eyes glistened in the light from the lamp. She fell silent for a moment and landed her gaze on the TV, or something just above it. Then she seemed to catch herself, took a breath. "See, you're lucky,

Vince. No kids, no dealing with the idea you'll probably never see them again. Better that way."

Dorella was amazed at the things Esther's eyes betrayed. She had thought the woman to be quite cold and uncaring, as indifferent as Dorella herself had been a century ago. Yet here were softness, reflection, pain. . . .

All of which were then gone so quickly, it was as if they had never appeared. Still, unlikely as it now seemed, a spark of humanity had flickered there before Esther had snuffed it out—another person Dorella had only just met.

"Can't you call them on the phone?" Dorella asked her.

"Oh, sure. But I won't. They don't want nothin' to do with me, and I'm not gonna go begging. Or praying, either. It won't change anything. I did everything I was supposed to do. Now, nothing comes back. That's just the way of it."

"Some things cannot be changed," Dorella agreed. "They are bound to occur, part of the natural order of things. Others, however, can be less certain, more pliable. The trouble is that there are no rules posted. You can guess reasonably, of course, but you can never be sure which is which until you try. Fate might be fooled, or altered, once in a while. But the only truth—"

"You are the weirdest thing!" Esther proclaimed, cutting Dorella off. "Where do you find that stuff?"

Dorella noticed even Vince was looking at her sidelong.

"What did you used to do for a living?" he asked.

Dorella avoided their eyes. "I came by a sound inheritance some years ago, which I've made do with. Otherwise, I like to read a lot, like you, Vincent. A lot of philosophy, really . . . and I'm very well traveled."

"Right," Esther said, rolling her eyes.

Vince tried to nod knowingly.

On the TV the young prince was battling the evil witch. She made herself into a fire-breathing dragon.

A grand display. Then the most foolish turn of events occurred—

A screeching call from the crow interrupted the entertainment. All three living room occupants were on their feet as the sound mixed with the pounding of footsteps on the floor above them. Dorella went straight up the stairs, with Esther and Vincent close behind.

They found the doors to most of the rooms upstairs opened. Dorella went past Lynn's room straight to her own. She discovered the crow perched atop the metal curtain rod over the window, still cawing frantically, eyes dancing as it kept watch on the three cats attempting to claw their way up the curtains. Dorella shooed them away as Vincent came into the room behind her.

"She's stoned," he announced angrily. "You should see the shit she's got in there. I got it away from her, but now she's on her knees looking for crumbs she maybe dropped on the floor. I'd love to know what the hell's going on."

He bent over and picked up a cat, tossed it into the hall. "How did these little guys get in here?" he asked.

Dorella walked to the edge of the window and looked out. She pointed towards the street. Vincent stood beside her, following her gaze. "That may be our explanation," she said.

A young black man, well-lit by street lamps, was disappearing around the corner below. He wore an ankle-length coat, a dress fedora. He looked vaguely familiar to Dorella.

"He must have broken in somehow," she said. "Do you think he knows Lynn?"

"Well, I'll find out," Vince said half under his breath. "She'll tell me if I have to beat it out of her."

"Now you're making sense," Esther commented from the hallway behind him. Dorella and Vincent came out of the room, Dorella glancing momentarily over her shoulder, favoring the crow with a nod before she closed the door. Good watch hound, she thought.

"We should check for a broken window or something," Vince suggested.

"I would hope so," Esther said in her most disparaging tone. "Still, one wonders. Isn't it more likely he just appeared, magically?"

Dorella, learning by now, held her comments.

They arrived at Lynn's room to find her sitting on the bed, smiling out of one side of her mouth like the Mona Lisa, fidgeting with one of her dolls like a baby. Esther looked at her coldly, then turned to Vincent and Dorella. She spread her hands to all of them. "After that," she said, "maybe we should all get trashed with little Miss No-Mind here. Or I can skip that part and just go have my head examined. Find out why I live with such people. Or maybe even how you live with yourselves. Or why I am cursed with these problems."

Everyone stared at Esther without remark.

"Maybe it's me," Esther said then. "What do all of you think?" She made a face like a gasping fish. "Of course, that's exactly it! All this is fine, and I'm not!" She began cackling like the evil witch in the Disney film. "I'm going craaazy!" She set off down the hall, waving her arms above her head.

7

The intruder had gotten in by climbing a tree at the back of the house, then leaping onto the upstairs porch. He had apparently found the door unlocked. Lynn, Vincent said, had done the honors herself. The temptation had been too great. The following day, everyone was mobilized.

Esther retrieved a saw from the basement and Vince spent the next afternoon cutting off tree limbs, then Dorella helped both of them nail the porch door and a number of the upstairs windows shut. Dinner was late. Lynn did her best to avoid looking at everyone.

After dinner Dorella followed her nightly ritual of feeding the crow. When she came back downstairs she found Vincent and Esther sitting in the common room.

"I've left the bird out in the hall," she said, finding a spot for herself. "So if you see it walking about up there, don't be concerned. It's on guard duty."

"Long as it don't come down here," Esther said, cringing for Dorella's benefit.

"Did you check on Lynn?" Vincent asked. Dorella nodded. "She seems fine, for now."

"She says she's back on the wagon for good," Vince said. "She was sort of shaky when I took dinner up to her, but toughing it out. I've been reading up on this kind of thing. I guess they mostly want more crack while they're on the stuff, but once they're off it things aren't so bad. After a few days, maybe a week, she ought to start getting over the worst of it. It's slow after that. She'll need lots of support. And eventually, decent work, somewhere outside the neighborhood."

"And what keeps her friends from getting to her in a week or two?" asked Esther. "Or are you both gonna move? Which means I have to look for new boarders. Which, actually, doesn't sound like such a bad idea."

"She told me her pals want her back to work. She owes them, but I gather she made some special runs for them, too, so she might be a little hard to replace. Anyway, they know she's got nowhere to go. Except to them."

"Everybody hates to lose a good dog," Esther said, flipping through the TV Guide, not looking up. Vincent frowned.

"I hope she does well," Dorella said encouragingly.

"I got her some sedatives," Vince said. "From a friend of mine. They'll help some, and she seems stronger about it now. We moved the phone into Esther's room and locked the door—I think she used it to set up that little visit we had. I doubt anybody will be sneaking up on us for a while."

"I'm glad someone's confident," Esther said.

"I doubt they intend to try that approach again," Dorella remarked. "In fact, I'm sure of it."

"What does that mean?" Esther asked.

There was a noise on the front porch, footsteps on the wooden planking. Someone knocked.

Dorella shrugged. "I believe that's them at the door."

8

Vincent was out of his chair before anyone could say another word. He rushed to the door, put his knee behind it, then pulled it open only as far as the chain lock would allow. The voices from outside were muffled, but Dorella distinctly heard them mention Lynn.

"She isn't in the business anymore," Vincent snapped, clenching his fist around the inside door handle. "Just get the hell away, or we'll call the cops."

Someone on the porch was laughing. Someone else made some reference to do with Vincent engaging in sex without a partner. Then the door shook, straining the chain with a sudden thrum, jolting Vincent who, much to his credit, stood his ground.

Dorella was finding the man to be quite a study. Though not especially brave or intellectual, he seemed capable of great purpose and conviction. Whether it was boredom or loneliness or some kind of desire that drove him to his decisions regarding Lynn, he seemed determined to help her, even if it got a little rough. It occurred to Dorella that, at one turn or another, mankind had always exhibited this capacity. From brave young mothers to the mightiest kings. She had seen human beings go to their deaths against impossible odds—sometimes even seen them prevail. Admirable, she thought, though over time it did seem to get them into far too much trouble.

"I'm warning you," Vincent said. "Don't start any shit. Be smart and just go away."

"You're right out of your mind," Esther called to him, her face terrifically grim. "You'll get us into a war with these criminals, and *we* don't know where *they* live. We either gotta beat them up or give them the girl and forget about it. And I don't think you can beat 'em up."

"Just shut up, Esther," Vince growled out the side of his mouth. "I can't believe even you would say that."

"Man's a certifiable twit," Esther complained.

A knife blade, wide, single-edged, with blackened gashes and circles along the flat edge, found its way through the door opening. Vincent jumped back, startled. More laughter followed from the porch.

"Tell the lady that Gitz was by to see her," a voice called in, one Dorella had not yet forgotten. "Just to talk. And that we'll be by again. Soon."

The blade slipped out of sight. Vincent used his knee to slam the door shut, then locked the deadbolt. He watched at the edge of the front window shade until he was sure the intruders were gone. Then he walked, hunched, to one of the sofas, favoring the stiff hip more than usual, and collapsed, breathing in gasps, hugging his arms tightly to him like a man freezing to death.

"Are you all right?" Dorella asked, watching him closely. Vincent shook his head yes as he tried to control his breath.

"Gonna blow that ticker yet," Esther prophesied.

Vince swallowed hard. "At least I have one," he wheezed. Esther picked up the cable box and punched the TV on.

9

Lynn sat on the bed petting two cats at once. They purred loudly, content with their spot on her lap. The third cat sat on the floor at her feet. She had on jeans, a bright green sweatshirt, and a bright look. Her hair was washed and pulled back in a loose ponytail that added freshness. Her eyes seemed clearer, black and shining, the dark surrounding bags of a week ago all but gone. Dorella put Lynn's lunch on the nightstand.

"You never do say too much, do you?" Lynn said, looking at her.

"Neither do you."

"Yeah, well, you spend a week this straight and stuffed into one little room and see what it does for you."

"I've spent a great deal of time alone," Dorella said. "It has always agreed with me." She paused to consider. "Tell me what is it like to get cracked?"

Lynn giggled at her. "Wow, what can I say to that? It's wonderful! It's fantastic! Better than that! And the whole time all you can think about is doing more. You don't want to give a shit about anything else. You ever done much drinking?"

"No."

Lynn shook her head. "Well, never mind."

"Why do you—did you do all the things Vince and Esther keep talking about?"

"It was easy, that's all. And fun, for a while. I like sex, I like getting wasted, I like money. Not so complicated. It never bothered me until I started getting sick of the whole thing, and bored, I guess. So I came here and tried to sort of cut down, you know, like quitting smoking or something. You can't really live that way, but you do anyhow, until . . .

"Well, then Vince let it bother him. And Esther

keeps ragging on me all the time. People like me tend to die an awful lot, too. You don't think about that, though. Then all of a sudden one day you do."

"I think I understand."

"You think maybe you could let me alone now? Nothing personal." She turned to look out her window. One of the cats jumped off the bed, then the other. They paced.

"Vincent seems to care very much," Dorella said.

"Maybe. Maybe he just wants a young piece of ass all to himself. He's got to want something, right? Everybody wants something."

"Different things. Not always what you might think. Sometimes all they want is a chance to be what they are." Sometimes, Dorella reflected, even if they really aren't.

Lynn eyed Dorella narrowly. "The old bag is right about one thing. You are sort of weird."

"Mrs. Mulvihill seems to dislike everyone and everything for one reason or another."

"Yeah, except her kids. You've seen the pictures. Of course, if I was her kids, I wouldn't come around here either. Who knows why I put up with her shit."

"Why do you?"

Lynn shrugged. "She lets me stay here."

Dorella stood wondering if Lynn was joking or expecting to make sense. Lynn reached for her plate. "I want to eat," she said. "Take the hint, lady."

Dorella honored her request.

10

Saturday morning Vince smiled at the three ladies seated about the breakfast table. He stood up, landing his gaze on Lynn, who was still wearing knee socks and an oversized T-shirt bearing the logo of a heavy metal rock band under a fleece bathrobe. It took a moment, but she smiled too.

"Why don't you stick around here today?" he suggested to her. "I'll go to the mall myself, bring you back a new book I have in mind. Some magazines, maybe. And one of those giant cinnamon rolls you're so crazy about. I don't think you should get back into traveling just yet. Let it rest awhile longer." Vincent tried to look cheerful.

Lynn's expression bunched up, but then relaxed. "Yeah, I suppose. Can you maybe just bring me a six-pack or something?"

"Why not?" said Esther over the top of her coffee cup. "It's a short wall, just jump over it!"

"You and your cheap analogies," Vince said. Lynn leaned back in her chair and snickered. Vince refused any humor. "You really want something?" he said. "I'll go and get you something. And then I can just tell you to go to blazes, and we can all admit that this past week only proved that one of us is an idiot."

"Both of you," Esther corrected.

Lynn stood up and put her hand on Vincent's arm. "Please," she said, speaking only to him. "I'm sorry. You're not an idiot. I've been a mess for so long, and I needed someone besides myself, and you did all that. I promise I won't fuck up anymore." She came around the table, stood there quietly a moment, then she hugged him. He closed his eyes and hugged her back. "See you when you get back," Lynn said.

Vincent nodded. He turned and headed for the front room.

"Isn't it nice," Dorella said, thinking out loud.

"Oh, get out of here," Esther said, taking dishes to the sink.

"A most pleasant prospect," Dorella remarked, and followed Vincent into the common room.

"She's impossible," Vince said. "The woman doesn't have a kind bone in her body." Dorella nodded. He finished buttoning up his coat and pulled his car keys out of the pocket.

"It takes all kinds," Vince added. Just a mumble.

"What takes all kinds?"

Vince looked dully at her, then shrugged in silence and stepped out the door. Dorella turned and went up to her room.

She arrived to find the crow gone and shook her head in mild exasperation. Her sister had surely been at work. Though she was never certain how much control Alibrandi's consciousness actually had over the bird, her presence occasionally surfaced enough to spell open a window, to turn a key. Dorella saw this generally as an encouraging sign, but nothing more. She had never been sure what had gone wrong with the spell she had used to save her sister, why she had never been able to undo that spell since; or how much of Alibrandi she had truly been able to save, how much remained?

She looked out the window, saw Vincent's car drive up Route 12. She watched a pair of small children along the street below, both too young to be out alone, alone all the same. A mongrel dog, black and brown and spotted white, came through a yard two doors away. The children ran after it, whooping and cooing. She glanced in the opposite direction and saw three dark and very recognizable young men appear at the corner and head for Esther's front door.

Just then the crow returned, sailing through the open window on a chilly March breeze that was filled with the voices of the men crossing in the yard below. The fearlessness of their approach was evinced by their rapid, emphatic banter. They had waited for Vincent to leave, Dorella guessed. And after a week without their young and useful assistant, along with whatever they felt she owed them, they had likely waited as long as they were about to.

Which left Dorella with a difficult decision to make. She had finally come to accept that it was her prerogative to intervene in human affairs, if she thought the situation somehow warranted it, and if she was convinced she wanted to. But almost without exception the practice had backfired, or at least raised as many questions as it had answered. In order to maintain her privacy, and lately her safety, she had been forced to become estranged from the very people and way of life she had grown close to. She was resolved now to keeping herself out of any conspicuous light, to keeping her true nature completely hidden.

All of which said nothing of the fact that, although she was coming to know Esther and her fellow tenants fairly well, they were not truly her friends. More like—acquaintances. Like people on a bus, or in a crumbling apartment building . . .

It appeared that so much close association with human beings, so much shared experience with them, was affecting her judgment more and more, and there was little to be done about that. Tempting though it was, she couldn't just turn her back. It was not unreasonable, on the other hand, simply to have a look, she decided, not for the first time. A brief, less distant moment of erudite observation. . . .

Dorella paused as she approached the top of the stairs. She heard Esther's voice, loud and clear, telling the visitors to go away. They beat at the front door and called to Lynn, who promptly asked Esther to let her handle it somehow. Esther told her to go right ahead.

Dorella could just see them through the landing's banister rails as Esther held out one open palm to indicate the front door. Lynn moved in that direction, clutching her robe about her.

"I got nothing to do with you, Gitz!" she yelled out. "Just piss off!"

"Oh, that ought to quiet them," Esther commented.

"How you feeling?" Gitz asked.

"Better than you," Lynn answered. "Fine."

"Get out here and let's have a look."

"No thanks!" Lynn shouted. "Just get off of me."
From her crouch at the top of the stairs Dorella

watched the girl take her hair in two fistfuls and stamp her foot, punctuating the phrase.

Esther had backed up against the edge of the love seat. She had her coffee with her. She stared down at the steamy liquid, perfectly still.

"That won't work," Gitz replied. "We got to do something. Way it is, I don't see where we got a choice."

Lynn began whimpering just audibly. She shook her head limply back and forth, let her knees fold slowly beneath her; losing courage, or strength, or hope? Esther sat there with her coffee and callousness, so separated. She seemed always primed to deliver royal criticisms from her self-proclaimed throne of perfection, but her concern had no dimension beyond that, so far as Dorella could see. How could a woman raise three children and yet be so unforgiving of all those she encountered? Like the cold arrogance of the old "gods," she thought. Like—

She heard a sudden smashing of glass, then the front door banged open. KJ came first into view, followed closely by Ray and Gitz. Esther was off the sofa and moving in the same instant. She framed a near-straight posture between Lynn and the intruders, then threw her coffee at them, just missing KJ. Next she turned half around and threw her arms about Lynn's upper body, then pulled her around almost behind her. "Just back up and get out of my house," she shouted at them, top of her lungs.

"Look, lady," Ray said, waving the knife at her. "You're just close enough to the grave so a good push won't matter."

"We're gonna talk to Lynn," Gitz said, taking a cigarette out of his coat, stroking it with two fingers in an almost sensuous manner. "We'll just take her outside."

"She doesn't need to talk to the likes of you. She's trying to keep a promise to herself, so she can get out of the garbage. And she's doing it! I'm not about to let you come in here and ruin it. You boys run along, and get your mothers to go work the streets for you, see how far that gets you. Leave her be."

Ray's expression had changed from a fallow grin to one of puzzled concern. Gitz ground his teeth and motioned to KJ, who nodded and circled around to the left, nearer Lynn. Then Ray smiled and faded right.

Dorella could barely contain her shock at the old woman. Here was Esther, suddenly sticking up for Lynn as though the girl were her own, risking her life to defend Lynn's newfound and largely untried ideals. Esther, as far as Dorella knew, had never done anything but berate the girl and Vincent along with her from the very start.

Of course, no one could change from an attitude of combative dislike to one of dauntless loving defense in a matter of seconds, human or otherwise. Which meant Esther Mulvihill was quite probably an out-and-out fake, unable to show her affection for anyone, even her own sons, in a normal fashion and she had come to deal with that in the only way she could.

Dorella turned, eyeing the crow, which stood on the runner beside her. She could feel her sister's presence pulsing within the creature as she hadn't in years. She touched the bird's matted black feathers and spoke to it, using words the animal could not understand, but words that spoke directly to Alibrandi. "Be there," she pleaded. "Hear me."

She commanded the bird to go and to bear her thoughts along. The crow gave a high octave screech and a bounce of its head, then leaped into the air and flew down through the open stairwell.

It swooped straight across the room, lighting atop the big TV set. Then it took to the air again almost immediately, flying clumsily now, carrying something large in its mouth and claws. The front door was still ajar as the intruders had left it. Too quickly for anyone to focus, the furious clutter of blackness was out through the opening and into the yard beyond.

Dorella waited, then smiled as she heard the window in her room scrape open. A brief rustle of feathers followed, then the bird stood beside her again.

It dropped its catch and pranced to one side. Dorella glanced away. She needed a few more seconds, but Gitz seemed to be in a hurry. So she spoke with concentration to that part of Gitz' throat that contained his voice, making the small fleshy cords lock in spasm. Gitz opened his mouth to talk but no intelligible sound was produced. Pain gripped his face.

She spoke next to KJ, concentrating on his legs until he began to wobble uncontrollably. Finally she worked on Ray's right hand, pinching the nerves where they ran in a cord through his wrist. The knife started to shake as he struggled to hold onto it.

Using those talents which were integral to her existence, she projected her thoughts outward across the vastness of space until she came to a place at the edge of existence, a familiar loop. With fingers she only imagined, she touched the cosmic thread and felt the strengthening power within the narrow string come flowing out, back across real time and space, channeling into her crouched body in a house on Route 12.

She reached down, picking up that which the crow had brought, and recited a spell as old as her art. With the passing of only seconds there came a new burst of noise at the front door—as three men entered the house.

They were each very well dressed, ranging in age from their late thirties to their early forties, all quite tall. Two of them had Esther's eyes, the third, wearing a dress military uniform, had her chin and nose. The oldest, slightly balding, wearing a charcoal pinstripe, pushed back the sleeves of his suit jacket.

"Hi, Mamma," he said.

They stood side by side no more than six feet behind the intruders. Gitz began making choking sounds as his voice suddenly returned. KJ stood up straight, eyes twitching wildly, as if he was waiting for his own newly returned stability to fade again, sighing with relief when it seemed it would not.

Ray had picked up his knife off the floor and tucked it back inside his coat, where his hand remained. He stared at the new arrivals.

Esther, eyes full of tears, brushed past all three younger boys as if they had disappeared. She fell into her oldest son's open arms. Lynn stepped around to the left of Gitz, putting the TV between herself and everyone else.

The three boys, visibly shaken, eyes darting about as though they half expected the roof to tumble in on them at any moment, circled around on an opposite tack past Esther and her sons. They avoided eye contact with everyone except each other. Gitz said something hoarsely, the others nodded.

Esther made a very clear announcement to all of them, something to do with broken bones, and the three intruders hurried out the door, across the porch and were gone without further comment, leaving a calm silence in their wake.

Esther and her boys suddenly burst out talking all at the same time, nodding to one another, making faces. Someone closed the door. Esther introduced everyone to Lynn in a sentence. Someone else made a remark about Esther and they all broke into laughter as they started down the hallway towards the kitchen. Even Esther laughed and wiped away the last of her tears.

Lynn stood by the TV, hands over her face, breathing deep breaths. She looked up through parted fingers as the front door opened again and Vincent stepped through it.

He was frantic and at once began asking if everyone was all right, warning Lynn that he'd seen Gitz and the others on the street outside.

"It's okay," Lynn told him. She grinned weakly, then spread her hands. "They tried to drag me out of here. Then Esther stood up to them. She said I was doing good, Vince, like she was proud of me. Like she—"

"Like she really cares," Vincent finished for her. "Sure she does." He came to her slowly. "I hate to ask," he said, "but what the hell actually happened?"

Lynn tried to tell him all at once—the sons, the choking, shaking intruders—he made her start again twice before he told her they'd better just go over the whole thing later on, when he could sort the details out.

Lynn looked at him then with tenebrious eyes. "I'm okay, anyway," she said. "For a while I didn't know, didn't believe it, but I just . . . I feel differently now." Her face brightened a bit. "Good," she said. "I feel good." She paused, looked away. "I know I owe you for that. And a deal's a deal." She turned her head back to him. "I think I know what you want, so whenever you're ready, you know, we can go upstairs, and it's all yours."

"Oh, for crissakes!" Vincent said, smiling, reaching out and taking one of her hands in his. "I've had a wife. What I never had was a daughter. You keep all that for when you need it. Just try to act like you're listening when I'm talking, and let me listen to you, and I'll be happy."

Lynn was still for a moment, just looking at him. She reached out then and threw her arms around him, hugging him as though her life depended on it.

Dorella gathered up the picture frame the bird had brought her and went up the hall to her room, beckoning the crow to follow. Once inside she opened one of her bags and pulled a few things out, making room. She took the gold and glass framed photo and placed it inside near the bottom, glancing at the curious outlines where the figures had been. Then she filled the bag up again and zipped it shut.

She would put the photograph back on the TV

before it was missed, of course. Just after Esther's sons had gone again—and been returned.

A day or two, which was the most that sort of spell was good for anyway.

No matter. It had already been enough.

Part Six:
THE TEST OF TIME

1

Within two days Galidar finds a place that is rich in ancient magical auras and natural wonder. It is a place well known to the old mind he now occupies. He works his way around to a good location, a long slope of low hills and ravines. From his little hill he can see every detail of Tse Bit'a i, the "rock with wings." It was here that the ancient tribes had once fled, chased by great enemy numbers, and were saved as the rock rose into the air, spreading its wings, carrying the people to safety in the place where it now rests.

Galidar sets about making a home. Deftly, crossing old bridges, reaching back and away into the negative, nether side of existence along newly established channels, he draws all the power his brief renewed practice will safely allow—and changes the desert.

He reconstructs wood from the fossil remains

buried in the earth, conjures a well from deeper still, then uses the water to make mud. Against the low hill, tucked into an opening in the rock, he builds a tiny hogan.

Because they are not illusions but creations of substance, the work takes great concentration and energy. Lesser spells of illusion would need constant renewing, and he thinks he may need all his powers for other goals in the days to come. He strains the limits of his inner self, of the body he inhabits. In the end he is satisfied, and he rests.

Days after he notices occasional stray Navajo ponies that graze on the sparse grasses in the shadow of the winged rock. He convinces them to stay near, teaches them to be his eyes and his ears. Again he rests and plans.

When it is time, he travels away visiting the nearby towns of Ship Rock and Farmington. He is searching for servants, and he finds an ample supply.

The Indian existence is a series of contradictions, the rich living alongside the poor, poor living poor generation to generation. Many lack direction or purpose. He picks two such individuals. He gives them what they lack.

They are both Indian, though not the same. One is Navajo and named Wagua; the other is Acoma and he is called James. They are young men in their early twenties. Both are addicted to the ancient drug alcohol. He casts a strong influence over their minds, then washes their addictions from their bodies.

These two will serve some purpose, but Galidar has other, more specialized needs that cannot be met here. When they are ready, he buys for the two men a used Jeep and gives them their first task, that of drivers. To the east there are fantastic cities filled with many people and millions of machines—places called Albuquerque and Santa Fe.

They travel to the former and arrive to find every

variety of human being imaginable. He needs only a few.

He discovers a young and resourceful woman who uses her body to earn her living and, he is able to personally determine, uses it very well. He finds too a vacant, hardened fellow who lives much of the time outdoors or in abandoned buildings and makes money cleaning yards and parking lots. His grace is that he is white—which may prove an asset—and easily manipulated, which is required. Galidar thinks at once of a task he might perform, but he requires preparation.

The spells are simple yet strong. Galidar fills the man's mind with his own thoughts, his special ideas, and places a protection on him. He tells the man to investigate, to seek out the source of the magic he has sensed, and to gather any tangible evidence as to who or what that source might be. He then sends the white man away to the Northeast.

This done, Galidar finds another disciple, a middle-aged business man who, when Galidar happens upon him, is in a bar contemplating suicide in the wake of an investigation by a government agency he calls the IRS. His name is Packerson. Galidar makes him a very special offer. It is an easy sale.

Finished, Galidar collects his followers and returns to the desert.

Here he masters the two Indians and the woman, molding them to be precisely what he wants. He makes something almost approaching a lesser apprentice out of the Packerson man, who is more aggressive than the others, more treacherous, and tolerably intelligent.

Through all this he waits, but the weeks pass and it eventually becomes clear that the man he has sent to the far coast will likely not return.

He feels that Packerson is ready, however, or as ready as he will conceivably get. So he sends him on a similar mission. And waits again. Eventually, Galidar decides that Packerson will also not be back. It is a troubling, irksome thing.

Still, Galidar can sense the power of the being he knows is there; still, his thirst for vengeance longs to find that source. And there is more. On occasion he can sense this power being plied, someone drawing from the great wells of the universe. The scent is compellingly familiar. It also guides him in his quest.

He knows it is preposterous to imagine even for a moment that, of all the magical beings in existence at the time of his final battle, the only one now remaining might actually be his final adversary. Might be, in fact, the one being in the universe that he *needs* to find. Easier instead to believe that she would have died a natural death, or been destroyed by others, or that the scent was only as familiar as his enraged imagination made it up to be. Yet he is almost convinced. . . .

With each failed attempt to gather facts through his agents, Galidar's frustration grows. But he also learns from his mistakes.

After much reflection he decides to proceed in a different, amended fashion. He is becoming more familiar with this new world and its ways. He gathers his apostles and makes another trip to Albuquerque, and tries something new.

2

On Saturday, as Esther finished up the breakfast dishes and Vincent and Lynn set off on their usual weekend run, Dorella was feeling especially right. She had promised herself, after all, and the day had finally come to make good.

She fed the crow breakfast, threw a spring jacket on over a tawny cotton dress, and followed the others out. Vincent offered her a ride downtown but she declined. It was a lovely, summery morning and she was firmly of a mind to take pleasure in such things.

The post office was some ten blocks straight up Route 12, all of it frequently intersecting some of the older streets in the city, some of the poorest. Diverse and fascinating, but harsh. The combination had yet to fail to intrigue her.

She thought it best to let the crow follow at a good distance, as the bird had often proved too tempting a target for area youths in recent months, a challenging change of pace from city pigeons. Even so she was no more than three blocks from the house when she heard a familiar screech, and surmised that all was not going as planned.

She turned to see a crow, *her* crow, madly dodging projectiles. The bird was in the midst of an evasive maneuver, swooping up in front of a tile warehouse store. As it tried to land on the roof, a pair of young boys gathered a few more stones and chased it from its perch.

Stones flew suddenly up, down, in circles and in figure eights, hitting everything in sight—except the crow. Another volley brought the same results.

The bird landed on a phone pole, squawking righteously at the boys, smug as their best efforts miraculously missed the mark again and again. Dorella called to the bird. It seemed not to hear, still enjoying the moment. Dorella spoke again, more quietly, and smiled as the crow let out a sudden shriek. It leaped again into the air, a small stone bouncing off the pole just next to where it had been. The boys saw only the bird's shadow—momentarily redirected—flying off in the opposite direction. The crow flew near Dorella and settled on a fire hydrant just ahead of her, waited for its shadow to join it.

"Just once I would like you to do as you're supposed to," Dorella told it as she passed. The crow appeared the very definition of remorse. Dorella walked briskly on, followed at a distance by a small black-feather cloud.

She arrived at the post office and went straight to

the private boxes. This was the first time she had been back here since mailing a postcard to Alison containing the box number. There was nothing inside. No reply. She sighed, her bright anticipation fading into nothingness.

Of course, she thought, and rightly so. A bright young girl like that could surely find better things to do than befriend an eccentric, middle-aged woman with notorious habits. She would be just out of school for the year by now. Probably husband hunting, if she had any sense, or looking into a proper career. Or both.

As for herself, Dorella reminded, there were certainly plenty of other prospective comrades about. Most people were special in one way or another—some more so, perhaps. Lately again, she had been reminded of that remarkable fact. She locked the empty box and went back out into the street.

Mid-morning was approaching now, traffic picking up. Dorella could see people strolling or standing along the sidewalks on both sides of the street. She stood and watched them for a while, looking about for the crow as she did, unable to spot it.

It struck her that her own people had never lived so close together, not like human beings. But they had always been . . . *aware* of each other. So many humans, though, seemed oblivious. Invisible to one another. Yet as individuals they were sometimes so concerned about others that they forgot themselves . . . like Alison, or Esther.

She decided that in this, like more than enough other recent puzzles, she would be some time finding all the answers.

She concentrated briefly, calling to the crow in silence from within. In return she felt a strong sensation of something wrong, very . . . no, *not* wrong. Something very . . . exciting!

She looked about furiously, but still she saw nothing. A potato chip truck abruptly pulled away from the curb directly across the street. Dorella spotted the crow perched on a trash can, hopping up and down enthusiastically, eyes fixed on the young, slightly plump, bright-eyed girl that was standing to the side of it. The girl was frozen in place, apparently awaiting the crazed bird's next move.

Alison.

3

They stood facing one another beside the waste basket for a long moment. Alison shook her head at last and tried a feeble grin, still intermittently eyeing the bird, which had quieted notably. "You're looking at me funny," she said.

"Perhaps a little," Dorella replied.

"What did you expect?"

Dorella shrugged. "A letter."

"I came in person instead. I staked out the post office."

"Why?"

Alison looked up and down the street, as if she hoped the answer might roll by at any minute. "I don't know," she said. "The last time I saw you, you'd just done some rather impossible things. I had a few questions, for you and for me. I still don't have any answers."

She paused for a moment. A look of mild trepidation crossed her face. "That demon was positively the most terrifying thing I could have dreamed of, and you destroyed it. And I saw you do for that young boy—things like that change a person. Can't you see that? It changes your perspectives."

"Maybe you're overreacting."

"Not at all! What else have I got? *Who* have I got? Look lady, I didn't have anybody I could call close in the first place, but then you come along, and you're like this weird big sister or something, and I think we're getting to be friends. Next you make the Wizard of Oz look like a game show, and then you vanish! And I'm supposed to pick up my life where I left off, which was the middle of nowhere anyway, and just toss it off to experience?"

"I'm no one you need to follow about," Dorella said. "I'm just a little . . . ridiculous, and maybe—"

"You're like nothing I've ever seen! You changed everything. For the better, I think."

Alison drew a breath, filling her lungs, closing her eyes briefly as new thoughts filled her mind.

"I saw things in such small context before," she went on. "I never understood that there might be more to life than my own little picture. I've never had so many incredibly scary and wonderful thoughts. I want to ask, I want to know, I want to fill this huge void you've created in me—and that I associate with you.

"But then you're gone, and I'm supposed to be just a pen pal or something, read your postcard and say, 'Oh yeah, a note from that Ms. All-Powerful again.' Have a nice day. I can't do that."

"Eventually," Dorella said, looking generally at the crow, "I'd hoped you would discover your own life, and live it. Just as I must. Just as everyone—"

"Oh," Alison said with a smirk, "what a bunch of shit."

The crow squawked an interruption and leaped from the trash can as three young children, bolting from their parents' side as they stopped to window shop, ran to grab it.

Dorella made a slight shift in the morning light, brought the sun's reflection across the store's window glass into the mother's eyes. The woman squinted and turned to check on her brood. One shout brought the trio around, off the chase.

Dorella looked up to find Alison frowning cynically at her. "You see," Alison said, "you're like the Good

Fairy. Or like Merlin the Magician or somebody. That crow is yours too, isn't it?"

"Merlin became little more than a politician as soon as he had an opportunity, and I have no such ambitions. In fact, he was—" She cut herself off. None of this was going the way she wanted it to.

Alison stared back at her, a question on her face that would not come to her lips. The crow made cautious little chirps. Dorella sighed, keeping the rest to herself.

"It *is* nice to see you again," Dorella said, sincere.

"You too," Alison replied, penitent, almost.

"Where were you headed?"

"Just . . . here."

Dorella sucked her lower lip, then caught herself at it. "I live just a few blocks from here."

"Oh?"

"I'm headed there now." She looked distantly up the way.

"Mind if I tag along?" Finger fidgeting. Indisposed.

"That'll be fine."

Dorella nodded, then set off immediately, Alison in tow. She signaled the crow. It took off, gliding out well ahead of them, circling, scouting their way as the two women moved along the street.

"Dorella?" Alison said, catching up.

"Yes?"

"Please tell me one thing. Just who the hell are you?"

"I'll explain when we get there," Dorella said. "Over coffee. It might take a little while."

4

They arrived at the house to find Vince's car still absent. Alison made comments about the immediate neighborhood, pointing up some of its grimmer aspects, comparing it to the corner where a crooked boy had once stared into her window. Dorella frowned at the comparison, then thought it over and softened somewhat. "Perhaps," she said, "but that isn't necessarily all bad. I've come to find this place rather fascinating."

"Extremes are the norm," Dorella added. It seemed impossible, she explained, that such an amalgam of individuals as was contained in these neighborhoods could live together at all and yet, though tenuously at times, they did.

"*Some* people might worry about getting robbed or raped or—" Alison stopped herself, looking curiously at Dorella. "Well," she admitted, "maybe not *everybody*."

Dorella led Alison in through the kitchen, expecting to find Esther there. She was surprised to hear an unfamiliar male voice as they entered the room.

He was seated at the kitchen table with Esther, a settled sort of man, darkly tanned, medium height and build, very dark hair, even on his hands. He wore loose, high-top athletic shoes, a heavy cotton shirt with each sleeve rolled up twice to the inside, safari trousers. A large black and gold watch adorned his wrist, a thin gold chain circled his neck. He appeared about thirty, maybe a little more, especially about the eyes. Serene eyes, Dorella thought: fixed.

"This is Michael Vallez," Esther said, looking up, extending a finger towards the man. "He'll be renting a room here with us beginning today."

Dorella looked at him and nodded in greeting. Vallez returned the same. She stared at him for as long as their eyes remained in contact, making every effort to peer inside at the stormy currents she feared might lie below such a tranquil surface. She saw nothing to alarm her, no darkness, no unnatural light. A nice, passably intelligent man. Almost too good, she thought, especially for this sort of arrangement. Almost like Packerson, at least in that way. . . .

Vallez spoke up: "I was working at a microwave filter plant down south. They laid almost everybody

off. There's supposed to be work up here, from what
I understand. Figured I'd try and find out."

Well, he's already passed Esther's verbal third
degree, Dorella thought—no small feat for anyone.
The easy manner with which he handled himself
seemed too natural to be the result of any recent magical subjugations or enhancements, and he sounded
nice. After all, she reasoned, not *every* villain was a
Dire; not *everyone* who seemed nice was actually an
evil agent in disguise.

Of course, not all of them *weren't*.

"Planning on introducing your friend?" Esther
asked curtly, being a curtly sort herself.

"Oh, of course." Dorella turned. "This is Alison
Kimbrough. I met her at a college where I used to
work."

"Just visiting?" Esther asked after that.

Dorella looked at Alison, who was looking right
back.

"She'll be staying, then?" Esther prodded.

"For a few days, I guess," Alison said, her voice a
bit hesitant. Dorella nodded approval. Alison grinned.

"Going to be crowded," Esther remarked so evenly
that there was no telling how to take it.

Esther pointed to the other chairs. They all sat
down and began to chat, citing house rules at first: no
late nights in the common room, no arguing with the
landlady, breakfast was *always* cereal, like it or not.
For the most part though, Esther and Dorella just
listened.

The talk grew more serious as it went on, and slowly
each of them let out some of the better and bitter
details of their lives. Alison talked about school, about
looking to the future, leaving behind the traces of the
past. Mike Vallez talked a little about the roller-coaster
state of various high-tech industries and the related
failings of those idiots in Washington; about living day
to day, and then about living in days gone by, the

horses his family had kept by the hundreds when he was a kid, the tiny local school.

Alison said she was getting over losing her Grandmother now, that it felt good to say that. Vallez talked about southern summers and southern friends. Esther finally joined in, retelling worn tales of what it was like working in a shirt factory and before that going to school while she was living on her great-uncle's broken-down farm. Dorella found it all very interesting, and grew more at ease.

She was nearly convinced now that Mike Vallez was probably genuine, harmless. Still, something about him didn't quite seem to fit. He was so smooth, so— practiced at talking with people, a man one might think of in terms of great experience and wit. Not trickery, she decided, or any sort of dark magic. He was no apprentice sorcerer or zombie attacker or even a normally aspiring criminal, come to that.

Still, she felt as if he were leaving something out; a criminal record perhaps, even a recent divorce, or the death of someone close.

He was not many things, but Dorella felt certain he was somehow more than he had so far described.

By the time Vincent and Lynn got back the group had adjourned to the big common room and were getting along like old friends. Though that, Dorella understood, didn't mean they actually were.

5

The crow leaped excitedly about as soon as it heard the knock. Dorella let Alison into her room to a trumpeting of unintelligible crow screech. Alison told the bird to be silent only once, and remarkably, silent it was. Dorella sat on the edge of her bed, Alison on the only chair. The crow flew down from its perch on the window table and landed at Alison's feet, then looked up at her with big crow-eyes.

"I like you, too," Alison told the animal. "You know, it strikes me I never learned its name."

"Just 'crow' seems to work well enough," Dorella said. "But it has you at a disadvantage. It already knows you, from the college. I had it follow you one night when you went to the old barn. It saw everything. That's how I knew you might be in over your head, and why I went there myself."

"No ordinary crow, then. Nor any ordinary lady."

"No," Dorella said. Then, "I mean, yes."

"So maybe you could start making some sense of all this. I couldn't sleep for weeks after what happened. I kept seeing Daniel gutted and devoured by that horrible creature, and the others all running and screaming; and you, suddenly out there, emerging from the fire like a goddess, destroying the demon. You're this nice, interesting, middle-aged librarian, right?" She bunched her shoulders, as though imagining a shiver. "And then you're not. I need to understand, and you're the only one in the world who can help."

"Which is mostly why you're here."

"No." Alison smiled. "It's hard to get new friends on short notice, especially slightly . . . 'ridiculous' friends."

They considered each other a while, nothing gained, nothing lost. "Are you going to tell me anything?" Alison finally asked.

Dorella sighed, nodded. "Where would you like me to begin?"

"You're so good with history. I'm even willing to bet you're some kind of time traveler or something."

"Of course not," Dorella quipped, nearly smiling now.

"Well, you're awfully touchy about Merlin."

"You never had to deal with him."

"You see?"

Dorella looked at her straight on. Alison's quiet grin disappeared. There was nothing else for it.

"He and I share a common heritage," Dorella explained. "I knew him well enough. I am one of the last surviving descendants of a race of beings from another place, another dimension you might say, who escaped here about four thousand years ago. My people are all children of the stars, *our* stars of course, but they were much like your own. We are, *I* am, at one with the stars. I can 'touch' them."

Alison looked at Dorella with wide eyes. "Touch what?"

"I have as part of my nature a means of reaching out into the depths of space, or through space—I've never been certain how it works—and 'touching' different parts of the universe. It is similar to what you call telepathy, only it's ... different."

Alison nodded numbly. Dorella frowned at herself. "We, my people I mean, use thought in a certain way, directing it in a specific manner, and are able to extend a part of our conciousness millions of light years away. There we have learned to seek out the rare primordial cracks that lie hidden among the stars—the wells of power."

"What—what cracks?" Alison beseeched her, squinting.

"They are a uniquely suitable, controllable source of energy. I think you call them 'strings.' But there are dangers. Only the smallest cracks can be safely tampered with, so one must always seek them out, and once found, remember exactly the paths and carefully cultivate a method of access in order to ensure a ready supply.

"The obvious temptation is to find a single great source, since that would allow one to gain instant, unequaled power in time of need: in a battle, for instance. But too great a source, or even poorly handled smaller ones, can become deadly. They can be the instruments of our own destruction. Each one of us must learn, from others and from our own cautious experience, to handle the energies that flow from these places.

"It takes hundreds of years to learn what can and

what must be done. And as in all such things, one's ultimate level of achievement depends on individual talents. Merlin was one of the oldest and ablest beings of his time, perhaps of anyone's time. He kept himself alive for several thousand years, during which time his strength and knowledge of the universe, along with his exquisite ability to draw from his chosen sources, became legend.

"Really, his one prominent fault was his preoccupation with human affairs and human destiny. He saw a great and personal value in mankind. It was something no one else understood then. Though I am beginning to now, I think."

"Of course," Alison said, looking at Dorella owl-eyed. She was a bright girl, Dorella knew, which could work both ways in a situation like this. She would know from recent experience that Dorella's story was likely real enough, but part of her mind must be screaming "foul" like crazy.

"My people have never been close," Dorella went on. "We never knew a tribal, hunter-gatherer period. We've always been loners, always wary of each other, and doubly mistrusting of anyone who might enter into an alliance with others of our kind or, during certain periods in history, with humans. There is much more."

"Oh, please go on," Alison asked, her expression unreadable now.

"There are those who draw power from the negative universe, the nether world where creatures like Daniel's demon friend originate.

"Much of this is easier to understand in terms of your own human religious beliefs. Your culture believes in God and Satan, and you have little but your own faith to go on. We have long believed that there are many 'positive' universes or dimensions but one 'nether' world. My people have always seen this in a more natural, physical sense: many universes of positively charged matter coexisting with one negatively charged universe where nearly everything is different, from the rules of nature to the creatures those rules have produced. Still, we see *this* existence as 'good,' and the other one as 'evil,' much the same as you do."

Alison sighed. "I expected something incredible. I suppose I should be happy to get it."

She paused, reflecting. "You said your people didn't think much of humans. What's wrong with us?"

"Very little, it seems. More than anything it was prejudice. Humans lack our stellar abilities, so we have always looked down on them, as our mothers taught us. It is much easier to note the grimmer aspects of another species when you are trying to sanctify your own, and quite easy to disregard the things that are good.

"You see, human beings love, they trust, they befriend in the deepest sense of the term; they share and give, and *forgive*. At the barn, when you saw me still there and so near the demon, you forgot all about your own safety. In your concern for me, you nearly sacrificed your own life; and before that, in your concern for a crippled street-boy you'd never truly even met, you did the very same thing."

"Don't remind me."

"Why not?"

"Oh, not really." She considered a moment. "You mean you or your people wouldn't? In a similar situation?"

"My people would pause briefly to consider their options, the values of action and inaction, then make a decision based on whatever formulation resulted. I am only slightly more ... inclined to err on another's behalf. Faced with clearly impossible odds, as you were, I doubt my own mother would have—"

"Oh, I don't believe that! Maternal instinct must be universal."

"Perhaps you're right, but we have a different maternal ilk than you. We do not marry. We form

only temporary mating arrangements and seldom bear
more than one child. The mother is then left alone to
raise that child, and generally divests herself of the
task as early as possible."

"You don't have any close elders to turn to, to look
up to? No twilight friendships?" Alison asked, obvi-
ously more puzzled by Dorella's description than Dorella had expected.

"No," Dorella said, searching for an analogy. At first
nothing would come. "We don't ever go to Grandma's
house."

"Oh." Alison sat digging at one thumbnail with
another. Dorella waited her out.

"It was stupid, really, what I did at that barn," Alison said then. "I wasn't thinking, and I didn't know
what the hell was going on. The truth is—"

"The 'truth' is something that it has taken me fifteen
hundred years to learn, and that you have always
known."

"How can anyone be that—old?"

"Youth spells, of course. Though even they have
their limits. Not that I've reached mine."

"You don't look a day over fifty."

"The best I can do nowadays. All spells are in some
way contrary to the natural order of things. Nothing
is without limits. I could temporarily maintain the illusion of any age, but to what point?"

"By 'spells' do you mean—magic spells? Like a
witch or something?"

"We have been known as many things through the
ages. We were the gods of man's early civilizations,
the wizards and sorcerers of later times, the witches
of a recent age. My people cannot take credit for all
the stories and deeds attached to those labels throughout history, but we are what those legends and myths
are based on."

"I don't understand how it's possible that no one
else is aware of you. Why is there no news of you? It's
not that I doubt anything you've said." Alison made a

point to put her hands up in front of her, double stop signs. "It's just that not much goes on in the world today that some news-hungry network or publication or TV talk show doesn't pick up on, even from a historical standpoint. And usually the more bizarre the better. In fact, I don't think there's *anything* they wouldn't chase. The other thing I can't help but wonder about is why your people wouldn't have taken over the world centuries ago."

"There were not very many of us, and as I've said, we were never a close, cooperative people. Indeed, we were too busy fighting each other. Only a few of my people survived the war that destroyed our own universe by escaping here to yours. It was a war between those who drew their power from the positive universe and the dark legions, those who had forged an alliance with the nether world. But the war followed them, reigniting in fierce, deadly flare-ups between the survivors of both sides. Today I fear there is virtually no one left. I sense almost no 'magical' energy at all. As for taking over the world . . . you're still not seeing this in quite the right light. Human beings, for instance, do not feel they have to 'take over' the world from chimpanzees."

"Oh . . ."

The crow was butting its head against Alison's leg. Alison reached down and began to pet the bird's head with two fingers. The crow leaned towards her, swaying on its legs as though it were intoxicated. "And that's how you feel?" she asked.

"Not really. Not anymore."

"So you're all alone, like me? Only it doesn't bother you very much, does it? Because you've always preferred being alone."

"That's not the same anymore either."

Alison nodded, silent. The bird stretched its wings lazily, causing Alison to draw her hand away. "Weren't you ever . . . close to anyone?" she asked.

Dorella faced the window. "Yes," she said, dropping

her voice nearly to a whisper. She turned her head, found the crow. "To my younger sister, Alibrandi. As I explained, siblings are extremely rare among my kind. The two of us were always close, *always*—at least by our standards—very trusting and supportive of each other. We made no boast of it; our mother viewed our behavior as something of an embarrassment."

"That sounds awful," Alison said.

"Not really. Anyway, it was a unique feature of my youth and one that let me notice the differences between my people and yours. The more important differences."

"Where is she now? Your sister, I mean."

Dorella addressed the crow. "Do I tell her?" she asked.

The bird bobbed up and cawed without hesitation.

"A few survivors of the dark legions were extremely powerful. Alibrandi ran afoul of one of them, one known as Galidar. He was much older than Alibrandi and more cunning. She fell victim to a trap he had laid for her. She fought back fiercely, forcing him nearly to exhaustion, but in the end it was not enough.

"When I found her she lay dying, drained almost completely of life and spirit. I tried to save her, but her body was beyond repair. Only the fading energy of her essence remained. There was no time, I knew that. I decided my only hope was to collect her essence and place it within the first living creature I could find.

"In the midst of the transfer, Galidar attacked. I had sensed a presence I thought was Galidar's, very near, but until that moment, I couldn't locate him. My warding spell saved me, but the transfer was affected, the spell was somehow changed. I was barely able to complete it. I turned and caught a glimpse of Galidar at the crest of a nearby hillside, and then something else, weakness. I saw an opportunity to strike him down and took it."

"So you killed him and saved her," Alison said,

more comment than question. She had resumed petting the bird, both of them finding some apparent comfort in the activity.

"More or less."

"More or less?"

"I had always thought Galidar destroyed. Yet coming here I was challenged by a man, someone trained in the ways of natural magic. He was sent to find me, or to find out who and what I am. He was an apprentice and he let slip the name of his master."

"Galidar?"

Dorella nodded. "I don't know what the truth behind all of that really is. There may be more than one explanation. But I must find out. If he still somehow exists it may explain why all my attempts to restore Alibrandi have met with failure. His existence, however faint, might be the barrier I have been unable to break."

"But if you killed him, how could he be alive?"

"I have no explanations for that. At least not yet."

"Then where *is* Alibrandi—exactly?"

"She is still a resident of the crow."

Alison jerked her hand away from the bird and looked down. "Alibrandi?" she croaked.

"Yes, more or less."

Alison pulled her leg away from the animal as well, adjusting her position on the chair.

"What I mean is, this *is* a crow. Quite an ordinary specimen, in fact. But hidden deep within it is the essence of Alibrandi. She hears us much of the time. Sometimes she can make her presence known, though less often these days than in the past. She is fading, slowly—I think permanently. If Galidar does still live I must find him."

"And when you find him, then what?"

"I must destroy him, though I'm sure he would be inclined to do the same to me."

Alison shook her head, made a face. She grinned feebly at the crow. "You know, if I hadn't seen any of those impossible things that night at the barn, I'd never believe a word of this. I still don't quite understand. I should have been taking notes."

"But you accept what I've told you?"

"Every unbelievable word."

"I've never attempted to explain any of this before. It is a comfort to find it so simple a task."

"Simple," Alison repeated, nodding, rolling her eyes.

Dorella waited until Alison looked at her. "Are we still . . . friends?" she asked.

The crow had again moved near. It began bumping Alison's leg with the top of its head again, looking up at her with plaintive annoyance. She reached down idly and resumed stroking its head and neck. "Yeah."

6

Mike Vallez sat in the living room sipping morning coffee and chatting with Vincent and Lynn, all of them deeply immersed in a discussion of city life—north versus south—and their own experiences in particular. Vallez made mention of how active the people hereabouts were, busier than they seemed in warmer climes, and how interesting he thought the residents of the house were, present company included.

At length they came to the subject of Dorella—and kept at it, as Mike Vallez seemed averse to moving on to another. Almost it seemed an obsession. Finally, in the face of growing irritation on the part of the others, Vallez relented and moved on.

About this time a crow was seen to swagger out from behind one of the sofas, then hop and flutter up the stairs.

7

The evening air was warm, the sun still up but just low enough so that the neighborhood trees and houses blocked it from view. Esther sat on the porch, pushing gently back and forth with one tiptoe, relaxing on a slightly mildewed vinyl and metal love seat hung from rusted chains. The spare breeze was filled with the smell of barbecues and lilacs. A robin dug into the lawn.

Mike Vallez listened while Esther made mention of the southside's declining condition, in particular the junk car that the Hawleys, who lived two doors down, still hadn't gotten rid of. Mike made sympathetic remarks, then he began to talk about everyone, especially Dorella.

He was interested in how long Dorella had been living at her home, in what Esther knew about the lives and pasts of all the tenants—especially Dorella, and in particular if anything unusual had happened around the place in recent months—purely, he insisted, because Esther seemed like a wonderfully unusual host.

When Esther looked doubtfully at him, he went on weakly explaining about people and destiny and how he'd always imagined the two might be related. As Esther's frown deepened he dropped it all together and went on to something else.

Just then a crow was noticed flapping itself free of the rain trough along the edge of the porch roof, swooping around the corner, vanishing from sight.

8

In the morning Mike Vallez managed, quite coincidentally of course, to come out of his room at the

precise time that Alison was leaving hers. He walked
with her down the hall, down the stairs. He asked her
how she liked living in the house so far and mentioned
how, after less than a week, he was settling in nicely.

She told him something about her own, rather neutral feelings, about her lack of intuition concerning a
direction in life. She said she liked it here, though,
because she was with her friend Dorella.

Vallez seized the conversation then, grilling Alison
about how she had come to know Dorella, what Dorella was really like, if Dorella seemed in any way a bit
unusual to her. When Alison balked at his questions
he managed to stop himself, then changed the subject
abruptly, pondering what was to be for breakfast.

Cereal, Alison thought.

In this particular case it was not necessary that a
crow be present.

9

On Saturday, when Lynn and Vincent went to the
mall, Alison and Dorella went with them. They wandered about, ducking in and out of stores, making one
or two minor purchases. They ate pizza and drank
soda and watched children race through the halls.

On the way home Dorella asked about Mike Vallez.
Everyone had something to say.

10

He had begun to accumulate a good deal of information, had managed to form more exact questions.
But one new question in particular was beginning to
bother Mike Vallez a great deal: why?

Not that he wasn't used to taking on jobs that were
strange in one way or another, or even on occasion a
bit unethical. You didn't ask a fellow why he wanted

to get the dirt on his wife's extracurricular activities, or what he wanted with details of his partner's after-hours errands; you simply took the money and did what you had to do—then you said good-bye and spent it. You didn't ever go back and ask the wife or the partner, either, even if it meant you could work for them both at the same time—double the money just wasn't worth it.

He'd helped a wealthy woman from Santa Fe get back her stolen jewelry once, but had never asked her why she hadn't simply called the police. A check was a check.

He had accepted the very generous fee offered by the old Navajo medicine man in the same spirit. He and his friends, cash and airline tickets in hand, had come to Mike's office, with the simple request that he fly to Pennsylvania and gather information on a woman the old Indian needed to know about. A woman he claimed might be in danger of being possessed by an evil, ancient spirit. They had no good description of her, and an address they were even less certain of, but that didn't make it impossible. Not at all.

All of this said nothing of the fact that Mike Vallez hadn't had a decent case in a long while, and saw none in sight. The money was even generous enough to allow him the added luxury of hiring a temporary girl to handle the office while he was out of town.

So he'd gone, found the P.O. box he'd been given, and through it had found—he was now convinced— just the woman the old Navajo had so vaguely described. But the more he learned, the more he wondered about the Indian's purpose, and his mind refused to let it go.

These were nice people really, the young girl, the old man, even in her way, Esther. And despite some peculiarities, real or supposed, Dorella seemed to fit in. She seemed—fine. A bit odd, a bit eccentric with her language, and not many women kept crows as pets, but otherwise . . .

She knew a great deal about history, but then again he knew a great deal about prying and about horses, for that part of his story had been quite true. *People have their interests, that's all*, he thought. Nothing he'd seen warranted covert curiosity, especially by some antique Navajo medicine man—anyway, nothing he'd seen yet.

He had noticed that there was *something* about her though, the look in her eyes sometimes, the expression on her face when people mentioned certain subjects, like religion or war or love—the way she seemed to look right through him at times. But that was all. No spirits. No weird.

That was the trouble.

He'd decided that once he was finished here and had returned his information to his employer, he was going to bother the old boy for an explanation as to exactly what the hell was really going on. This once, for whatever reason, he just couldn't bite it all back.

Meanwhile, of course, he had a job to do.

11

The old doors on the upstairs rooms were as easy to get into as a child's toy bank. Finding the right moment to do so had proven the only difficult part until finally, after nearly two weeks of waiting, the opportunity presented itself.

That morning Vincent, Lynn and Esther had all gone shopping together, reportedly planning to make a day of it. More importantly, Dorella and Alison had decided to visit the local public library for something like old time's sake. At midmorning, alone in the house, Mike Vallez judged the situation to be exactly acceptable and let himself into Dorella's room.

The woman didn't have many clothes or other belongings, almost as if she were a transient drifter or someone on the run. In the corner of the room he discovered a large, dark brown canvas-style bag that contained some of the oddest items he could have imagined.

Beneath bits of faded, mostly threadbare clothing, he found larger, more refined garments apparently hand-embroidered in intricate patterns and dyed in dark, rich colors. These removed, he found a handful of stones, rough and unimpressive, at least to his eye, and also a handful of dark red-and-black speckled stones, some lying loose, some fashioned into amulets, each of them identical in size—each one, no doubt, quite valuable.

He picked up two of them, looking them over, touching their smooth surfaces. They seemed almost warm to the touch and certainly heavier than he had expected. He shrugged wistfully and put the stones back in the bag. Whatever his purpose, he wasn't here to rob an old woman.

There were other items: some very old books, none of them in English, an assortment of twist-tie baggies containing everything from shells and twigs to dried flowers and several different dark and light powders. Other bags held what looked like sand; another, bits of ground crystal; another, something that might have been tea leaves.

Wrapped in a soft gray cloth he found a collection of the most unusual figurines, each somewhat similar in size and composition, yet each one portraying an entirely different figure—figures that could not be clearly identified even with the most imaginative observations, though at a glance they resembled animals . . . almost.

The figures made him feel uneasy as he held them and turned them over in his hands, as if they held some terrible secret or spoke of some impending doom. He wrapped them again and set them back inside the bag.

The prize turned out to be a painting. He found it rolled tightly and tucked inside a hard leather tube. He pulled it out carefully and unrolled it to discover a portrait of two hauntingly beautiful young women. They wore long black gowns that hugged their exquisite figures and colored roses in their thick, black hair. The taller of the two, on the right, wore a thin, gold embroidered sash, the one on the left a gentle mauve shawl that hung about her shoulders and in the back touched her waist.

Each of the women wore necklaces, one a stone pendant like the ones Mike had found in the bag, the other a series of beads and disks that the artist had gone to the trouble of painting to resemble brightly colored glass. He'd seen the gown before, too. The woman on the right, he realized, was a very young Dorella. The woman in the painting with her might have been a sister.

He gently rolled the painting again, slipped it into the tube and put it back. At the bottom of the bag, wrapped in a felt jeweler's pouch, he found the second necklace.

Mike began to wonder if Dorella might not be the descendant of European royalty, or possibly a semi-retired stage or screen actress, or an heiress . . .

Or some crazy kind of cult freak, though that certainly was the least likely answer. As he contemplated the contents of the bag it became clear to him that Dorella was possessed of a complex, mysterious past and had no desire to bring any of it to light—for whatever reason.

That assessment gave rise to a host of questions and an eagerness to get to the bottom of them, but it did nothing to help him resolve a problem he'd started with, that of discovering what on earth she could have to do with the Navajo medicine man.

It came to him that in his rush to welcome minor

fortune he had managed to overlook certain facts about his employer. He'd never gotten a full name out of the fellow, and the two men that had come with him may have been Indians alright, but one looked more Acoma than Navajo. And both of them looked nearly ruined—drawn, hollow faces, empty eyes—the look of the bottle.

He'd never been given a phone or address to use. The old man had insisted instead that Mike personally deliver his information at a special rendezvous point, near a mountain known as Ship Rock on the Navajo reservation, and had promised a small bonus to make the added journey worth his while.

Something to hide and nothing good to say, Mike thought. Seldom a good combination.

Dorella, on the other hand, seemed well-liked, friendly, honest. She simply didn't talk about her past very much. But then again, he hadn't really asked her about it.

He had no intentions of taking sides, especially when it might mean hurting no one but himself at the long end, but he was beginning to want to know just what the sides were.

He was dragged suddenly from his thoughts by the sound of footsteps off the runner, tapping the wooden hallway floor. He got the bag closed just as the door came open behind him. He'd already guessed who it was.

As he spun around Mike Vallez was greeted by a flurry of black wings and sharp, knotty claws all in his face. The bird dug and tore at his upthrust hands, then leaped off to dive again.

Mike used the opportunity to turn and lunge for the open window. He wrenched aside the little metal pins holding the screen in place. The frame slid up just as the crow's strong talons raked the back of his neck. He heard someone—Dorella?—shouting something at him. He looked out the window at the lawn two stories below.

What the hell am I doing? The thought flashed in his mind, bright red—but it was overruled by a massive jolt of adrenaline suddenly boiling through his bloodstream as the woman shouted again in chorus with a deafening screech from the crow. The bird's claws found purchase on his shoulder in the same instant. He jumped.

12

It always seemed that when people were falling on TV, whether they were stunt men or Olympic athletes or parachuting sky divers, they somehow managed to wave their arms and aim their bodies just so, until they brought themselves around to the right position for a perfect landing. Mike tried—a commendable effort—but attained extremely poor results.

He found himself diving earthward absolutely out of shape, turned head first, tipped to snap his neck cleanly on impact. He questioned his life, his sanity, his chances of getting a scream out before it was too late—then realized he was already doing that. He clenched his eyes shut.

And nothing happened.

He reached out with his arms, then his legs, moving them about in all directions, but felt nothing—no earth, no air rushing past, no thud.

He opened his eyes. All around him he saw a featureless, dull-gray and white nothingness. Heaven, maybe, or purgatory or—

But it was *something*, he decided. He could see it, everywhere, anywhere he looked. Substance without form, depth without dimension. He tried to move again and noticed that his actions did cause a reaction, though slight. He arched his back and swung his limbs, and his body began to rotate. The direction was arbitrary but as he kept on, twisting, swinging this limb or that in a deliberate manner, he gradually found he could move whichever way he intended. Like swimming, but much less dramatic. Like astronauts floating about in weightless orbiters, but somewhat more substantial.

He thought how great it would have been to be able to maneuver like this a moment ago, when he was falling—

But he *wasn't* falling anymore. He wasn't in any pain. He thought to check whether he was dreaming, or worse. A pinch was supposedly proof of the former, but how could one verify the latter? He tried a pinch first—which stung nicely. So he wondered . . .

Then someone tapped him on the shoulder and he felt his nerves explode. He turned too quickly, twisting his body at the middle like a screw, then kept going, completing a full circle of rotation.

"You!" he said, wrenching his neck in a futile attempt to face the right way.

She held her arms folded in front of her, a long expression on her face.

She was upside down—or he was.

"Me," Dorella said.

13

Vallez had an obvious log jam of questions pressing to burst past his stunned expression. Dorella had no patience for it.

"I will put you back exactly as I found you," she told him, "an inch from your death, or you will tell me what I need to know."

"Of course," Vallez said, getting his throat working. "But could you tell me—"

"I could, but we're not here for that."

"Where *is* here?"

"A man with a broken neck asks no questions."

Vallez looked at her, wide eyes replaced by a quick composure. "Sure." He swam in a manner that caused his body to pivot until he and Dorella were face to face. This seemed to help put him right in several ways.

"Who sent you?" Dorella asked. "What are you after?"

"I'm a private investigator." He glanced away, examining the endless something/nothing all around, shrugging, barely, to himself. "I was hired to find someone. You, I think. To learn everything I could about you. I'm telling the truth, just in case this is the hereafter. Just in case this is real. I just want to know—"

"Who hired you?"

"Don't know, exactly."

Dorella fixed him with a frown. "Guess."

"What I mean is, it was some old Indian, a Navajo, a medicine man, he said. I never got his name."

"Describe him to me."

Vallez looked at her, tipped his head. "Old. Indian."

"You're not doing very well."

"Look, I'm trying to cooperate, but if I give you every detail, and word gets around I'd do that, I'll never work again. Not that I've got work anyway, but there are principles involved, my principles."

"This is not the hereafter, Mr. Vallez. Not yet."

"I know." He smiled thinly at her. "But I've got this feeling about things. About you. I'm good at that, looking a person over, watching them, seeing through the posturing and getting a full picture in my mind. I don't pretend to know who or what you are, or what the hell is going on, but I don't see you killing me off cold-blooded like that. You're too . . . too nice."

Dorella smiled back. "You don't know me that well."

Vallez shrugged. "So sue me. But in the meantime, couldn't you please give me some idea what all this is about?"

He was a fool, Dorella thought as she considered, as he continued to overwork his torso in an attempt to stay in place. A century ago he'd have already been a part of history. But he had already supplied her with a great deal of information—a medicine man would be a fine enough pretense, Dorella thought.

"We are in that space which exists between normal dimensions, between the levels of existence. You were about to die. There wasn't time to work a proper spell, so I was forced to use a special—knack—I have had since I was a child, and just the right amount of force, to push you just outside the dimension you know as reality.

"Fortunately, it takes very little energy to get here, or to get back. I have not yet decided what to do with you, but since I can leave you here almost indefinitely, I'm in no hurry to. Another method of getting all the details from you, I think."

Dorella began to rotate with no apparent physical movements. When she was fully inverted her body turned slowly away. "You'll keep well enough here until I return. You may go wherever you wish for no direction is far and I can find you easily enough."

"Please, wait!" Vallez launched into a freestyle broad stroke, making little headway behind Dorella. "Don't do this. I'll be good. I'll help."

Dorella drifted away, her speed increasing as she slid out of sight like an airliner after takeoff. No response. No good-bye. Vallez opened his mouth to yell again. It was already too late.

"What the hell happened to you?"

"I just stepped out for a moment," Dorella said.

Alison made a puzzled face. Dorella reflected a moment on what the poor girl must be thinking. She'd just seen Vallez fall screaming out the window, seen Dorella lean out after him and then just vanish. If she'd looked out she would have found Vallez missing as well. Then, before she'd had time to wonder, Dorella had rematerialized out of nowhere in the middle of the room.

"Our friend Mike Vallez is out of business for a while."

Alison's eyes grew wide. "He's still alive?"

Dorella nodded. "I put him in a place just beside reality, a dimension between this world and others. He may even find his own way out eventually, if he's as resourceful as he thinks he is. He is playing a game. I am not. Come with me."

With that Dorella strode out of the room, Alison and a still-panting black crow following close behind. She made straight for Vallez's room. The door clicked and opened even before she reached it. "Just returning a favor," she said and slipped inside.

Vallez's belongings consisted of one large suitcase and a gym bag; only the suitcase had been fully unpacked. The suitcase offered only clothing and toiletries. The gym bag netted a pair of GM car keys with a parking-lot claim ticket attached, and half a round-trip airline ticket good for his return to Albuquerque, New Mexico. She placed both items in the pocket of her dress and turned to Alison.

"I feel a need to begin a journey west," she said. "I don't expect you to go along. In fact, it's probably best if you stay here. Use my room, of course. No one will mind. If for any reason you leave before I return, just leave word with Esther and I'll get in touch."

"Sure," Alison said, nodding too much, like a bob-up in a car's back window. Then she changed the motion to side-to-side. "Are you crazy or something? Have you ever heard the saying 'in for a penny, in for a pound'?"

Dorella looked at her. "No."

"Never mind. Listen, you just don't know what it's like to know you. I didn't follow you here so you could say 'stay' and then run off again. I'm not the dog—or the crow. Whatever you're up to I'm sure I'll find it plenty interesting enough. I still want to learn from you, and learn about you. Anything I can soak up just hanging around. Anything you'll teach me. If I stay here I'm going to miss all the best parts."

"If I find who I'm looking for, I won't want you along."

"You mean Galidar."

Dorella nodded. "If he does somehow truly exist, there is no measure of what might happen, and little doubt that whatever does happen will be unpleasant."

"I can stay out of the way if I have to."

"I can put you with Mr. Vallez until I return if I have to."

"I know!" Alison stood silent, looking Dorella straight in the eye. "But I don't want you to."

"I know." Dorella held her gaze. "You'll do exactly as I say?"

"Of course."

"But what else would you say?" Dorella shook her head. "Very well. I know you'll just mope anyway."

"Endlessly."

Dorella turned and swept back out of Vallez's room, bound for her own, signaling Alison to follow. "Come along," she said. "We have a plane to catch."

Part Seven:
A TENABLE FATE

1

Alone in the dark, dry quiet of his adobe, deep in the midst of meditation, Galidar feels a shift, something almost too subtle to describe. Movement, he thinks.

Somewhere, somehow, something has changed.

2

Bringing an "empty" animal carrier onto an airplane proved only slightly more difficult than it had on a bus, though the presence of frequently passing flight attendants created an unforeseen burden. Dorella was forced repeatedly to renew the spell that allowed the bird to absorb all the visible light waves falling upon it.

Alison kept a constant watch from the aisle seat.

Through team work the bird went unnoticed, though the drain on Dorella's energy did not.

"I'm fine," Dorella explained when Alison asked. "I'll hold up until we get there. Keeping the creature quiet has proven the worst part. It doesn't seem to like this particular variety of flight any better than I do."

With that the crow gave a crusty squawk. Dorella, in turn, sent it cowering with a quick and deadly glare.

A little girl about eight, wearing braided hair and a blue corduroy dress, came walking by with her mother, headed towards the lavatory. She snatched her hand free of her mother's grasp suddenly and leaned past Alison to get a look inside the cage. Dorella gasped and bore down. The bird seemed to fade into nothingness.

By now the girl's mother had a grip on her hand again and began pulling her along, apologizing for the interruption, scolding the child about always bothering everybody on earth. The girl appeared positively stricken.

"What could it hurt," Alison asked, when the pair had gone, "just to let her see the crow?"

Dorella breathed a sigh and the crow reappeared. "It's quite a long story," she muttered.

"We still have two hours 'til New Mexico."

"Umm," Dorella acquiesced. "That ought to be just about enough."

3

The New Mexico sky was bright with fevered, parched sunlight. They stepped from the cool air of the terminal building and made their way along walkways to the parking areas, wading in the sea of cars until they reached the spot that matched Mike Vallez's parking stub: Row F, Slot Six. A sun-bleached maroon

Pontiac 6000. In the glove box they found the registration.

The car belonged to Mike Vallez Investigations, Inc., so it was reasonable to assume that the address listed there was Mike's office. They found other items: a camera, a Bic lighter that didn't work, wadded fast-food wrappers. A pad of yellowed paper lay on the console. Two versions of what was apparently a want ad for a secretary had been scratched on it. The trunk was empty other than the temporary spare. The obvious course dictated a trip downtown. Dorella let Alison drive.

Once they were out of the slot Alison turned the car's air conditioner on. The two women waited for comforting coolness to flow from the dash vents. By the time they reached the main road into town they were still baking.

"For an investigator," Alison remarked, "Vallez creates more puzzles than he solves."

Dorella smiled, then turned her attentions to the car. She closed her eyes and said a few words, using language more appropriate for dealing with mill works and ox carts, making little changes in the style and putting in a few ad-libs near the end. In all it was an incantation few of her ancestors would have approved, though the air from the vents quickly grew cold.

They drove through a city that Dorella found hardly peculiar: streets and houses and office buildings, all quite interchangeable with their Northeastern, even European counterparts. Not unlike the streets of other cities in other times, in other lands. . . .

Once again she had the rare notion that it was only the individuals that gave the patterns meaning—who, not what. Intriguing, intricate ideas, she thought, though there might be enough time to see them through.

They bought gas and a county map at a quick-fill, then hunted down Vallez's office, which they found to be an old but well-preserved three-story office building on the edge of downtown, near a giant furniture warehouse. They parked the car in the small lot around back and left it running, A/C on, with the doors locked, so as not to cook the crow while it waited for them. They went in through the building's rear door.

The tiny foyer offered no ledger, so they started on the first floor, checking the names on every door, noting that many of the doors were bare. On the second floor they found an office marked M.V. INVESTIGATIONS and tried the knob. It wasn't locked. Dorella hesitated.

"They *should* be open," Alison remarked at a whisper. "It's Monday. You don't have any sixth sense or something you're not telling me about?"

"No. We don't know who might be here." Dorella shook her head. "But I *would* sense something, I think."

"Okay, after you," Alison offered. "Age before beauty."

"I've heard that," Dorella said. "What about, 'Last one in,' or whatever it is?"

"What about it?"

"I don't know." Dorella swung the door open wide.

"Morning," said the woman at the desk: a metal secretary's desk containing a phone, an ink blotter and a note pad; a blond woman in her thirties, tanned too dark, skin showing a premature shrivel from the sun, or from tribulation. She wore a mauve crepe blouse trimmed in white. She was holding a copy of the *Star News*, and as she put it down Dorella noticed how thin she really was, all bones beneath the light material of her blouse, only her tan keeping her face opaque. She held her left eye in a particular squint, as though concentrating on some new, inconceivable aspect of her visitors, but on closer inspection Dorella realized it was the result of a poorly mended tear that ran from the lid up into her left eyebrow.

The woman grinned briefly at them and straightened in her chair, a small attempt to appear pleasant. Dorella saw already that there was little truth in her wan expression.

"Rita," she said of herself. "I'm afraid Mike isn't in today. Maybe I could take a message for him."

"In fact, we need information," Dorella replied. "Mr. Vallez is presently working for a Navajo Indian and is in Pennsylvania. Please tell us all you know about this."

Rita's calm gaze seemed to falter slightly. "Why, no. Of course I can't!" she said, her voice cracking. "That's all very, ah, confidential."

"How long have you been working for Mr. Vallez?" Alison asked, circling the desk slowly, looking everything over.

"Not long."

"How long is that, exactly?" Alison pressed her.

"A—a few weeks. Do you actually know him?"

"Oh yes, very well," Dorella said.

The woman turned suddenly skeptical. "Why don't you give me your names, addresses and phones numbers, then I'll have Mike get back to you. He can answer all your questions. *I* ain't gonna."

Dorella caught a flicker of perception in Alison's quick glance. They both turned back towards the receptionist. Or whoever she was.

"Sorry," Alison said. "I'm afraid your pal Mike—"

"Thank you, Rita," Dorella said, stepping in front of Alison, cutting her off. She walked forward to the desk and held out her hand. "We will have to come back another time. It was very nice meeting you."

Rita stared up somewhat blankly, then grinned, thin mauve lips riding up over gray teeth. She took Dorella's hand and shook it limply—then froze in place.

Dorella gazed deeply into the woman's eyes, searching the upper layers of her consciousness for information. She frowned inwardly at what she saw. A shell, dark and cold within, ignorance buoyed by indifference, spunk fueled by want. Whatever Rita was doing here, it had nothing to do with an affinity for office management.

No magic had been used to imbue her to her mission, yet Dorella doubted any would have been required. Certain individuals, human or otherwise, were quite utilitarian; commonly, readily for sale, often at very reasonable prices.

Dorella didn't need to buy Rita, however, she only needed a short-term lease. "Good night," she said, and squeezed the other's hand. Rita slumped back into her chair, her torso collapsing across the desk as Dorella guided her there. "Let us see if Mr. Vallez keeps proper records," she announced. Alison headed for the larger desk and twin filing cabinets in the adjoining room.

All of Vallez's files were stacked neatly inside the filing drawers, none of them in any particular order. None of them, after a lengthy search that left Alison and Dorella standing amidst a sea of paper, seemed in any way connected to Dorella or mysterious Indians. They searched the desk, the note pads, even the small, noisy refrigerator in the corner (which contained only two bottles of Coors and an open can of Pepsi). The room's single closet contained a gray-blue sports coat, a white windbreaker and a short stack of old magazines, *Playboys, Reader's Digests*.

"It's really hopeless," Alison said finally, rubbing her eyes with the palms of her hands. "The guy's a schmuck." She sat on the floor, leaning against the big wooden desk, toying with the phone cord that hung off the edge. Dorella came over to her, rested a hand on the desk.

"I'd say you're right," she said. "A schmuck."

Alison stood up and looked around, drumming fingernails on the wooden surface. A fluorescent lamp stood on one corner of the desk. She picked it up, found only dust beneath it. Moving the phone produced the same results. She shrugged, then added a sigh.

Dorella caught herself doing the same thing. She straightened and picked up the square green ink blotter that covered the center of the desktop. Underneath it she found a folded, badly faded dollar bill and a worn fingernail file. She let the blotter back down. Alison snatched it up again. She picked up the dollar bill and opened it, laid it flat.

Dorella saw it now, the pen scratchings along the border. The words "Medicine Man" and "Ship Rock." The two women looked at each other. Dorella put the bill in her pocket and then headed for the outer office.

Thumbtacked to the paneled wall near the front door was a map of the State of New Mexico. Dorella began looking it over while Alison grabbed the note pad off the receptionist's desk, fished a pen out of a drawer and joined her. She began making a sketch of the desert.

"I don't know what we'll find out there," Dorella told her. "You should think of yourself. For a change."

"I know. I told you I wasn't missing all the fun parts. Anyway, I happen to know you can't drive." She tossed the pad and pen at the receptionist, reached up and tugged. The map came free of the wall. "Let's go," she said.

Dorella shrugged, then sighed—and followed her out.

4

The battered Jeep makes a thin trail of rising dust as it pounds along a narrow bead of earthen roadway, crossing the desert towards the small adobe. Galidar stands outside the entrance to his tiny house, letting the sun feed him with its warmth; he had been cold for more than a thousand years and has yet to find fresh annoyance in such comforts.

The car stops as close as it can, pulling over near the Rock. Wagua emerges and covers the remaining distance on foot. Even in bright daylight his eyes look as though they have been baked nearly shut. His gait lacks energy. Galidar waits him out, concerned more with the message the young Indian carries. He thinks it is the most activity this poor fellow has done in some time.

"Rita called," he says, panting—wheezing, more like. "Some people came by. Two women, one older, one younger. She thinks the old one may be the same person you sent Vallez to look for, and maybe now she's coming to look for you. She don't know what happened to Vallez."

Galidar considers him serenely. Rita is far better at sex than she is at thinking, he knows, though he suspects that in this instance she may be partly correct. Rita would have no way of knowing which one of the women was his adversary, either one of their appearances could be no more than a seeming. But he has sensed something recently, further movement—has concentrated on it all morning. A presence, shrouded and deflected as expected, but seemingly, recently, very *near*. He is almost certain of it. "Where are the two now?"

"She says they asked a few questions, then left. I got people watching the roads, especially roads this way. I got word already that maybe they were seen heading for the reservation along I-64. Maybe coming here, probably going into town, though. We're waiting. We could set something up if you want, catch them between—"

"No. If this is who we suspect, then they will not stay in town. She will sense something here, just as I am aware of her. They will turn off, into the desert, and that is what you must look for. Then you will report quickly to me. I must know exactly.

"There are things I want you to do in preparation of their arrival. Gather the others. I will give you instructions for them as well." He eyed Wagua assessingly. "I will keep it brief."

The younger Indian nodded, open-mouthed, and tried hard to concentrate on every single word.

5

The land was marked by sandstone monoliths that rose from the flat earth, pointing at the long blue sky like stubby fingers. Occasional clumps of housing passed, much of it fairly new, though most of it was simple and very often identical.

Alison drove on, following the road towards a little town called Ship Rock in the northwestern part of the reservation. They were nearly there, a little while out of Farmington, trailing along beside the San Juan River, when Dorella made Alison pull over and stop.

"He is not there," she announced, gazing intently into the scrubby countryside. "Not directly ahead. He waits to the south."

"You know, I've been wondering about this setup," Alison told her. "And I bet you're right." She reached between the seats and pulled up the map, unfolding it. "You see this," she said pointing. "This is the *town* of Ship Rock, right here, but also over here and to the south, is a geologic landmark which is *also* known as Ship Rock." She reached down again and retrieved a pamphlet they had picked up at a gas station in the city. The pamphlet contained tourist information about the reservation, its people, its finer points. "There's a picture of it here," she said. "It's way out in the desert, in the middle of nowhere. So I didn't think it could be the Ship Rock we wanted."

Dorella thumbed her chin, eyeing the map, then turned to face directly southwest and closed her eyes. For a moment she was completely still.

"The pull is very strong. I haven't felt anything like it in—in a very long—"

She stopped then, opening her eyes. She stared at the desert again, keeping quiet.

"We can turn off," Alison said, "take Route 666, then take the desert roads." She pointed the route out, thin lines on the map. Dorella nodded, drooping her shoulders in capitulation.

"You act like you already know something's going to go wrong," Alison said. "And the more I learn about your instincts, the less I like it when that happens."

"It's not too late for you to be sensible," Dorella said, turning, looking at her. "You could stay in town, perhaps, at least until—"

"Yeah," Alison said. "Right." She chuckled wryly, then put the car in gear and launched it onto the dull, dusty pavement.

Dorella placed a mild spell upon Alison, quite inconspicuously, which was intended to protect her from minor irresponsibilities of fate—a snake bite, the falling sky, a flu—a minor precaution, she thought. After all, not everyone could be so reckless.

6

From a distance, Ship Rock resembled a man buried in the sand up to his arm pits, each arm outstretched: the head and shoulders of some massive alien monument. The land was stubbled with a mix of nominal dark shrubs that did little to make the rusty browns and stormy grays of the rocks stand out. Ship Rock was the biggest thing in sight. Dorella turned to Alison as they approached it.

"Drive off here, that way," she said, "around the other side of the rock. I feel the source of the magic is there, or something of it is."

Alison cautiously eyed the sandy way. "What if the car gets stuck out there?"

Dorella shot her a narrow glance. A look Alison was apparently quite familiar with.

"Okay, never mind," Alison said, then complied. The little car bounced and rattled through the rough terrain with remarkable footing. Alison tried to stay out of the shallow gullies and circumnavigate the clumps of near leafless brush clinging to the desert. At one point, coming down from the last in a series of hard bounces, something in the transaxle made a cracking, ringing sound and the car ceased to move.

Dorella climbed out, stood looking at the car disparagingly, then spoke to it softly, like a coachman forced to comfort his team during thunder. Directly she got back in. Alison tried the shifter. The car lurched forward.

"Certain physical things," Dorella confided, "are not so difficult. Though machines necessitate a certain amount of—creativity." Alison only smiled.

Dorella continued to guide their way, slowly rounding the wing of the rock, driving out over the more heavily ravined surfaces on the far side. They found an adobe house half hidden in a gully some distance away. Made of much mud and little wood and sewn with brush, the colors and configuration of the tiny adobe made it almost invisible. Very remote, very inconspicuous, Dorella thought.

Nevertheless, as they drew near, Alison was quick to point out that theirs was not the only vehicle to make tracks on this piece of the desert lately; Dorella only nodded.

"Maybe they were made by tourists," Alison suggested.

"Or by someone here waiting for us, I rather suspect. Galidar, for a fact, was never fond of doing everything by himself. Not so long as other, less glorious hands were readily available. I have already met several of his more recent—friends. It is possible some of them are here."

"Swell."

They sat staring at the adobe, windows down, letting their bodies adjust to the outside temperature. A hint of breeze touched their faces. "What's our plan?" Alison asked, her voice somber now.

"We get out and see who is home."

"I should have thought of that." Alison opened her door and slid slowly out. Dorella turned and checked the crow, found it sitting contently in its familiar carrier, eyeing her with vague indifference. She thought to let it out—aerial reconnaissance was always an asset—then decided to wait, seeing no immediate danger in this vastness of being snuck up on, and stepped out.

They moved into the ravine with great caution, minding their footing, keeping silent. There were no windows in the little structure and just one door. The only other opening was a hole in the roof, too small for a man to fit through, intended to allow the smoke from cooking fires to escape.

Dorella stopped Alison and stood completely still. She reached out then, "feeling" the way ahead, but could sense no one. Yet the aura of magic was still evident, a radiance without warmth. She slowly moved forward to the entrance and motioned to Alison with a slight flip of her head. She reached out and pulled the door flap open, and the magical aura grew more intense.

Easing herself in, squatting to navigate the short doorway, Dorella found the adobe's interior unoccupied. Candles were set about the walls. No furniture was present. She spoke to the candlewicks and flame caught on their tips. In the fresh light she viewed the room's details: a scattering of bowls and pots, a locked trunk against one wall, a small metal tub filled with water. The most interesting item in the adobe lay at her feet.

"There's something like this in the brochure," Alison said, wiggling in beside her, following Dorella's stare. "It's what they call a sand painting. The medicine men use them."

Dorella examined the fine detail of the painting, the flat colors. There were stick figures in the middle, vaguer patterns all around, and an odd background latticework of patterns that worked only to spoil everything else, so far as she could tell. A ring of painted feathers pointed outward from the middle like the petals of a daisy. These were enclosed finally by three brightly colored rings.

As she looked, Dorella saw something in the latticework that bothered her, a subtle image, she was sure, that was not directly apparent unless viewed with the corner of the eye. She sought to change her angle and moved left, then back around to the right, finally circling the painting almost completely. She found the narrow confines of the hut a formidable obstacle, and did all she could do to keep from stumbling into the painting itself. Alison came along behind her—but did not fare as well.

With a sudden yelp Alison pitched forward, arms whirling, and landed in the center of the sand painting, which instantly caused the fierce tendrils of the magical trap within to swarm up and about her with radiant dark energy.

Dorella forced herself back against the earthen walls of the adobe, nearly blinded. Now she saw the small protective spell about Alison burn bright and die as it was instantly devoured by the ravenous trap.

She could see it clearly now, expertly woven into the painting, a geometric trap indifferent to the passing of a random mouse, or even a normal human being, yet designed to catch anything magical that touched it.

As the deadly thing rose and took shape Dorella was able to identify its creator by its distinct elemental aura, to taste of it and recall its poison, a distant yet unforgettably foul flavor she knew belonged to Galidar.

Somehow, in some form, some impossible incarnation, he *must* still exist. She had seen his smoldering body, felt his essence fade from it, but there could be no mistake now. The worry was real. The terrible danger, to her or to anyone unfortunate enough to fall under his manipulative attention, was *real*. A thousand years, she thought; still it was much too soon.

Alison seemed physically untouched by the magical trap, seemed largely unaware of what had transpired, but soon enough there would be numerous threats Dorella must reckon with, physical threats which Dorella knew she might be unable to avert. There was no time to belabor the point, and no point in waiting for the worst to happen. Galidar found his own kind occasionally formidable, but humans were as web-wound flies to a spider. She had to do something at once.

Alison turned to her, holding her palms out apologetically as she looked up from the artistic damage her feet had wrought. Dorella waited while the claws of the trap vanished back into the painting, while Alison smiled, sheepish, and stepped off to the side, out of the ruined painting—the waiting trap.

"I'm sorry," Dorella told her, and gently pushed.

Alison's eyes opened wide, and then she was gone.

7

Everywhere off-white nothingness—

Alison screamed, put her hand to her mouth to make herself stop, then drew a shivered breath. Where had the world gone? she wondered. Where had *she* gone?

She feared for a moment she might be frozen in place, then wondered if instead her mind simply refused to mobilize her body. She forced herself to breathe more deeply. She blinked. A spell of some kind, she decided, holding her prisoner. She had the impression of being back in the womb—which, she reasoned, denoted the possibility of eventual release.

She was brought abruptly back to herself as someone tapped her on the shoulder. She jumped—an action which caused her to rise—or fall—several feet. She noted with extreme curiosity that as her body slowed and stopped it remained perfectly in its new location and did not fall—or rise—back towards . . . towards where she had been.

Alison looked around and "down" and was again surprised as she laid eyes upon Mike Vallez.

"Nice of you to pop in," he said, grinning like some ridiculous, mischievous child.

Alison gazed about at her surroundings again. She waved her arms a bit, then a bit more, until she was facing almost directly down at Vallez. "How do I get . . . there?" she asked.

"Just sort of . . . walk. Like this."

Then he moved, strolling through the air like an awkward god, circling out, then back in. He reached out his hand to her. Reluctantly, she took it.

"Come on," he said.

"Where?"

He turned and walked her down to about the location she had originally been in—so far as she could tell. She felt all turned around inside, as though she were having attacks of claustrophobia and acrophobia at the same time.

Vallez stopped, stood looking at her, holding her left hand with both of his now. "Right here," he said. "Now, let's not move, and we might be able to work this out. Or, I should say, work *us* out."

Alison was beginning to get her equilibrium. She blinked hard again, then shook her head and frowned. "What are you saying?" she asked, loading her voice with annoyance. "Not that I feel I ought to listen."

"Oh, forgive me for being amiable," Mike said, letting go, holding his hands out like a preacher. "You're the first—the *only* person I've seen for—for however long I've been in—in wherever this is. You'll have to give me that."

"I'll tell you what I'll give you, you son of a bitch. You came to spy on Dorella. You're some sort of half-assed private dick, I happen to know. You work for a sorcerer named Galidar who wants to destroy her! You—"

"Hold it a minute! I was hired by some old Navajo medicine man. An information-only, nobody-gets-hurt job. He paid in advance. And very well, I should add. And that's all there is to it."

Alison glared incredulously at him. "So you have no idea who he is or what he's up to?"

"I still don't. He never said anything about destroying anybody or did anything to make me think he could if he wanted to. And nothing at all about sorcerers. So maybe you could tell me what *you* know."

"About what? Dorella? Galidar? You?" She looked away. "I know Dorella is acting weird about all this, even for her, and that isn't good. Whatever else I happen to know is probably best not shared with you or your two-peso secretary."

"Hey, she's just a temporary. I can't even remember her whole name right now. Look, I admit I was sent to learn something about your friend, but what I've learned doesn't make any sense. Not the least of which is that she is capable of putting me here and that makes her anything but a nice, eccentric, half-lost lady, which is sort of what I was led to believe. I'm also quite capable of figuring out that some simple old Indian would not be pulling something like this with someone like her, if that makes any sense—and I'm not sure it does.

"I can imagine maybe they're old friends, or that they're just the opposite, but I can't tell you who or what either one of them are. I'm convinced I haven't been handling things very well, if that helps, and I'm definitely open to suggestions."

Alison softened her posture somewhat, seeing at that moment a vested lack of harshness in the other's face, a reflection of vulnerability in his eyes. Perhaps she had hung around Dorella long enough to learn her knack for seeing truth in people, or perhaps it was a latent talent of her own. But Vallez didn't look at all dangerous anymore, more like a puppy who had missed the papers.

She still wanted to think of him as a snake, but perhaps . . .

"I don't have any . . . suggestions," she said. "I don't quite know why she put me here, though I believe we're safe enough, at least the way she explained it to me when she was telling me about you. Maybe that's it: protection, safety. And on the spur of the moment, the same way it was with you."

"Spur?"

Alison nodded.

"I'm definitely impressed all the same. I'd like to see her work when she's at her leisure."

"Oh, I have," Alison said, reflecting back. She frowned as memories overlapped, as her perspectives grew muddled. "I still think putting me here against my will, right in the middle of things, was a miserable trick." She looked at Vallez. "In your case, though, it was undoubtedly warranted."

Mike grinned sarcastically at her. "Be that as it may, I wonder if we might use this little break to start a brief discussion. You know, you tell me who or what the hell your friend Dorella actually is, and who you really are, and what the hell is going on. Stuff like that."

"I suppose it won't make much difference now that we're in here."

"It will to me."

Alison only stared at him.

"So go on."

"If I asked, would you tell me whether you're still on Galidar's payroll?"

"Please, I may not be as clever as I thought I was, but give my mother at least a little credit."

He had a slightly different look now, Alison saw, stronger, yet remarkably unpretentious.

"Dorella explained that this was some kind of way station between dimensions," Alison said. "She also said you'd likely be able to find your own way out . . . eventually. She thinks you're bright somehow."

"I am. In fact I may be onto something. When Dorella left she went back to approximately the place where she came in, then inverted herself, and simply walked out. I think that may be a key. But I haven't been able to find her exact point of entry—which I think is another key. My own point of entry is not something that I think I would want to find, even if I could."

"It *is* very easy to get disoriented in here," Alison said, wistfully gazing about. She let her shoulders slump. "This could take forever. I can't imagine where I might have entered anymore."

"I can," Mike said, almost cavalierly. "I witnessed your appearance. That's why I've tried to keep us in the same spot." He put his hands on Alison's shoulders and turned her forty-five degrees right, then assisted her in turning upside down. Once she was stationary he mimicked the procedure.

"You haven't told me anything I really wanted to know yet," Mike mentioned, waiting until she looked at him. She held her hand out, let him take it again. "No," she said. "But there's a very good chance I will."

They stepped forward in a motion.

"One other thing," he said mid-stride, almost as an afterthought. "Where were you when she popped you out?"

8

Ponies talk. They tell him of the strangers coming across the desert.

When the strangers arrive he is long away, high in the ruffled mountains to the southwest. Here he waits deep in concentration, his mind trained on his tiny desert home, on the car as it approaches there, and especially on the being he trusts is inside.

He has instructed Wagua and James to follow the

car at a good distance, to give the occupants time at his house, then to move in and finish their tasks. He knows what they will find if all goes as expected—as planned.

He rests atop a bluff, looking out through a high walled canyon which faces Ship Rock. He makes some few comforts for himself, a lean-to behind a ridge of tall, sheltering rock, and bedding beneath its shade. A fire to cook a rattlesnake that has obligingly wandered past his camp. He watches the sun descend across the clear, blue-white sky, letting his ancient spirit baste in its fusion-wrought radiance. He protects his tender mortal body from its harmful spectrum with a common, simple working—common to a different era, he notes.

He has found this newer world to be a place where magic holds little sway, where men admire, respect, hate, *fear* mostly themselves, and where the last of his kind have abated somehow. He has observed this mien even in the limited minds of his own new soldiers, and in the girl, Rita.

For everything that the universe is or ever will become, it seems, there are men who seek explanations; men who expect that, once found, those same explanations will somehow manifest themselves in human destiny. They reach for the power of the gods yet discard or discount any primitive, untidy mentions of darker forces. He has always found that those who do not look back are easily approached from behind. So in some respects, they are no wiser at all. He sees an advantage in this.

As he sits on the rock, Galidar lends thought to the future, to a time when he will extend his studies of modern man and his world, of his own influence over them both. He has many plans for the days ahead, but they are all contingent on the paramount task before him now, on removing the weight of vengeance from his mind—the craving it fires inside him.

He thinks again of the time of his fall—he is vividly

reminded of the sight and scent of Dorella. A hateful passion begins to overwhelm him; he lets it come, lets it strengthen his vehement resolve—though only for a moment. He must exercise control. There is not much time.

Galidar bears down squarely upon the plains beyond the mountains, the barely perceived rock that punctuates the desolate surface. It is at that moment that he feels the trap spring to life.

He detects the sudden presence of the trap's victim, senses magic being devoured by the trap's lethal appetite. This time the power he has stored in the trap seems to be more than enough. He is all but certain that his plan has netted him the one being he has hoped it would—that Dorella is his.

As the magic-laden trap retreats into itself Galidar thinks of his soldiers, Wagua and James, who are, he expects, already driving near in their truck, closing in. They will find only one whole, living person upon arrival, the human girl who is Dorella's companion. They will give her a small bottle of liquid to drink, a potent concoction he has created which, if the girl has any magical talent at all, will cause a bright reaction that he will sense, and that the two Indians, by her brief convulsions, will easily witness.

If the test is positive they will bring her to him. If there is no reaction they have been instructed to question her, for there may be secrets she will know, secrets that, per his own special guidelines, they must force her to tell. This done, they will find for her a suitable resting place in the vast New Mexican desert.

Before leaving they will closely examine the sand painting in the adobe and confirm the softly imaged lines of life essence radiating within its angular design matrix. He must know she is there, secure, powerless. Waiting for him.

He has given much thought to the many ways he might end her wretched existence. The final, ultimate choices are aligned in his mind and selection from among them remains his only task. It is a most joyous one.

Tonight, once he has heard from his observers, once he is certain, he will go to Ship Rock and be finished with it.

9

The trap showed signs of great ingenuity and fine expertise. The many finer lines of the painting were clearly visible, displayed like dim neon tubing by the fresh energy they contained. Galidar had always been a vexingly clever sort, Dorella reminded herself. She must let caution walk before her now.

She turned and made her way out of the little hut, crouching again through the doorway, emerging into the hot afternoon sun. She went around back of the adobe and climbed up on the earthen mound that was a part of the ravine, then stepped off onto the wooden roof. She needed to think, to consider the whole situation. He would come now, she thought, from somewhere, in some form, and she must prepare for that.

She reached inside herself, then out across the space between the stars, sailing beyond the arm of the galaxy into the endless depths of creation. She located the one small, familiar, stable string in the near universe, then joined with it, touching its inner fury with the fingers of her mind. Near here, just beyond a huge elliptical galaxy that dwarfed the many clusters in the region, she could sense again the prickling aura of the massive string she had found in her youth. She concentrated on it with her most tenuous touch, unable to resist this slight indulgence, yet unwilling to chance anything more. She felt its terrible forces, an unimaginable concentration of the core fires from the birth of the universe; not a crack, this one, but a great rift.

Dorella shuddered inwardly at its seductive potential,

its sheer limitlessness. To her knowledge none of her kind had ever found, and certainly never used, this rift—at least none that had survived. Often she had been tempted, but always, *always* she had resisted. And endured.

She let the awareness fade from her mind and fully concentrated instead on the tiny, aptly potent string she had already made contact with. She drew cautiously, safely from its energies. When she was done, she sailed back into herself, back again to the desert of New Mexico.

The old wizard was doing his best to shield himself from her senses, just as she had done, constantly renewing the spells that might mask a low, purposely subdued aura. But Galidar had certainly been the one to set the trap and was no doubt aware of its recent activity. He would act in some manner. She was aware of the intensity of her anticipation as this last thought settled with her—centuries of anticipation—everything brought sharply into focus; it reminded her too much of fear, so she tried to refuse the thought.

A flicker of movement caught her eye, dark spots barely visible on the heat-shimmered horizon. She stood up, fumbling about with select ancient phrases, nudging her memory into service as she searched for the proper words. The third attempt had a ring of authenticity to it and she felt the spell take hold. Her vision promptly improved and the distance seemed small; her hearing improved momentarily and she found the drone of a small truck adrift on the hot breezes.

She reached out to the truck, examining everything there with senses no human being had ever possessed. There was no magic, no Galidar. Not yet. Still, these newcomers seemed to have a particular purpose, heading straight for the rock as they were. Perhaps they would prove a good source of information. . . .

With a fresh effort, Dorella concentrated her energies on the door of the little animal carrier still inside her car, causing it to pop open. She beckoned the crow, speaking to it with her mind, lending it a sense of her intentions. The bird took flight, leaping through the car's open window, and sailed quickly into the bright, ocher distance.

One other task remained. She worked a subtle, superficial illusion, a veil over the truth, and covered herself with another, younger woman's image: Alison's.

Dorella sat back down, letting her legs dangle off the adobe's low roof, and watched them come.

10

They came the last leg on foot. Two young Indians each dressed in light-colored, long-sleeve shirts and faded jeans, each wearing wide-brimmed, western-style hats to shade their heads from the sun. One of them stopped to examine the Pontiac as they passed it, the other, in the lead, kept his dark eyes trained steadily on the adobe and the sitting figure atop its roof.

Their minds were easily read, Dorella found, the surfaces telling more than enough of what lay beneath; they spoke of misfortune and misdirection—of much texture with little substance. Not awfully bad men, Dorella assessed, but there was little good left in them and much of Galidar's influence.

When at last they stood on the crest of the ravine, level with her and less than two meters away, Dorella smiled and gave a little wave.

"You are the witch's companion," the lead Indian said.

Dorella cocked her head, considering them. "Very well," she said. "I am that."

The same Indian instructed the other man to stand watch over her, then he climbed down and disappeared into the adobe. The second Indian had slightly more rounded features, was less convincing as a deadly henchman than the first. Dorella asked him for his name. He was reluctant to reply at first, but Dorella found it an exceedingly small task to sort that out. "James," he said finally. He said his friend's name was Wagua. She asked him where Galidar was. He said he didn't know. It seemed to be the truth.

Wagua came back out and regained the top edge of the ravine. He reached around to the small of his back and pulled a stubby revolver from his belt.

"What did you find?" James was asking, apparently anxious, his mind clear again.

The other man made a tight face, glanced briefly at the adobe's entrance. "I think it looks the way he told us. The lines are there. They don't look so bright though, not like I thought they'd be. No trace of a body."

"Maybe there isn't supposed to be," James concluded, making a face at the desert. "The witch isn't here."

Wagua looked at him and shrugged, then nodded and turned back to Dorella. He raised the pistol, bringing it to bear. James struggled a piece of paper from the tight pocket of his jeans and unfolded it, then handed it to Wagua.

"And the bottle," Wagua said. James went back into his pockets.

"We got something for you," he said, taking the bottle from James, "and some questions. You answer them. Simple."

"Then you'll kill me, of course," Dorella said.

Both men looked at each other.

"Your pants are undone," Dorella said.

Both men looked down. She closed her eyes in brief concentration. Wagua was glaring at her when she opened them.

"I will kill you *now* if you don't cooperate," Wagua said tersely.

"Be careful you don't shoot yourself instead, my poor friend," Dorella told him.

Wagua scrunched one eye in momentary perplexity as he glanced down at the handgun and saw that the barrel was facing directly at him, despite the still normal configuration of the grip and trigger. He turned the gun around in his hand and found that the weapon resumed its normal shape—and found it pointed, quite properly, at himself again. A third attempt returned the gun to its impossible front/back condition. He closed his eyes hard—a painfully tight expression—then opened them again, then shook his head at the lack of improvement.

Wagua swore an oath in Navajo, then handed the backwards pistol to James in a violent motion. He undid the snap on the leather sheath that hung from his belt and withdrew a short, single-edged hunting knife. James, in a delayed response, drew a similar blade of his own.

Wagua came forward, stepping down the slight slope ahead, then stepping up again onto the roof of the adobe. He glared at Dorella, gritting his teeth, clenching his fist as he held the knife out threateningly—and winced.

He looked down to find himself in a predicament similar to his previous one, this time clutching not the grip of the knife but the blade. Blood oozed down his palm and dripped from his wrist. A twisted, fearful look came to his features.

"Oh, here," Dorella said. "Let me take that from you." She reached out and took the grip, then pulled the knife free. Wagua shuddered back in open-mouthed, silent anguish as the blood dripped from his trembling hand. Dorella reached out again and touched him, speaking to him in a soft, even voice. He closed his eyes with a sigh and crumpled to the roof.

James, in an obvious sudden change of heart, dropped the peculiar pistol, lowered his own knife and turned to run. He stumbled—though it was not quite apparent over what—and went down clutching at his ankle. Dorella dropped the knife, then moved off the roof onto the ridge and stood over him. He was holding the injured limb, moaning, looking up at Dorella in frightened anguish. She stared at him a moment as he fought to control his whimpering, then she did a very small, very simple thing to him. He looked down at his ankle with amazed relief.

"Come along," Dorella instructed him. "I'll just bet you know how to drive."

11

Wagua came to in vague mystery. Hot sun baked his back. His temples throbbed dully. He pushed himself up with his forearms. Sand had adhered to his sweaty face. He leaned over to one side, went to wipe his cheek and saw the long cut, already scabbed over, that crossed the palm of his hand and ran to his index finger. Then he remembered.

The fogged vision before him became recognizable as Galidar's adobe, and the sun—the sun had hardly moved, which meant this might be about the same time next day—or only an hour or so had passed since—

But his hand!

He had been on countless binges, survived countless mornings after; he thought to trade this moment for any one of those, and yet—and yet he felt rested, as though he had slept for ages. He yawned, stretched, squinted anew at his surroundings. She was gone, of course, whoever she was and so was James.

He got himself up and wandered gingerly about. He found his pistol nearby, from all indications quite normal again, and put it back in his belt, then recovered his knife. He climbed down and ducked his head into the adobe, making sure it was empty, then climbed back to high ground and scanned the horizons.

The afternoon was getting late, shadows reaching

long across the scrubby dry earth. The truck was still there, parked near the other side of Ship Rock, just visible beyond the jagged ridge. He made straight for it.

When he reached the truck he found the hood open, the distributor cap and wires melted onto the engine, the battery cables melted through. He'd never seen anything like it.

Can't even play the radio, he brooded. He dug the canteen out from beneath the passenger seat, then sat on the driver's side and sipped—and tried very, very hard to think. Directly, though, a sound caught his ear and fortunately removed the need.

He stood up on the seat cushion, put his hand above his eyes and squinted into the distance until he saw a car approaching. He watched it become a tattered gray Volvo that rolled up finally beside the truck. A woman got out: Rita.

She was dressed in a blue and beige sun dress, thin straps at the shoulder, cleavage showing all over the place; an effective distraction from the plainness of her face.

She greeted him absently, her eyes searching the desert.

"Why have you come?" he asked.

"I'm just checking up on you guys." She went on studying the vicinity, a perplexed look coming over her. "I think the woman and the girl I met in Albuquerque are headed here, and I thought—"

"I know all about it. Never mind. You're too late."

Rita scowled at him. "They've been here?" she asked.

Wagua nodded dully.

"Where's Galidar?"

"I guess he knows about it already. At least, I guess he *thinks* he does. He had this sand painting in the adobe, it was supposed to catch her, but I'm pretty sure something went wrong." He looked at his hand again, saw only a fading scar. "I saw the painting, it didn't look like he said it would . . . exactly."

"Show me the painting," Rita snapped. "You couldn't see dark at midnight." She turned impatiently and set off towards the adobe.

Wagua scrambled after her, trying to keep up. He hadn't realized until just then how hungry the day's events had made him or how weak he had become. He set his mind on new priorities, then became disheartened as he considered the time involved in the drive back.

They had nearly reached the adobe when something odd occurred just in front of the door, a distortion of the air, a slight change in temperature. Shapes came at them out of nothingness, growing clear an instant after that, becoming two human figures—who stood quite unsteadily, gaping about, hanging onto each other. Wagua, in a sudden rush of cognizance, remembered the pistol and drew it. Rita stood smiling beside him.

"I didn't think I'd see *you* out here," she said, addressing Mike Vallez. She looked at both of them sidelong for a moment. "How the hell did you just do that?" she asked.

They stared at her. Rita's expression clouded. "No matter," she said. "I don't know what's going on, but I think it's best if we let Galidar sort it out for himself." She bit into her lip, hesitating. "We just have to find him."

"It's okay," Wagua said. "I'm supposed to meet him in the hills. I know where. Me and James were—"

"Where the hell *is* James?" Rita asked him.

"I wish to hell I knew."

Rita shook her head. "Great." She moved back out of the way. "Everybody go." She waved Alison and Mike on with one hand, motioning to Wagua with the other, urging him to keep them covered. When they reached the car she got Wagua to drive, then got the other two to crowd into the front seat beside him, so that she and the pistol could keep an eye on them from the backseat.

She stood waiting for them to get settled, looking about the desert in dull contemplation. A shadow flitted across the ground and swept on towards the Rock. She looked up. A young buzzard, she decided, flying high. Though in a way it more closely resembled a crow.

Part Eight:
TRUMP

1

There beneath a setting sun that burns in the long canyon below, there on a bluff among the pointed shadows, they come to him. He waits impatiently, nearly ashamed of his mood. Slowly, finally the car arrives.

The young Indian and the woman Rita bring others; the man, Vallez, has changed somehow since the time when he was hired. Galidar finds in his eyes a queer light, a mix of bright colors and dark shadows that swirl and churn in unavailing, trite human currents. Vallez's loyalties are no longer tied to the money Galidar has paid him; he is no longer sensible, from either viewpoint.

The other is a girl whose name is Alison and she is quite bold. She tries to hide her fears, her worries, her inner disappointment. Still, he can sense that all these are there. He asks about Dorella, her whereabouts, her condition, what plans she has made. Alison tells him nothing of value. Galidar finds this an impressive, almost admirable trait; largely, though, it is a particular nuisance.

He invades her mind, pushing her consciousness aside, crushing her resistance, going as deep as he can. She is not easily overwhelmed, her center secured in too much inner bedrock to be badly shaken by his attack. But he learns.

By the flavor of her thoughts alone he can sense that Dorella is a very real part of the girl's life, and that Dorella has indeed come here, to this place, to *him*. He also becomes aware of Dorella's present confidence, made obvious through the reflection it has left on this young girl's psyche, and inside himself he cannot help but smile.

Dorella has no doubt forgotten, having lived and aged through all these centuries, how badly she would have fared against him had it been an even match, one on one.

He learns too that Dorella has in some sense befriended this girl and he smiles again; it is a scoff. He has no respect for the arrangement to begin with and even less understanding of it. Regardless, he begins to see the possible, special values this arrangement might provide.

He decides that whatever the girl and Vallez mean to each other, or whatever they want from anyone else, it is of minor concern. As long as they are here and can be kept available as bait, he needn't lend them further attention. His priorities are clear.

Leaving Wagua and Rita to guard the others, Galidar goes behind the rocks and enters his lean-to, then sits in quiet meditation. He enters a deep trance and, pushing just so, places a part of his being in contact with the world of eternal darkness. He draws from the energies that fire this anti-universe and renews his oaths paying homage to the nether-beings who have been his mentors, those to whom he has ultimately pledged himself when the time of his own eternity comes.

He returns completely to the mountain then, to his lean-to, to the business at hand. He feels the power of the energies within him with a glutinous satisfaction. Not in a millennium has he had such strength, wielded such raw might. He steps out into the orange light of sunset. His hands and face feel sunburned; his skin shivers with a chilling, sweaty heat. The old body is badly taxed by the power it contains, but he senses it will last for some time. Enough time.

He takes a moment to repair some of the initial physical damage, to fortify where he can. There are other bodies available, of course, should it come to that. It may not.

Then something touches his awareness—a faint, sudden sense of magic.

In the air—

He looks up high into the dimming sky and sees a bird circling there. No ordinary creature, this. A bird, but more. Much more. He gathers a fragment of his vast, fresh reserves and concentrates on the animal. There is a magic sense about the creature, but it does not, as he might have expected, carry those particular characteristics unique to Dorella.

He finds a taste, a feeling that is nearly as familiar, yet different and puzzling.

He cannot quite remember. The essence is so faint, so small, as if tucked away into some tiny space. . . .

Galidar looks to the others and sees an unexpected blaze of fear in the eyes of Alison. She too has seen the bird, has seen his own observance of it. She knows *something* he does not and that presently he *must*. He moves towards her. She struggles to move away, but Rita has tied her hands as well as Mike's, as a proper precaution. She helps to hold Alison now, keeping the young girl from running or even dropping to the ground to avoid his stare.

He touches Alison and enters again into the surface

of her conscious mind. Thoughts run and hide there, but he can find many of them before they get away; he holds them long enough to get a proper look. The bird—crow, he sees, is very special to the girl and, it is clear, to Dorella.

It is an odd sort of riddle, and even with these facts before him, he cannot exactly ascertain the nature of the arrangement. No matter. It is the cream for an already very rich dish.

The next step is a ridiculously easy one. Standing away, raising his arms, he speaks—and strikes the crow from the sky.

2

James took Dorella to a locally concocted ranch-style home somewhere southwest of Ship Rock: no siding, three rooms, a small bath with no door, no utilities. The place hadn't been lived in for some time, nor had any of the half dozen similar houses scattered near and about in the shadow of a low rocky hillside. James said he would take a walk with some jugs and bring water back. Dorella decided that it could wait. She had a greater, more urgent thirst.

Carefully, insistently she touched James' mind, helping the young man to relax in a ragged armchair, to yield and await her further guidance. She looked at him in the dusty shadows, his face softly orange, half-lit by a shaft of fading sunlight through the empty window beside him.

His kind had always interested her the least, men without passion, or without the will to risk it, seek it. Yet now, for no clear reason, she wished she had the time to lend him something of that, to guide him to some of the missing pieces of his life and give him something real he could hold onto—a vision, a confidence in himself, the way Alison . . .

Then the light changed, the sun eclipsed completely

now by a high ridge in the distance. Pulling James along, impressing her own consciousness upon him, she let thought flow between them, let him feel the air flow in and out of her lungs, let the world come to her and talk to her and touch her, and so him. In return, from within him she could sense her enemy.

Galidar would be waiting for her, looking for her, building an army perhaps, setting a trap—or many. Waiting with the knowledge that he had nearly triumphed before, even under the worst conditions, and would have every advantage in this. She would construct the best plan she could, build spells and traps of her own, each capable of ruining the most horrible assaults; she would reconcoct the dual killing spell she had used those centuries ago; she would hope that these might prove effective when the time came. But that was all she could do, all that she had.

Haste in such affairs was a deadly indulgence, but her mood was such that she welcomed the chance, any chance to meet Galidar again in battle, to release the tensions and angers and anxieties bursting almost painfully inside her. She wanted finally to have done with it.

This night those thoughts began to control her, sweeping her away, sweeping James along with her. She saw the possible events to come as her sole destiny, more important now than caution or odds or life itself. It was a thing almost of substance, clouding, influencing her thoughts, driving her forward in spite of—

Galidar was here, somewhere in the desert. She had felt it strongly, a massive concentration of dark energy that flowed from the nether reaches to some single point, shielded too well to pinpoint, yet impossible even for Galidar to completely hide—a vast dark cloud that obscured the horizons, looming and ominous. The Indian would know. She must continue with him.

With a measured effort she levered all this aside, paring her attentions until there was only the darkened, cooling house and James. She realized he was crying.

Then she saw everything, all of it brought to the surface by James' terrors and tears, memories and emotions dripping down his sun-baked face like acid rain. She saw no father he had ever known, a mother who seemed all too wonderful until the tuberculosis had taken her when he was not quite a young man. She saw other boys going to schools off the reservation as they grew older while he, already imposing on the resources of elder family, stayed on—and on. She saw the same kind of loneliness she had found in Alison at first, though more desperate, more debilitating.

Pulling a small white candle from her pocket, Dorella gathered warmth to its wick until a flame lit the deepening night around them, until shadows and images flickered like anxious ghosts in every corner, across every surface.

James looked up and saw his mother's face.

He rose from the chair, all the way up, standing as straight as he knew how. Thin sounds echoed behind his mind, noises from an old, exactly remembered house. He found the scent of his mother in the hot wind, saw the sunlight pour onto the colors of the blanket she'd made and laid over the back of the sofa. He reached, put his arms around the woman before him.

She whispered something that drifted through his mind with the memory of cooking stew, of visitors smiling, the words coming to him in his mother's own gentle Navajo. She told him to be proud inside, to be outwardly strong, to remember that she would always be a part of him and he a part of her, always one, together as they were now. She seemed to be everywhere in his thoughts, bringing with her everything he could think about, and the darkness seemed to fill with a warm, simple light. He felt a glow, a softness, then a rising drowsiness flowed into him—and she asked him to sleep.

Dorella blew the candle out, shook off the fog from
her consciousness. She had never done anything quite
like that before, she mused, feeling strangely unexpectedly refreshed by the experience. She had no idea
how much good it might do, though stranger still, that
seemed less relevant than expected; the trying alone
seemed somehow to be enough. She sat in another
chair, her mind filled with the images she had gathered from James' head: the face of the body Galidar
now used, the places he and Galidar had been
together, everything but the way to the place where
he was now. A carefully constructed block? she wondered. Or he simply didn't know.

But at just that moment, her mind attuned to the
distance, to Galidar himself, she was suddenly aware
of a sound—like the sound she had heard in her mind
months ago on a bus-stop corner, in a small town half
a continent away—the inward double scream of the
crow.

This lasted only an instant. Long enough, just, for
Dorella to sense exactly where it had come from.

3

James led her off to the lee of a scrubby hill. She
let him go then, let his mind begin slowly to clear.
He would be fully cognizant by the time he returned
home—or back to the town of Ship Rock, or wherever
he was going—which was a choice that only he could
make. She had a sense, though, for the man. A rather
good sense.

She turned and walked into the clear, then stood
alone on the far side of the hill, hesitating. Some small
part of her mind was going begging for negatives—
most of which made perfect sense. Why shouldn't she
simply run and keep running, content to survive in
such a manner rather than face possible death as an
alternative? Why, when deep inside she knew she was

trying to save a sister that was probably too far diminished to afford any reasonable hopes? And certainly Galidar's plans for the world, whatever they were, were none of her business . . .

She set her feet in motion beginning a short journey to the sharper hills taking form with the sunrise in the near distance. The echo of the crow's cry still rang in her mind, along with the rage it had kindled within her, rage that threatened to overcome her and even now threatened to take control.

She went back to the stars, to the familiar well of power, and gorged herself, stretching her capabilities beyond rational limits, beyond the point where, if memory served, she was endangering her very life. But she had learned over so long a time on earth, had built up tolerance and ability, and gained the talent to control and contain more energy than she had once dreamed possible.

She had practiced for centuries, yet had never dared utilize her full potential, always resisted the temptation to test its bounds.

But whatever drove her now was stronger than any sensibilities—a harsh mix of fears, desires, loves, hatreds, a desperate sense of inevitability and rushing tempo, and perhaps . . . duty.

She trembled as she approached her destination, a wide-mouthed, yet quickly tapering box canyon. The canyon was formed on either side by two very high rock ridges and by a high facing wall that stood mostly hidden in shadows which the coming sun had yet to dispel. She stayed to one side, squinting into the cool, sheltering darkness, watching for anything. Soon, high along the facing wall, she saw something move.

She was still too far away to gather any detail. She tried a seeing spell—with no effect. Something was blocking this mild effort, like a blanket thrown over everything. Blankets, however, were naught but thread and thread could always be unraveled.

She moved on, choosing her path carefully, listening

and watching with all of her senses before continuing. She worked her way up the floor of the canyon towards the big, dark wall ahead of her.

When she was halfway there, Galidar made himself known.

4

She heard his voice in her mind. Not words exactly, but a sound like the blowing of freezing winds through the empty limbs of winter forests. She felt his tone at once: powerful, hateful, vengeful. Serrated thoughts. She answered him in kind, calling back to him through the warming morning air, making her signal plain and clear at first; then, with a particular effort, adding her own reproachful tones, finally tinging it with a wrinkle of dry humor at the thought of him.

Then the voice was gone. She could see a small fire burning on the ridge at the head of the canyon, smoke rising like loose pigtails. A lone figure was silhouetted atop the rocky wall. Bright sky stood behind him. The sun was not yet visible, but when it cleared the ridge it would be squarely in Dorella's eyes. A worry, she thought, though that might prove to be the least of them.

She went forward again, step after step, knowing she was far enough along now for almost anything to happen. Wishing, or at least part of her was, that it would.

The canyon's width began to narrow, its fifty-meter-high walls crowding about her, closing in. The effect was eminently intimidating, she noted, allowing Galidar credit for his choice of locations. The facing wall was still some three hundred meters away. She doubted she could traverse that distance without incident. Questions sought to overwhelm her. Already she could sense something stirring all about her, the faintest shimmer on the waters of reality. Or was it her own mind drunk with tension and anticipation—

There, she thought, just ahead of her now, a trap of some design hidden in the dark abyss, looming. Or it wasn't.

Then yes. Yes it was—

The thing rode out of the deepest well of shadow and came straight for her. A scaly beast thrice-tall as a man, it stood on two sharply taloned feet, flexing massive, stumpy calves and thighs. Its body and shoulders were thick, its neck brief and seemingly too thin to accommodate the beast's great melon head—which was all jaws and eyes at a glance, eyes that oozed black syrup, jaws and teeth that flowed with blood as the creature opened wide.

As it drew near it raised its claws and mauled the air, then dropped as though something had forced it back down, and she suddenly saw that the creature bore a rider high on its back, clinging to its neck.

This little demon was a common sort, reddish brown and generally quite human in shape with the exception of a head that much resembled that of a wild boar. Fangs curled at either side of its snout, framing black, glossy eyes. Its pig ears twitched as it brought its mount to within thirty meters of where Dorella stood. She held the pair steadily in her gaze, eyeing the rider in particular, as she waited for it to decide its move.

A sound like steel being dragged over concrete came from the small demon's lips as it hung its snout in the air and raised its meaty red fingers above its head. It bellowed at the sky, shaking with a seizure-like frenzy; then its call went silent. Directly, other shapes began to appear in the blackness behind it, moving up.

A company of ancillary demons, Dorella saw, some no taller than school boys, some taller than three meters, each one a consummate emissary of the nether world, each one gruesome in its own right.

Some went without arms or legs or even heads, others were assembled in an irrational manner, an amalgam of hideous parts more strange even than those of their mounted leader. She saw bits and pieces of many creatures, known or imagined, from this world and from every time in history. Each found a way, dragging, loping, bleeding, oozing and breathing a deathly foul stench in their fore, to bear down upon her.

They came screaming, crying, howling, calling to her in voices that pierced her mind and tore at her heart with razored, icy edges. She felt a weakness that came from somewhere deep inside, her own fear and trepidation turned against her. Yet her strength did not falter and she gave no ground.

At a round swing of their leader's arm the forward-most line of demons, more than a dozen in all, fell to the ground and burst into flaming balls. They took up rolling towards her, gaining speed as they went, bouncing over rocks and rises on the rough ground and leaving bits of red-orange flames in crackling trails behind them.

The fireballs converged as they drew near, growing brighter as if by association, appearing then as a tightly set string of enormous flaming beads. They allowed no outlet. They would allow no retreat. There was very little time.

Dorella spied a large outcropping of rock far to her left and spoke to the molecules that made up the great mass of stone. She began to draw electrons from the rocks while still forcing the material to maintain much of its shape. When little more could be drawn she pulled the invisible cloud of energy across the canyon to the opposite wall, to a similar parcel of rock she had chosen, and forced the electrons in. She then stripped all of the protons from this second group of rocks and sent them back across to the left side of the canyon, then kept them there. She held all the particles in place, her will set against the newly wrought, furious forces around her, waiting for the right moment.

The line of fireballs blazed up before her, crossing the line between the two sections of rock, and at that instant, she let go her control.

A brilliant flash of white/blue current seared the air just in front of her, the manifestation of a bolt of lightning that drove straight through the balls of demon fire, leaving in its wake a wide trail of absolute vacuum—air pushed aside and sucked away by the twin bolt—which instantly snuffed the demon flames out.

A thunderclap echoed through the still canyon air, followed by a cool, empty silence. Dorella breathed a deep breath, then made her way towards the demon horde.

5

Urged on by their mounted, squealing leader, the rest of the demon pack surged forward, saturating the canyon air with unearthly, raving sounds. They bore no metal weapons, no man-made machinery, but hell's own arsenal was well-displayed among them. Some of the creatures quickly sprouted additional claw-tipped limbs, others spat flames and acids and an assortment of poisonous fluids which sizzled and charred everything in their path; still others doubled in size or split into multiple smaller demons, each snarling and scurrying with dreadful ferocity.

Dorella drew on her strengths, looking into herself to the stored energies of the cosmos. She found the combined strength she needed and cast a multiplication spell, not unlike the one used by another demon, Arynome, not so long ago, a spell to even the odds.

She copied herself exactly once, first appearing double beside herself, then doubling again to make four, then redoubling to eight, sixteen, thirty-two—until two hundred and fifty-six Dorellas stood together in a tight line. Each one called out a different demon's name, names learned over centuries of studying the ancient texts, during months gathering knowledge at the college library back east, and even through an occasional brief association.

One by one, as the role was called aloud, they stood down from the charge, no longer commanded by the powers of Galidar or guided by the demon general riding among them.

This done, the legion of Dorellas called the legion of demons by name a second time and commanded them to attack their swinish leader. Turning en masse, swarming upon beast and rider, they each obeyed. Gnashing teeth tore stout legs out from their sockets, clutching claws ripped scaly meat from cracking bones. The riding-beast shrieked with a volume that pierced the mind and shook the foundations of the canyon before it died. The horde bore down upon what remained of their leader, ignoring its own agonizing howling as they disassembled its body, then made a meal of him.

The mob came up ravenous and insane with the taste of blood. It took only a word of prodding to start them at each other. In a motion they attacked.

Chunks of meat and bone and severed organs flew everywhere, a shower of scales and tails fell about the ground as chorused screams filled the air. Gruesome death covered the canyon floor as the genocide reached its apogee, then began to die. Blood flowed continuously forming dust-sprinkled streams that ran and bubbled across the ground, pooling into the low spots. In a moment the worst was over. Larger bits of demon still moved in places, upper torsos and detached limbs. A handful of nearly intact creatures stood victorious amidst the carnage, their chests heaving, jowls dripping with blood and gristle, eyes bright with the glow of madness.

One Dorella clapped her hands twice and the remaining demons turned and faced her. She fixed them with a baleful glare—and started forward. The demons paused, then turned as one and vanished as quickly as they had first appeared.

Dorella was forced to squint as the first direct rays of sunlight broke over the top of the ridge. And there was something else, a fresh discharge of energy that surged outward from the ridge as if ignited by the sun itself. She walked forward, back into shadow, stepping over dirty red puddles and mounds of bone and meat. The terminator of darkness and light followed her as though intending that she go first.

Dorella took stock of her resources. She was somewhat drained by the demon encounter, though not distressingly so. It was clear to her that she might need a quicker solution to the next unsuspected event, one that did not require tailored concentration and execution—a way out, somehow. But extraction spells, spells that accomplished large, rapid motion or hard deception, required much preparation and too much energy. So she set about building a different kind of spell as she went.

Stray light began to brighten even the deepest shadows, revealing details of the towering canyon wall ahead of her. She saw that it was not—at least not now—a natural wall at all, but appeared instead to be a man-made, steel and concrete dam. At its base, still half-cloaked in darkness, she could just make out a row of giant floodgates. High along the top the dam was crowned by a shining steel railing. Standing there, enshrined from behind in brilliant sunlight, she saw a figure and knew it to be Galidar. Her eyes gave her no clue, but in her mind she held no doubt.

She thought she could hear him calling to her, almost a voice, almost a touch, though she could not gather any meaning from it. She blinked and he was suddenly gone.

It was then that she noticed the cracks. They wound down from the top of the wall, spreading out like the limbs of a growing tree, like the many streams of blood drying in the sun behind her. In an instant they grew to cover most of the face of the dam, advancing still, and the sound of giving concrete reached her ears.

Water leaked near the top, then down along the lower reaches. Puddles formed at the base of the dam. As she looked closely she could see the floodgates coming open now, all of them at once.

New, super cracks appeared near the base as the tired gates yawned open. The entire face of the dam began to break into pieces as millions of gallons of water formed a spray, then a torrent, bursting through the air and down the wall, drowning the desert below.

Chunks of concrete rolled towards her, carried forward on a rising wave. She could smell the flood in the air, the scent of moisture and algae and fish and rotted trees. The dam seemed to give way completely then. Fresh thunder filled her ears. The ground shook beneath her feet as a wall of water charged upon the desert. Dorella saw the entire display as completely remarkable.

Almost, she believed it.

Closing her eyes, looking deep into her own mind to find the link to her optic nerve, she stopped the flow of energy from Galidar's spell and regained her own true sight. When she opened her eyes she saw only the desert, the canyon, the shadows that had nearly evaporated beneath the climbing sun.

She called to him now, using a voice-of-the-mind she was certain he would hear, and demanded he reply.

She waited, half expecting at least some answer after all these centuries; certainly there were a number of things she was eager to say to him, a number of things he might say to her. But there came only the quiet breeze of the desert morning. She sensed no magic near about just now, not before the facing wall at least. She wondered if, perhaps, most of Galidar's carefully prepared tricks were behind her.

Setting her jaw, Dorella strode forward once more.

When she looked again to the top of the wall ahead she could see him, just as before, backlit by the sun. An old body it seemed, at closer range. Bent slightly, withered and not like Galidar as she remembered him at all, but Galidar nonetheless. She was certain.

A small stand of rock rose to his right, smoke from the fire made a shadow against the bright sky as it drifted up from somewhere behind the rock. I've interrupted breakfast, she thought, spiteful, hopeful.

She walked another few meters, watching the high motionless figure, then felt something tug at her stockinged leg and run the nylon. It let go as quickly, and she realized it had been a purely mortal, purely ordinary piece of fine wire, invisible in the ambiguous light until it snapped and coiled to either side. A simple trip wire she saw, used by man for centuries as a warning device, or the trigger to a trap.

A deafening volley of explosions broke high across the tops of the ridges to either side. The dynamite must have been buried deep in the rocky edges, rigged for simultaneous detonation. As she looked up she uttered the final words of the extraction spell.

Tons of stone and earth came crashing down, bringing with it a thick cloud of dust that filled the canyon and overflowed its walls, billowing up into the sky—a cloud thick enough to obscure most anything, dense enough almost to walk on—though that was not, in this instance, strictly required.

6

The breezes, in their own good time, thin the dust that will not settle, carrying much of it off. Galidar stands silently on the edge of the cross-ridge, looking down at the mountain of rubble that covers the canyon floor. He feels nothing of elation yet; he waits, he watches.

At the center of the pile, a small rock no larger than

a softball begins to tremble noticeably. Abruptly it takes flight. It sails upward at increasing speed, swift as can be seen, and drives straight for Galidar's head. Directing his mind's will with the movement of his hand, he reaches out and bats the offending bit of geology away. He looks about again and is suddenly blinded. The sun, it seems, is no longer behind but is straight in his eyes. He turns only to find it still behind him as well, still exactly where it had been.

He turns again facing the canyon and raises his hand to shield his eyes. In that instant he sees another airborne rock, but too late. He ducks, saving his face, but the rock catches him in the right shoulder and spins him half around. He staggers, letting the damaged arm hang limply at his side, and sees yet another rock, several times the size of the others, headed towards him. It is followed by countless small and large stones that form a wedge-shaped cloud.

Galidar rallies, bringing his powers to bear, and forces the projectiles from their flight, sending them spinning off in all directions. Struggling, he copes with still more rubble as another wave, chunks as big as a man, soars in.

The sun still stabs at his eyes from both directions as he turns and ducks and bleeds a little from his shoulder. He guesses he has been stationary too long and moves to one side, but does so too late. A rock of melon proportions catches him full in the chest and knocks him to the ground.

He lays there a moment moving his good arm, calling out a series of spells in a desperate angry voice, straining to produce an effective volume. He makes quick repairs, sealing the fractures in his ribs, stemming the flow of blood where his lung has been torn. When he is able to pull himself to a near sitting position he sees, by virtue of this new angle, the root of his difficulties.

Suspended in the air above the canyon are the hard edges of a great mirror, perhaps four meters across, polished smooth on the near side, yet on the back retaining the rough sandstone appearance of the rock it has been culled from.

He gets to one knee and scans the desert below. Then, heeding a prickly chill that begins to walk the back of his neck, he looks up and to the right, to the high ridge at the top of the canyon wall; for the first time in more than a thousand years he stares directly into Dorella's eyes.

7

She stood atop the ridge that flanked the left-hand side of the canyon, less than fifty meters from Galidar's position, nearly level with him. Working feverishly she called the mirror away and sent it around to the sunward side of Galidar. She let most of its sandstone composition crumble away to dust until only a very thin curved layer of smooth material, convex on both sides, remained. Finally, adding the remaining phrases as fast as memory would permit, she forced all of the material transparent—a thin, hovering sheet of glass.

Dorella adjusted the glass slightly until it acted to focus the solar rays blazing through it. The tightly focused beam fell squarely upon Galidar's back. Smoke sprang instantly from his clothing. A scream quickly followed at his lips.

Galidar turned into the beam and sent a gush of dark energy directly to its source. On impact the glass shattered and fell, showering down on the hills below. The old wizard whirled about, collected now, and faced Dorella again.

His eyes flickered with unnatural light, his body shook as though on the brink of a seizure. He filled his chest with all the breath it could gather, then threw his hands forward, shouting in a voice that shot the canyon, and let go a furious discharge of concentrated energy, shaping its incarnation as it came forth.

Before she could move she was caught in a fierce blast of frigid air that froze her flesh on that side and forced her off balance. Dorella reacted even as the chill reached her, pushing back, calling upon the burning hot energy of the cosmic core fires that flowed through her. Her body began to thaw and she pushed again, combining her might with a cursory reflecting spell, returning at least some part of Galidar's arctic attack to its source.

Following this she mounted her own counterattack in the form of a wave of blistering heat sent roiling at Galidar. But when it reached him he held it back, shielding himself by sustaining a countering spell of his own. She pushed again, harder. He answered with equal force.

Dorella was suddenly aware of the tremendous drain from her sustained effort. She felt her energies reaching alarmingly low levels and found it all but impossible to believe.

All the gathered energy and all the practiced control of a lifetime, driven by the rage and purpose she felt inside her now, all her years living in this world and still she could not defeat him; still she could not best his best.

Yet Galidar too had begun to weaken; she could feel it in his struggle, sense it in the changing colors of the aura produced by his massive use of dark magical powers. But the source of his energies seemed overwhelming—negative power gathered and refined, "prepared" by comrade nether legions, then fed to him in such a way as to allow unthinkable control—control that let him survive focused forces that would easily have destroyed another being.

Still, she sensed a limit as the contest extended into minutes, as the tides worked back and forth between them. She reasoned that even in Galidar only so much power could ultimately be stored, only so much could be channeled through him. He was fading just slightly. And it was possible the nether world or the body he had chosen could not accommodate his fantastic appetite much longer.

She felt him reaching back into himself, through himself into the dark universe, pulling in as much new energy as he possibly could, burning himself up in the process—

While a part of her turned as well and again made the leap, finding the string loop, touching all of its fires at once. She took all she could, brought all she could carry, and spent all of it nearly at once. She pushed and felt him give, then felt him pushing back with a titanic effort. The clash of two such eternal forces rent the air between them and threw a confusion of steam and charged bolts of energy in every direction. Still, neither seemed to prosper by it.

She saw a new, stranger light in Galidar's eyes then, saw him motion briefly with but two of his fingers—

Then a voice, thinly audible as it echoed across the ridge, called Dorella's name. A human voice.

The contest was suddenly interrupted, both she and Galidar breaking off at the same time. The voice had come from just behind Galidar and he had plainly expected it. Slight movement caught Dorella's eye.

More figures came into view coming around the side of the sheltering rock spire to Galidar's right. She recognized each of them: the Indian who had attempted to hold her at gunpoint the previous afternoon; Rita, the girl they'd found at Mike Vallez's office in Albuquerque; then Vallez himself, hands apparently tied behind his back; Alison walking beside him with her hands behind her too.

The Indian had gained back his gun and was keeping it closely trained on Alison and Mike. In her hands Rita held only a length of rope which trailed behind her. As they moved forward Dorella saw that the other end of the rope was tied about the neck of something black and limping—

The crow's eyes met Dorella for the length of a blink, long enough for Dorella to understand that the mind of her sister was very close to the surface now, fighting for an effective level, for a means, a chance— the one chance of a dozen lifetimes—to strike back.

Dorella paused then, distracted by the question of how Alison and Vallez might have come to be here in the first place, why they were not still in the space between worlds where she had placed them? Galidar would know how to gain access there just as she did, but he had no reason to look. And with no idea of their exact location, it would be like looking for two stones in an ocean.

Unless they'd figured their way out on their own. . . .

In any case, she decided, given the present arrangement, it might not be a bad idea to push them back again, out of harm's way.

She made the effort, reciting the short spell, and found both of them and the crow surrounded by a sphere of protective energies, a very potent warding spell which Galidar had no doubt spent a good deal of time creating. She might manage, using all her remaining strength in a single effort, to penetrate the spell's boundaries and tear it away. But such an effort would leave her spent and all but defenseless.

No, she reasoned, *I must focus on the source.*

Her thoughts broke as Galidar called her name, using it like a tether, pulling at her with great force. She resisted, acknowledging him with his own true name in return, pulling back. Galidar backed down slightly, then spread his hands.

"You have grown generous in your years," he said. His voice carried with an unnatural volume and had a quick, almost amused timbre to it. "On the one hand you face me with greater powers than I would ever have expected; yet at the same time you seem to have developed this most puzzling, extremely fortunate affection for a certain human being. An obsessive affection. Foolish, of course. Madness, perhaps. But a gift to me nonetheless."

"Madness is a thing you know well," Dorella responded, keeping him centered in her vision while watching the others at the corner of her eye. Galidar faced her unaffected.

"The girl, Alison, will of course be destroyed, along with the disappointing bit of meat you see with her." He brought his hands together now, clasped them tightly before him. "Or you will surrender yourself to me," he said, his eyes narrowed to slits. "That is their only hope. You have not long to make your choice, else I will make it for you—and for them."

Dorella stared him back, saying nothing.

"You cannot hold out against me for long. You know this to be true."

Dorella's mind was racing ahead, swirling with spells and tricks, searching for anything she might use to amend the situation. But every thought seemed so trite and transparent and a simple business for Galidar to counter. She knew that no matter what she tried, even complying with his demands and offering herself to him in complete submission, Galidar would still not allow Alison or Vallez to live for long. He would use them, at least for a time, to serve or amuse himself until they lost their will or begged for death's final escape. The fear rose up in her throat like a hard ball, threatening to choke her. She had used every trick, spent more power than she had ever dare command. And yet—

Yet there had to be something else. And she had to find it now.

She looked the ridge over, the rocks, the sky, fighting the sun in her eyes.

She looked back and suddenly noticed that Rita and the Indian were outside the protective spell surrounding Alison and Vallez, and her spirits rose a little.

These other two were on hand to assist, to herd the captives about and keep them in line, but they were not a vital part of Galidar's plan. He wouldn't need their help to destroy just two human beings. He didn't need—couldn't afford—to expend precious energies protecting them from some stray fragment of Dorella's wrath.

She observed that the Indian not only had his gun with him, but also his hunting knife. Hiding her activity as best she could, she drew on her remaining reserves, channeling energy, quickly building a very special, precisely molded spell. Then she refocused her mind and body—all of it save a very small, trigger-ready portion—on Galidar.

"Very well," she announced. "I will lay my defenses aside. Might you be willing to discuss one or two last, small favors in return?"

"Perhaps," Galidar replied, forming a slightly bent grin. He seemed to relax just the tiniest bit. She saw him turn an eye for a brief moment to his captives, to the anguish he surely expected to find on their faces and the expected admiration on the faces of his aides. As he looked back to her, Dorella commanded the knife, forcing it loose from its sheath, and sent it flipping through the air at blinding speed.

The blade sank into Galidar's back just below the rib cage, half around on the left side. The wizard turned suddenly, looking back first to Wagua, raging, clearly intent on obliterating the man. Then, in half of the same instant, he seemed to come to the obvious truth of the matter and whirled back on Dorella again.

He clutched at the knife, knees buckling under him. He looked off momentarily, pain washing over his face, and in that instant of distraction Dorella struck again.

She used a dual spell similar to the one she had used against him so long ago. The first part of the spell was designed to fuse each molecule of hydrogen and carbon in Galidar's body into reaction, while the second part worked from the first—its own catalyst— and finished the job by destroying the essence that was the spell's true target. The spells had been altered slightly, shifted to a wider spectrum, strengthened by minor enhancements learned over so much time. Still, it was the second half of this same spell that had failed once before. She had destroyed the body but not, somehow, the thing that was still Galidar.

The only explanation was that he had utilized some sort of protection spell; or more likely a reconfiguring spell requiring only a few key words to make it complete. There was no way even now to be certain, even with her spell's improvements, that he did not still have some similar, adequate spell of his own on hand.

She had to catch him quickly, while he was occupied by the physical problems, before he had time to effect a proper defense against her main attack. Before he had time to plot another move.

Using nearly all her reserves, tying them to her carefully perfected spell, she let loose a blistering, concentrated bolt of positive energies—energies that would use the sudden fusion fire they created to ignite a second flame—like sparks touching hydrogen gas— a fire to consume Galidar.

The force of the release rocked her body. The brightness of it rivaled the sun as the energy leaped the distance between them and struck at Galidar. But he was not so vulnerable as she had hoped. Somehow he had managed to see her move and realized her purpose in time to react. He staggered back, nearly toppled by the assault—but he did not fall and he did not ignite.

She saw then the tightly constructed shell of a deflecting spell as it blazed a brilliant cobalt near his body, red-hued at its perimeter. Then it turned to crimson as it held up under the remainder of Dorella's assault, throwing off the energy she continued to pour into it. Almost, it had failed. Almost, she had done it. . . .

Galidar reached around slowly with his right hand and pulled the knife from his back, then worked, one eye to Dorella, to stop the hemorrhaging. He straightened then, stepped heavily forward again and slowly brought his hands up before him.

"So you make your choice!" he called to her. "And theirs as well."

He turned his head just slightly to his left, then dropped his left hand just enough to hold it straight out, fingers pointing directly at Alison. His hand suddenly jumped, and so did the crow. As the wizard's killing spell left his fingertips the bird was in the air, dragging its rope up behind it, finding just enough slack to fly between Alison and Galidar.

It took the spell full on, glowing for a barely perceptible instant with a crimson halo of its own. Then it dropped to the ground, putting slack back in its tether.

Alison screamed and fell over the crow, kneeling on all fours, covering it with her body. She called out, pleading with it to move, sobbing between drawn breaths. She glanced up at Galidar and cursed him with words Dorella could not exactly make out—though they carried well her intent.

The bird lay still. Then Dorella looked on in frozen horror, seeing more than Alison could, more than the small and lifeless physical body of the crow—a faint movement in the air above it, a vagueness of color. Released finally from the prison of the bird, Alibrandi's essence rose and shimmered above the tiny black body, above Alison, bright and beautiful, even now.

Alibrandi turned her head slowly, as though that slight movement alone required the greatest effort, as if she had no strength at all. There was no substance, only a faint semblance of the whole essence that had once been Alibrandi. This was all that was left, all that there had ever been, Dorella saw, forcing herself even now to accept that most of what was Alibrandi had died nearly ten centuries ago.

Then Dorella's eyes found her and the two stared into each other for a severed moment of time—for all the time there would ever be in the universe. Dorella saw that her sister understood everything, that she had always known her own hopelessness and yet, through the centuries, seeing and sensing and living through all that she and Dorella had shared—the people and the lives they had encountered—Alibrandi had been affected in a profound manner, had become almost . . . human.

She had given her life to save Alison, selflessly with no forethought, no hesitation, just as Alison would have. Just as Dorella knew, sharing her heart with Alibrandi, letting all the years and layers of internal confusion and baggage be swept away, what she herself was prepared to do.

Against Galidar she could never be sure of success, and yet she had come here, come knowing. . . .

"*You nearly sacrificed your own life*," she had said once, scolding Alison.

"*You mean you or your own people wouldn't? In a similar situation?*"

"*Faced with clearly impossible odds, as you were, I doubt my own mother would have,*" Dorella had replied.

The last energies of Alibrandi's spirit poured out to Dorella, filling her with the memories of life, the sum of a whole. Dorella cried out to her, the sting of tears burning her eyes. She tried to touch her back, but the time for that had already past. The last image of Alibrandi was gone.

A blackness filled her mind, a pounding dark ache that seemed to come from there and spread to everywhere else. She had never known such a hurt, such a penetrating sense of loss; it was as if she, not her sister, had died. She saw no pain as greater, no hope for any end to it—

No act unthinkable.

Galidar called to her, drawing her attention, shouting something twice, laughing at her, at her bird-turned-sister and now turned forever into nothing. He had been watching just as she had, had seen the image and recognized exactly who it was, and seemed delighted in his unexpected victory.

She tried to think, reeling from the spinning soup of hatred and longing and disjointed insanity that filled her now, an intense confusion which seemed to be the only thing that made any sense to her. Some part of her sensed that Galidar would strike back, would use everything he had and destroy her as he had her sister, his victory made complete: a victory he would have for as long as he existed.

And she could *never* allow that to be.

Dorella drew back into herself and made the leap one last time, traveling out into the reaches of the universe, in search of the energy she needed. She found her string, her own special loop; all the power she could hold, yet not nearly enough. A silent scream rose up within her, frustration and anguish and pain and rage boiling through the last fragments of reason and restraint—a voice screaming that the existence of Galidar *must* end, that *nothing else mattered*.

She sensed again the massive fissure that lay just beyond the huge elliptical galaxy, the rift she had never dared encounter with more than the most tenuous touch—yet it was so close to her now, there, just a little further out. Power enough to split whole worlds. More power than any being in the universe ever could imagine; more than she, with all her years of learning, could ever possibly hope to control. A part of her knew that to make contact with it and draw from its fires would be suicide. Every other part of her being screamed in blinded defiance.

She reached out, completing the path, and touched the limitless well.

Sunlight exploded again in her eyes, images flashing, mind racing. Almost too late she saw Galidar launch his assault upon her. She threw up her own reflecting spell, felt it falter, a flaw in the hasty incantation. She staggered as the fire of his attack began to reach her.

Then she glared back, shouting Galidar's name with all of her breath, and countered using the dual spell, letting all the energy of the massive super-string flow through her and into it.

The spell pounded Galidar like a row of hammers, smashing first through his reflecting spell, then smashing into his body, setting off a fusion reaction, igniting every part of him. And Dorella used the force to fuel an added spell—to push Alison and Vallez out of harm's way, into the place between places. Finally, binding with Galidar's essence, the spell ignited a second blinding spiral explosion. Energy poured forth, beyond her control now, beyond anything meant to be.

She saw the ridge erupt just as a wave of pain unlike any she had ever known poured through her, ripping her apart from the inside out. As the force of the explosions reached her, something inside gave way and the energy within her ceased to flow.

She felt her body falling, tumbling backward, down, away from the sky and the light. She felt no pain anymore. Then the world faded and was gone.

8

There is timeless darkness, complete absence, total immersion; yet there is something . . .

Like dreaming.

There are faces that come near, then go by, unclear, possibly familiar. She stops a face as it passes, a man carrying a bag. He turns towards her and still she cannot see detail, only gray outlines. She tries to talk to this person, but nothing comes. Failing this, she hopes that these faces instead might speak to her, even though they have no visible mouths. It seems, through some sense other than sight, that this person *is* trying to say something, trying very hard in fact, but she cannot hear a word.

The person pulls away, pushes one hand down into the bag, fumbling about, then comes up with a mirror. He holds it up and she sees that she has no face as well.

9

There is distant shouting. She sees that she is on a street, long and lined with faceless, interchangeable people and buildings. Suddenly the street begins to empty. The people all seem to know just what to do, just where to go, and just exactly why. She feels a terrible sense of ignorance and fear and anger at being somehow left out of this great disclosure. She wants to see what they see, to hear what they are listening to, to talk to anyone willing to acknowledge her.

Then they are gone and it comes to her that she is entirely alone, without a clue, without a face. . . .

Shouting begins again, or a roar, getting louder. A hurricane hits the street, shaking the buildings, pushing her about violently. She falls to her knees, then onto her side, then tumbles down the way, grinding her body against the concrete as the wind forces her over again and again. Then she sees something, hears something—a face that is whole, above her, close, a voice.

It is Alison's face, Alison's voice.

Then someone else.

She tries to say something to Alison but nothing comes.

She remembers she has no mouth. . . .

The other voice belongs to Mike Vallez. She can see him now at the corner of her vision.

"Her eyes!" he is saying, excited, pointing. "Look at her eyes."

She is terrified that she doesn't have any.

She tries to blink, to nod, to move anything at all. Nerves crackle like braids of shorting electrical wiring.

Tiny fires burn by the millions all through her. She senses that the ground beneath her is jumping, rattling, then considers that it might instead be her own body, its reaction to the pain.

The movement itself causes a firestorm of fresh agony that makes her cry out, though still somehow no sound of it finds her ears. She screams again and again and again, and finally it comes.

10

"You were out for a while," Alison said. Dorella could feel the young girl's hand stroking her hair. It made her head hurt all the more. She said nothing.

"We carried you off the base of the ridge," Mike said, a weary smile. "How do you feel?"

Dorella tried to talk again, tried to move anything. She remembered to breathe, finally managed a deep breath, then choked when she tried to whisper, fighting a fresh wave of little fires. There were words in her head. Only garbled rasping came to her lips. Alison grinned and leaned forward, kissed her forehead. Dorella realized Mike was holding one of her hands in both of his.

She felt heat in her face, moisture on her cheeks. Salt stung at her eyes—herself crying, again. She closed her eyes as tightly as she could, sobbing as she had never done, as she had never known she could until—

"He's gone," Alison was saying. "There's not a trace. We came back from that other place, I don't think we were gone very long, and we looked around up there. There isn't anything."

Dorella tried to look, to get her bearings. She saw sun, rock. It wasn't worth the effort.

"Half the ridge is gouged out," Mike said. "You did it, lady. You did great."

Nearly, Dorella thought. He hadn't seen Alibrandi's

image; he knew nothing of the price that had been paid or the injury that would never heal. Though surely Alison must. . . .

"Try to move your legs," Mike asked. She did. He looked at Alison and nodded.

"You look like shit," Alison told her, sounding grim, apparently trying not to. "Radiation burns we think, or something like that. A lot of the skin is blistered. We have to get you to a doctor as soon as we can."

Dorella eased her eyes shut again. She was too weak now, the guts of her burned too raw . . . but she had to at least get a bit of her body repaired, enough so human medicine could be avoided.

But there was nothing there. She knew it without trying, knew that trying would work against her like tearing at a deep, open wound—would make her bleed in ways even she had little understanding of.

No, she told herself strictly, *let them care for you. Let them, or you will finish Galidar's own work for him.* She looked up, nodded, and winced.

"I found their cars on the other side of the ridge," Mike said. "I drove one of them around as close as I could. I'm afraid we'll have to carry you to it from here. We wanted to make sure your back wasn't broken. You think you can handle it?"

Dorella nodded again. They took her by both arms and gently lifted. She shut her eyes and set her mind against the pain. She tried to walk, kept trying until she felt the cushion of a car seat pushing up underneath her.

She faded then, slipping into timeless darkness, into total immersion. Yet there was everything. . . .

When she woke she was among doctors, all of whom seemed very nice and efficient and very far away. They gave her something to make her sleep again, and she concluded that it was probably a good idea.

11

When she awoke again she was in a small, dimly lit room, resting comfortably on a bed that smelled of fresh sheets. She breathed in and recognized the dry scent of air conditioning, the tang of cleaning liquids.

She moved. Most of the interior fireworks had gone out, though much of her exterior still seemed very tender. Dressings were wrapped about her head and arms, around one leg. In all, however, she was not entirely displeased.

She decided to tend to personal matters first, physical things being the easiest, injuries being quite unacceptable. She chose a modest, straightforward skin healing spell, directing it to only one of the affected areas.

It was then that she learned all of the magic was gone.

12

"Maybe it's only temporary," Alison suggested, her voice sounding bright. She leaned across the little round breakfast table in Mike's cramped kitchen, patted Dorella's hand. "You seem to be healing well enough otherwise."

"Have you ever lost your whatever-it-is before?" Mike asked. He looked at her still full cup of coffee, frowned, reached back to the counter and grabbed the pot. He dumped the old and gave her fresh.

"I don't know of anything like this ever happening to anyone else," Dorella said. "And there is no one to ask. There isn't anyone else at all. . . . "

She trailed off, staring at the grease stains on the wallpaper behind the stove, thinking in bits and pieces. She found such things hard to concentrate on.

She hadn't been able to get close to her feelings since she had come to in the hospital, more than a week now. Each day she grew stronger, yet each day was otherwise the same.

"I sort of know what that's like," Alison told her, showing dark emotions in her bright eyes. "I'm sorry."

"No," Dorella said. "I'm quite lucky to be here at all. I went too far." She paused a moment, closing her eyes. "Or maybe just far enough. I don't know. I know that what I did was very—"

"Incredible," Alison interrupted. "What you did was incredible. You can't stop and think at a moment like that. I'd have tried to do the same thing myself."

Dorella looked at her, and for the first time since coming to, she smiled. "Thank you," she said. Alison raised an eyebrow.

"So, what do you figure you'll do?" Mike asked matter of factly, or he was trying to sound that way.

Dorella considered this a moment, the many things it implied. "I don't know," she said, quite honestly. "Unless there is a change I think I am going to grow old, like you. And I suppose I'll have to figure out a way to survive. On my own."

"I could stick with you for a while," Alison spoke up. "You know—show you the ropes. I don't have anyone else, either," she added, shrugging absently, resigned just the same.

"Well," Mike Vallez said, grinning as he caught her eye, "I've been meaning to talk to you about that." Alison made a face Dorella couldn't see. Mike's grin widened.

"All the same," Alison said, turning back. "I go where the lady goes, for a while anyway. That's that."

Mike sat back in his chair. "Then where does the lady go?"

Dorella shook her head, despondent, finding this question much larger once she got it out and looked it over.

Alison said, "Home, of course." She patted her

purse where it rested on her lap. "We have round-trip tickets, remember? Mrs. Mulvihill is probably worried silly."

"You'll never hear the end of it," Mike added, frowning.

"She is a hurdle, isn't she?" Dorella quipped.

"Says the same of you," Alison said, averting her gaze.

Dorella closed her eyes again, letting her thoughts find their own way, listening to her heart beat with life inside her; she could no longer touch the stars, but they were there, still out there, all of them.

There was little to pack. And it had never taken long. She could easily be home by morning.

FALLEN ANGELS

Two refugees from one of the last remaining orbital space stations are trapped on the North American icecap, and only science fiction fans can rescue them! Here's an excerpt from *Fallen Angels*, the bestselling new novel by Larry Niven, Jerry Pournelle, and Michael Flynn.

* * *

She opened the door on the first knock and stood out of the way. The wind was whipping the ground snow in swirling circles. Some of it blew in the door as Bob entered. She slammed the door behind him. The snow on the floor decided to wait a while before melting. "Okay. You're here," she snapped. "There's no fire and no place to sit. The bed's the only warm place and you know it. I didn't know you were this hard up. And, by the way, I don't have any company, thanks for asking." If Bob couldn't figure out from that speech that she was pissed, he'd never win the prize as Mr. Perception.

"I am that hard up," he said, moving closer. "Let's get it on."

"Say what?" Bob had never been one for subtle technique, but this was pushing it. She tried to step back but his hands gripped her arms. They were cold as ice, even through the housecoat. "Bob!" He pulled her to him and buried his face in her hair.

"It's not what you think," he whispered. "We don't have time for this, worse luck."

"Bob!"

"No, just bear with me. Let's go to your bedroom. I don't want you to freeze."

He led her to the back of the house and she slid under the covers without inviting him in. He lay on top, still wearing his thick leather coat. Whatever he had in mind, she realized, it wasn't sex. Not with her housecoat, the comforter and his greatcoat playing chaperone.

He kissed her hard and was whispering hoarsely in her ear before she had a chance to react. "Angels down. A scoopship. It crashed."

"Angels?" Was he crazy?

He kissed her neck. "Not so loud. I don't think the 'danes are listening, but why take chances? Angels. Spacemen. *Peace* and *Freedom*."

She'd been away too long. She'd never heard spacemen called *Angels*. And— "Crashed?" She kept it to a whisper. "Where?"

"Just over the border in North Dakota. Near Mapleton."

"Great Ghu, Bob. That's on the Ice!"

He whispered, "Yeah. But they're not too far in."

"How do you know about it?"

He snuggled closer and kissed her on the neck again. Maybe sex made a great cover for his visit, but she didn't think he had to lay it on so thick. "We know."

"We?"

"The Worldcon's in Minneapolis-St. Paul this year—"

The World Science Fiction Convention. "I got the invitation, but I didn't dare go. If anyone saw me—"

"—And it was just getting started when the call came down from *Freedom*. Sherrine, they couldn't have picked a better time or place to crash their scoopship. That's why I came to you. Your grandparents live near the crash site."

She wondered if there was a good time for crashing scoopships. "So?"

"We're going to rescue them."

"We? Who's we?"

"The Con Committee, some of the fans—"

"But why tell me, Bob? I'm fafiated. It's been years since I've dared associate with fen."

Too many years, she thought. She had discovered science fiction in childhood, at her neighborhood branch library. She still remembered that first book: *Star Man's Son*, by Andre Norton. Fors had been persecuted because he was different; but he nurtured a secret, a mutant power. Just the sort of hero to appeal to an ugly-duckling little girl who would not act like other little girls.

SF had opened a whole new world to her. A galaxy, a

universe of new worlds. While the other little girls had played with Barbie dolls, Sherrine played with Lummox and Poddy and Arkady and Susan Calvin. While they went to the malls, she went to Trantor and the Witch World. While they wondered what Look was In, she wondered about resource depletion and nuclear war and genetic engineering. Escape literature, they called it. She missed it terribly.

"There is always one moment in childhood," Graham Greene had written in *The Power and the Glory*, "when the door opens and lets the future in." For some people, that door never closed. She thought that Peter Pan had had the right idea all along.

"Why tell *you*? Sherrine, we want you with us. Your grandparents live near the crash site. They've got all sorts of gear we can borrow for the rescue."

"Me?" A tiny trickle of electric current ran up her spine. But . . . *Nah*. "Bob, I don't dare. If my bosses thought I was associating with fen, I'd lose my job."

He grinned. "Yeah. Me, too." And she saw that he had never considered that she might not go.

'Tis a Proud and Lonely Thing to Be a Fan, they used to say, laughing. It had become a *very* lonely thing. The Establishment had always been hard on science fiction. The government-funded Arts Councils would pass out tax money to write obscure poetry for "little" magazines, but not to write speculative fiction. "Sci-fi isn't literature." *That* wasn't censorship.

Perversely, people went on buying science fiction without grants. Writers even got rich without government funding. *They couldn't kill us that way!*

Then the Luddites and the Greens had come to power. She had watched science fiction books slowly disappear from the library shelves, beginning with the children's departments. (That wasn't censorship either. Libraries couldn't buy *every* book, now could they? So they bought "realistic" children's books funded by the National Endowment for the Arts, books about death and divorce, and really important things like being overweight or fitting in with the right school crowd.)

Then came paper shortages, and paper allocations. The science fiction sections in the chain stores grew smaller. ("You can't expect us to stock books that aren't selling." And they can't sell if you don't stock them.)

Fantasy wasn't hurt so bad. Fantasy was about wizards

and elves, and being kind to the Earth, and harmony with nature, all things the Greens loved. But science fiction was about science.

Science fiction wasn't exactly outlawed. There was still Freedom of Speech; still a Bill of Rights, even if it wasn't taught much in the schools—even if most kids graduated unable to read well enough to understand it. But a person could get into a lot of unofficial trouble for reading SF or for associating with known fen. She could lose her job, say. Not through government persecution—of course not—but because of "reduction in work force" or "poor job performance" or "uncooperative attitude" or "politically incorrect" or a hundred other phrases. And if the neighbors shunned her, and tradesmen wouldn't deal with her, and stores wouldn't give her credit, who could blame them? Science fiction involved science; and science was a conspiracy to pollute the environment, "to bring back technology."

Damn right! she thought savagely. We do conspire to bring back technology. Some of us are crazy enough to think that there are alternatives to freezing in the dark. *And some of us are even crazy enough to try to rescue marooned spacemen before they freeze, or disappear into protective custody.*

Which could be dangerous. The government might declare you mentally ill, and help you.

She shuddered at that thought. She pushed and rolled Bob aside. She sat up and pulled the comforter up tight around herself. "Do you know what it was that attracted me to science fiction?"

He raised himself on one elbow, blinked at her change of subject, and looked quickly around the room, as if suspecting bugs. "No, what?"

"Not Fandom. I was reading the true quill long before I knew about Fandom and cons and such. No, it was the feeling of hope."

"Hope?"

"Even in the most depressing dystopia, there's still the notion that the future is something we build. It doesn't just happen. You can't predict the future, but you can invent it. Build it. That is a hopeful idea, even when the building collapses."

Bob was silent for a moment. Then he nodded. "Yeah. Nobody's building the future anymore. 'We live in an Age of Limited Choices.' " He quoted the government line without cracking a smile. "Hell, you don't *take* choices off a list. You *make* choices and *add* them to the list. Speaking of which, have you made your choice?"

That electric tickle ... "Are they even alive?"

"So far. I understand it was some kind of miracle that they landed at all. They're unconscious, but not hurt bad. They're hooked up to some sort of magical medical widgets and the Angels overhead are monitoring. But if we don't get them out soon, they'll freeze to death."

She bit her lip. "And you think we can reach them in time?"

Bob shrugged.

"You want me to risk my life on the Ice, defy the government and probably lose my job in a crazy, amateur effort to rescue two spacemen who might easily be dead by the time we reach them."

He scratched his beard. "Is that quixotic, or what?"

"Quixotic. Give me four minutes."

ROBERT A. HEINLEIN

"Heinlein knows more about blending provocative scientific thinking with strong human stories than any dozen other contemporary science fiction writers."
—*Chicago Sun-Times*

"Robert A. Heinlein wears imagination as though it were his private suit of clothes. What makes his work so rich is that he combines his lively, creative sense with an approach that is at once literate, informed, and exciting."
—*New York Times*

Seven of Robert A. Heinlein's best-loved titles are now available in superbly packaged new Baen editions, with series-look covers by artist John Melo. Collect them all by sending in the order form below:

PRAISE FOR
LOIS MCMASTER BUJOLD

What the critics say:

The Warrior's Apprentice: "Now here's a fun romp through the spaceways—not so much a space opera as space ballet.... it has all the 'right stuff.' A lot of thought and thoughtfulness stand behind the all-too-human characters. Enjoy this one, and look forward to the next."
—Dean Lambe, *SF Reviews*

"The pace is breathless, the characterization thoughtful and emotionally powerful, and the author's narrative technique and command of language compelling. Highly recommended."
—*Booklist*

Brothers in Arms: "... she gives it a geniune depth of character, while reveling in the wild turnings of her tale.... Bujold is as audacious as her favorite hero, and as brilliantly (if sneakily) successful."
—*Locus*

"Miles Vorkosigan is such a great character that I'll read anything Lois wants to write about him.... a book to re-read on cold rainy days." —Robert Coulson, *Comics Buyer's Guide*

Borders of Infinity: "Bujold's series hero Miles Vorkosigan may be a lord by birth and an admiral by rank, but a bone disease that has left him hobbled and in frequent pain has sensitized him to the suffering of outcasts in his very hierarchical era.... Playing off Miles's reserve and cleverness, Bujold draws outrageous and outlandish foils to color her high-minded adventures." —*Publishers Weekly*

Falling Free: "In *Falling Free* Lois McMaster Bujold has written her fourth straight superb novel.... How to break down a talent like Bujold's into analyzable components? Best not to try. Best to say 'Read, or you will be missing something extraordinary.'" —Roland Green, *Chicago Sun-Times*

The Vor Game: "The chronicles of Miles Vorkosigan are far too witty to be literary junk food, but they rouse the kind of craving that makes popcorn magically vanish during a double feature." —Faren Miller, *Locus*

MORE PRAISE FOR
LOIS MCMASTER BUJOLD

What the readers say:

"My copy of *Shards of Honor* is falling apart I've reread it so often.... I'll read whatever you write. You've certainly proved yourself a grand storyteller."
—Liesl Kolbe, Colorado Springs, CO

"I experience the stories of Miles Vorkosigan as almost viscerally uplifting.... But certainly, even the weightiest theme would have less impact than a cinder on snow were it not for a rousing good story, and good storytelling with it. This is the second thing I want to thank you for.... I suppose if you boiled down all I've said to its simplest expression, it would be that I immensely enjoy and admire your work. I submit that, as literature, your work raises the overall level of the science fiction genre, and spiritually, your work cannot avoid positively influencing all who read it."
—Glen Stonebraker, Gaithersburg, MD

" 'The Mountains of Mourning' [in *Borders of Infinity*] was one of the best-crafted, and simply best, works I'd ever read. When I finished it, I immediately turned back to the beginning and read it again, and I can't remember the last time I did that."   —Betsy Bizot, Lisle, IL

"I can only hope that you will continue to write, so that I can continue to read (and of course buy) your books, for they make me laugh and cry and think ... rare indeed."   —Steven Knott, Major, USAF

What do you say?

Send me these books!

Shards of Honor • 72087-2 • $4.99 _____
The Warrior's Apprentice • 72066-X • $4.50 _____
Ethan of Athos • 65604-X • $4.99 _____
Falling Free • 65398-9 • $4.99 _____
Brothers in Arms • 69799-4 • $3.95 _____
Borders of Infinity • 69841-9 • $4.99 _____
The Vor Game • 72014-7 • $4.99 _____
Barrayar • 72083-X • $4.99 _____

Lois McMaster Bujold:
Only from Baen Books

If these books are not available at your local bookstore, just check your choices above, fill out this coupon and send a check or money order for the cover price to Baen Books, Dept. BA, P.O. Box 1403, Riverdale, NY 10471.

NAME: _____

ADDRESS: _____

_____

I have enclosed a check or money order in the amount of $ _____.

MAGIC AND COMPUTERS DON'T MIX!

RICK COOK

Or . . . do they? That's what Walter "Wiz" Zumwalt is wondering. Just a short time ago, he was a master hacker in a Silicon Valley office, a very ordinary fellow in a very mundane world. But magic spells, it seems, are a lot like computer programs: they're both formulas, recipes for getting things done. Unfortunately, just like those computer programs, they can be full of bugs. Now, thanks to a *particularly* buggy spell, Wiz has been transported to a world of magic—and incredible peril. The wizard who summoned him is dead, Wiz has fallen for a red-headed witch who despises him, and no one—not the elves, not the dwarves, not even the dragons—can figure out why he's here, or what to do with him. Worse: the sorcerers of the deadly Black League, rulers of an entire continent, want Wiz dead—and he doesn't even know why! Wiz had better figure out the rules of this strange new world—and fast—or he's not going to live to see Silicon Valley again.

Here's a refreshing tale from an exciting new writer. It's also a rarity: a well-drawn fantasy told with all the rigorous logic of hard science fiction.

69803-6 • 320 pages • $3.50

Available at bookstores everywhere, or you can send the cover price to Baen Books, Dept. BA, P.O. Box 1403, Riverdale, NY 10471.

ELIZABETH MOON

THE DEED OF PAKSENARRION

Anne McCaffrey on Elizabeth Moon:

"She's a damn fine writer. The Deed of Paksenarrion is fascinating. I'd use her book for research if I ever need a woman warrior. I know how they train now. We need more like this."

By the Compton Crook Award winning author of the Best First Novel of the Year

Sheepfarmer's Daughter
65416-0 • 512 pages • $3.95 _____

Divided Allegiance
69786-2 • 528 pages • $3.95 _____

Oath of Gold
69798-6 • 512 pages • $3.95 _____